PS-4one

S0-BUB-543

# THE AMNESIA PARADOX

---

## UNLIKELY SPIES 1

## NOELLE GREENE

To a
fellow
romantic —

Noelle Greene

This is a work of fiction. Names, characters, organizations, places, events, and incidents are either products of the author's imagination or are used fictitiously.

Text copyright © 2017 Noelle Greene

All Rights Reserved

ISBN 978-0692820025

Cover designed by Scarlett Rugers Design
www.scarlettrugers.com

# 1

JACKSON LEE HAD WONDERED all along if he was on a fool's errand. His suspicions were confirmed when her taxi took off, leaving him high and dry in front of the American Embassy, less than a minute after arriving.

He had called in favors. Ignored the State Department travel advisories. Postponed his next assignment. All for that welcome.

Rose glanced back at him with a perplexed expression. Oh, she was good. A consummate actress with talent completely wasted on vaccinating the world's rug rats. Or whatever it was she did.

He wasn't inclined to give her the satisfaction of a chase. At least not right away. He knew she wouldn't get far. The next street over was tantamount to a parking lot. Plus, he needed a minute. That first sight of her had caught him off guard with an oddly physical impact, like a hard thump to his chest.

This reaction would be relief of course, just relief that she was okay. Mostly okay. He hadn't expected her to look so different. She'd been so busy saving the world that she had lost weight, likely ten or fifteen pounds. She used to have a generous ass. Perfect, to his mind, though she had never thought so. Now her butt was as flat as an ironing board.

The bigger shock was how vulnerable she'd appeared as she walked haltingly across the uneven cobblestones. He'd seen that lost and desolate look on her face only once, many years ago. But by the time she called out and started running across the courtyard, any uncertainty had vanished.

He'd almost laughed when she ordered him to hold the taxi. That was the old Rose—a bossy little thing. No problem giving orders to anyone and everyone. Her eyesight sucked, so unless she'd started wearing contacts—she likely hadn't even recognized him yet. Or so he'd assumed.

Then, right to his face, up close and personal, she'd had the gall—or presence of mind?—to pretend she'd never laid eyes on him before. She hadn't been expecting him, he knew that much. Impressed despite himself, he wondered wryly why she hadn't been recruited by one of the intelligence agencies. He should have known to expect the unexpected. She was like no one else. Always had been. The strongest-willed person he'd ever known. Disciplined and stubborn. Also generous and loyal. To a fault.

Qualities lavished on everyone except him.

He narrowed his eyes in speculation as her taxi lurched out to the main boulevard blaring Afro-hip hop. The changes in her annoyed him. She'd become so conservative, with that unruly red-gold hair braided into submission and makeup hiding the freckles that dusted her nose. A plain buttoned-down blouse and chinos had replaced the boho skirts she used to love.

This new Rose was neither fish nor fowl, neither hipster nor prepster. Scary-skinny and fundamentally altered in some way he couldn't put his finger on, she wasn't the same girl. Something was amiss, something more than the political turmoil and violence that plagued this tiny corner of West Africa. Maybe she really was ill, as her mother feared.

He'd been right to come. Whether she wanted his help or not, she was going to get it. Even if Rose were in perfect health, security concerns here were real and ongoing. In the last six months, two aid workers had been kidnapped and one murdered. From the reports he'd read on the plane coming over, he'd concluded that the more things changed here, the more they stayed the same. The cast of characters rotated but not the fundamental issues.

There were the ever-present warring factions with similar names—Freedom this and Democracy that— fighting in different regions. Some were affiliated with extremist rebels, some with political parties that opposed the current regime. Some were local militia groups, armed citizens who patrolled their communities. They took justice into their own hands because they didn't trust the military or the police, often with good reason.

Jackson turned to scan the embassy compound with a practiced eye, noting the restive crowd waiting in line and the Marine guards armed with assault rifles. You could almost smell the anxiety here. The guards were expecting trouble. However, he knew from experience that days, even weeks, could pass before anything interesting happened.

His meeting with the science envoy wasn't for another hour. He'd been hoping for some decent coffee. Maybe a meal. He thought about catching up with Rose later. After all, he knew her hotel—and the room number. He'd have no trouble finding her. No reason why the difficult conversation couldn't wait till tonight.

Still, he'd come *this* far. He'd promised her mom that he'd check on her and do his best to convince her to go home for Christmas. Mrs. Slater had been kind to him when he'd desperately needed kindness and stood up for him even when—especially when—his father did not. So he'd keep his word.

Work could wait. The project he'd been assigned to wasn't going anywhere. Besides, if there really was a coup attempt, work would grind to a halt while the government cracked down on the rebels. Within a day or two, a few insurgents would be paraded in front of the cameras and then off-camera, executed. After that, order should be restored fairly quickly and the country would go back to business as usual.

Decision made, he hailed another taxi and folded his legs into the cramped back seat.

As he'd expected, they screeched to a stop in a traffic snarl a mere two blocks from the embassy. He located Rose's taxi about twenty car lengths ahead. Piece of cake, really, even if he hadn't recognized the enormous furry dice dangling from her driver's rearview mirror. He'd stared at that doo-dad all the way in from the airport.

Arriving had been the easiest part of this journey. Too easy. After a long, uncomfortable flight—he never had enough leg room—he had breezed through customs in record time. The agent had stuttered in disbelief that Jackson wanted *in* to a country on the brink of civil war. Not surprisingly, the departure lines he passed on his way out were long and fractious, teeming with ex-pats and locals fortunate enough—or crooked enough—to have the means to escape.

He rubbed his jet-lagged eyes with the heels of his palms. Judging from the street vendors now swarming the idling cars and trucks, they'd all be here a while. The vendors were making the most of a captive audience.

He flagged down a woman with a heavy basket balanced on her head. A Cameroonian immigrant, judging by her dress's striped fabric. She plucked two water bottles from her basket and then exchanged the bottles for his cash. She did all this with a smile and without spilling a single item from the basket. It was only when the woman walked away that he saw a sleeping baby strapped to her back.

He passed one bottle up to his driver and downed the other himself in two long gulps. Five stifling minutes passed with very little progress. The traffic jam had settled into hopeless gridlock and the fan mounted on the taxi's dashboard just moved hot air around.

Jackson fought to stay awake. Tropical heat did this to him every time. He hadn't slept more than a couple of hours in two days. The hell with it. He closed his eyes.

~

Rose pegged the tall guy at the embassy gate for a tourist. He had been too disheveled to be a diplomat, too old to be a student, and he looked as disoriented as she felt. Like he'd only just now discovered he'd picked the wrong time and place for a vacation.

Not only did he not hold the taxi for her, he stood there gawking while she ran over and lunged for the door handle. Even after she dove in and told the driver the name of her hotel, the American didn't budge from the curb.

His intense stare had taken her aback. Deep brown eyes met hers and she briefly registered an unkempt, not-quite beard and full lips twisted into something close to a sneer. He was younger than she'd first thought with long, dark hair and features that indicated mixed ancestry. As her taxi pulled away, his expression was both watchful and oddly exhilarated.

Whatever. She had bigger problems than a clueless American tourist.

The flutters in her stomach became big, beating wings that flapped against her rib cage. If she never had another adventure in her life, it would be too soon. The worst part about all this, aside from the terrifying prospect of losing her mind, was how alone she felt.

The craziness at the embassy had not helped. There'd been long lines of expats needing help and natives desperate for U.S. visas. Every one of them, including her, was waiting to see the lone duty officer. And every one of them, including her, thought that they should be at the head of that line. She had finally given up and decided to go pack up and book a flight. If her memory problem didn't resolve on its own, as her hasty research had suggested it might, she'd see a doctor back home.

A home she couldn't remember.

She'd woken up this morning with a black hole where her memories should be. Until she tore her room apart to find her passport, she didn't even know her own name. Her first guess was that someone had slipped her a roofy last night. However, she'd neither seen nor felt any evidence of that. She'd woken up alone in a neat, unrumpled bed in an ordinary hotel room. There were no signs of sexual activity, consensual or not.

Recreational drugs or alcohol abuse were an obvious potential culprit. But she felt fine, physically, with no hint of a hangover. If she'd partied hard last night, wouldn't she feel shitty? She didn't even have a headache. The only evidence of drugs she'd found was a prescription bottle, filled at a pharmacy in California. A common anti-malarial drug, she'd since learned.

During a quick search on the hotel lobby computer, she'd also discovered that any number of things could cause sudden amnesia. The term "psychotic break" had jumped out at her. She still wasn't sure what that actually meant. Did it mean *she* could be psychotic? Contemplating that possibility chilled her to the bone, despite the hot dry wind that blew through the taxi's open window.

The ride back to her hotel would not be a short one. Long lines of vehicles were doubled up on the boulevard, squeezed side by side in lanes meant for one. Cars, minivans, and rickety tricycle taxis jockeyed for position, maneuvering to advance only a foot or two.

Her driver turned his radio down. "The traffic is worse than usual, miss. Protesters were blocking the streets in the old quarter until a short while ago. We will move along soon."

"What were they protesting?"

He studied her in the rear-view mirror as if weighing his words. "Our president has been in office for over twenty years. He promised an election by the end of the year. Now it's mid-December and there is no election scheduled."

The traffic did not improve. As they drew closer to a roundabout, Rose saw that a truck had broken down, blocking not one but two lanes. They inched closer. People were getting out of their vehicles, curious about the hold-up. Several men shouted and gestured at the truck driver, who still had not emerged from the truck's cab.

"The foolish man is just sitting there," the driver complained, "waiting for someone else to do the work. Miss, you will be better off walking to your hotel."

"How far is it?"

"About one kilometer."

He must have seen her anxiety because he laughed a big, gusty laugh and met her eyes in the mirror. "You will be safer on your own two feet than in my city's traffic."

Embarrassed, she said, "It's just—I don't know the way."

Without further discussion, he grabbed his mobile and made a call. He spoke rapidly in what must be a local dialect before he disconnected. "You will have a guide miss. My young cousin will meet you at Bonhomie Street. Just ahead. He will show you the way to your hotel. His English is very good."

Sooner than she would have thought possible, a boy of about ten appeared on a far corner. Upon her driver's answering wave, the boy plunged across the crowded boulevard. Rose held her breath as he made his way to the taxi, nimbly dodging two scooters and a goat.

"This is our Raymond," the driver said. "He is a good boy. You will be safe."

She believed him. Her instincts were operational, even if her memory wasn't. The driver's kindness affirmed that there were good people here, people she could trust.

"What do I owe you?"

"Nothing, miss."

She paid him anyway—in the dollars that he seemed to prefer—and thanked him.

"You are very welcome. I wish you good health and happiness."

She smiled and held out her hand, unsure of the proper etiquette. It must have been the right move because he clasped her hand in both of his as if they were old friends, then shooed her out of the taxi.

He called to the boy, "Stay on side streets and watch out for the Red Boys."

The boy—Raymond—took firm hold of her hand and said, "Do not worry. I know a shortcut to the Continental Hotel."

As they crossed the wide boulevard together, Rose observed the pandemonium, amazed that no one else seemed concerned about the dangerous mix of vehicles and pedestrians. Not to mention the random goats that wandered through the lanes, bleating pitifully. People were everywhere, hawking cigarettes, candy, fruit, and drinks to the idling cars. Many of the sellers were women and more than one had a child strapped to her back.

The noise, exhaust, and heat radiating up from the pavement overwhelmed Rose. She wondered—for about the fiftieth time today—what had possessed her to come to this country? Visa paperwork in her hotel room had indicated she'd been here for months, working for a non-governmental organization as an aid worker.

In the line outside the embassy this morning, rumors and anecdotes about overnight gunfights and riots had swirled around her. If this place was as unstable as everyone said, she should have gone home by now.

An uncomfortable thought occurred to her. What if she were the sort who didn't believe rules applied to her? Even less appealing—the possibility that she was a martyr in the making, saintlier than thou and too dumb to heed official warnings.

She'd find out. In the meantime, she would operate on the assumption that her reasons for being here weren't stupid or self-serving.

"This way," Raymond said, tugging her toward the far sidewalk where a growing crowd watched the roundabout drama.

The onlookers shouted good-natured advice to the men still attempting to persuade the truck driver to get out and help. By now, most drivers had hopped out of their vehicles. Some were venting their outrage at the truck driver, some were buying snacks from the women with baskets on their heads, and some were just shooting the breeze.

Rose stepped onto the curb. That's when her world blew up.

An enormous concussive blast reverberated through her body and pitched her forward. She went flying.

A rushing noise filled her ears. Slowly, slowly, she became aware that she lay on her stomach. Awful smells filled her nose and mouth and she tasted blood. Her neck seemed to be wet and her hands and knees stung. When she opened her eyes, she found herself in hell, an intensely hot yet strangely quiet hell. Close by, something metallic burned, so noxious and acrid that the air she breathed felt toxic.

Still flat on the ground, she turned her head, afraid of what she'd see. A burning hunk of metal sat in the center of the boulevard. It took a moment for her to recognize the skeletal remains of the stalled truck. A dozen cars were scattered across the roundabout. Some actively burning. Others missing doors.

Had it been a bomb? A missile strike? She'd heard nothing coming at them. Now she heard only a constant buzz.

People ran back and forth. Some stepped over her. A couple of women were on their knees, wailing. Rose couldn't actually hear their screams but she didn't have to. There were misshapen objects in her sightline. Human body parts she didn't want to identify. Labeling the bloody limbs would make this nightmare more real. And it couldn't be real.

The black smoke lifted, revealing at least a dozen bodies in the street and on the sidewalk. One or two were children. Some moved. Some did not. She prayed Raymond was not one of them. He couldn't be far. He'd been holding her hand.

Someone shook her arm. She nearly passed out in relief at the sight of the boy crouched beside her, bleeding from cuts on his arms and legs but very much alive. She tried to tell him how glad she was to see him.

His lips moved in reply. She attempted to read them without any luck. He kept yanking on her arm and she kept trying to tell him she was okay.

Finally, she realized he wanted her to get up. She pushed herself to a sitting position and, with his help, stood. She blinked and got her bearings, thinking that even an explosion hadn't jarred her memory back into working order.

Across the boulevard, a taxi—her taxi—had flipped over and pancaked. The car's roof was completely crushed. She thought about the driver's warm smile and warmer handshake. He wouldn't have had a chance. When he'd shooed her out of his taxi, he'd saved her life.

Raymond pushed her into a side street where the air was clean. It hurt to walk but he pushed her onward. She didn't want to see anything ghastly so she looked at her feet, putting one foot in front of the other. She noticed Raymond had lost his shoes. When she stopped and tried to give him hers, he swatted at her hands as if she were a troublesome toddler and kept on pushing her to move faster.

On some level she knew she was in shock. Just as well. She didn't want to think about the smiling driver, the screaming women or the small, still bodies on the ground. She didn't want to think at all. They walked several blocks, swept along in a tide of people. The high-pitched noise in her ears still hadn't let up. She began to have second thoughts, wondering if they should have stayed on scene. Her injuries were nothing compared to others and maybe she could have helped.

The answer came a few seconds later. A second explosion hit and rattled the windows around them. The blast vibrations upset her more than she would have thought possible. Her instinct was to drop and curl into a ball. She tried to do just that but Raymond wouldn't let her.

He prodded and shoved and they kept going, darting up alleyways, taking shortcuts. She saw her reflection in a shop window and was vaguely surprised to see dried blood around her nose and mouth. She wiped her face with the back of her hand and then gave up. It wasn't bleeding anymore.

Motorcycle cops whizzed past, one after another headed to the blast site. A couple of police cars. But where were all the ambulances? She saw only one.

Shopkeepers were pulling down metal shutters and locking up. No one paid any attention to her or Raymond. Everyone was in a hurry. Residents seemed to know the drill: make yourself scarce, get behind closed doors, and lay low.

She studied Raymond's stoic face. He seemed to be taking all of this in stride. Had he known about the second bomb? And if so, why hadn't he known about the first one? Or had he simply anticipated the evil because he knew the terrorists' playbook? Detonate the first bomb. Wait long enough for emergency responders and Good Samaritans to come running, wait for more victims, and then detonate the second.

A little boy shouldn't have to know this. He shouldn't have to take horror in stride. The fact that he did upset her anew. Tears rolled down her face as the impact struck her—an impact of a different sort. She'd just seen a demonstration of evil in its purest form. Violence in the name of some cause—and she didn't care whether the cause was political or religious—was evil. She knew it in her bones, a conviction rooted in something other than her unreliable brain.

A rush of cleansing anger washed away the sadness. It was a physical thing, her anger, and at the same time, oddly familiar. Her body knew this rage—and while not exactly welcoming it—she recognized the emotion. She blew out a long breath and straightened her shoulders.

By the time they entered the modern business district, entire city blocks had emptied out. Fewer and fewer cars passed by and soon the only vehicles they saw were official-looking jeeps and trucks filled with armed soldiers and the occasional police SUV speeding down the shockingly empty streets and boulevards.

They walked a long way. She still couldn't hear jack-shit and consciously enunciated her next words. "How far is the hotel?"

The boy didn't acknowledge her. Could be his ears were as messed up as hers. She shook his arm and tried again but his attention was on a group of people up ahead. She squinted to see what had caught his attention. She obviously needed those glasses she'd found in her backpack. Just as well she hadn't bothered to wear them because they would have broken after…

She stopped short and frantically checked her shoulders, though she already knew what had happened. The backpack was gone.

*Shit.* Her passport, her wallet, her money. Gone. She was screwed. Without the passport, she couldn't leave the country. She'd have to go back to the embassy as soon as it was safe. Whenever that might be. The compound was likely locked up and locked down.

Then, for the first time since the blast, she heard something. Someone was saying her name. Soft and deep. Like an intimate whisper. *Rose.*

She looked around. Her mind must be playing tricks on her because her hearing had not yet recovered. Even now, a shopkeeper slammed a metal shutter over his storefront with enough force that all the surrounding windows shook. She knew because she felt, rather than heard, the shutter hit the ground. How was it possible to hear someone call her name?

She heard it again. *Rose.* More intense this time. No, that wasn't an actual sound. More like an echo in her head. That explosion really had done a number on her.

Meanwhile, Raymond pulled her on, avoiding eye contact with—she now saw—a group of young men on an opposite corner. The men—all under twenty, except for the biggest guy—crossed over to their side of the street.

Some of the men who swaggered toward them were dressed in camouflage and red berets. Some were in street clothes. Some held automatic weapons. Some held sticks or long knives. They weren't policemen on patrol. They weren't government soldiers, at least she didn't think so. Nor were they rushing to help bombing victims. However, they were definitely looking to mess with someone.

She remembered the taxi driver's last words. *Watch out for the Red Boys.*

Raymond pinched her arm. Did that mean "be quiet" or did it mean "run like hell?" She couldn't tell. It was too late to hide or run anyway. All she could do was follow his lead.

The largest and oldest of the gang wore full combat gear, from heavy boots to camo fatigues, along with a jaunty red beret. Despite the weapon over his shoulder, he had a round, friendly face. His body language when he addressed Raymond was non-threatening. He smiled and patted the boy on the shoulder. She relaxed slightly. They knew each other.

The teenager standing behind the smiling man was another story. Much skinnier and meaner looking, he grabbed Raymond by the ear and scolded him. Raymond tolerated this briefly, then wriggled free and returned to Rose's side. The rest of the men—boys really—laughed.

When she attempted to speak up, Raymond pinched her again. Hard. Then he stepped forward, talking, gesturing and waving his arms dramatically. Telling the story of the explosion, she supposed. None of the Red Boys appeared the least bit shocked, although their round-faced leader nodded sympathetically from time to time. With a final flourish, Raymond pointed at her and mimed blood coming from her nose.

Revulsion, then fear, replaced the indifference on the men's faces. As one, they backed away from her by a good ten feet. Which puzzled her. These men were no strangers to bloodshed. Why would they be squeamish? A bloody nose was trivial. Given that terrorists were blowing up their city, for God's sake.

The smiley-faced leader asked Raymond a question and then glanced over at the teenager to confirm the boy's response. The teenager nodded grudgingly and shot Rose a hostile look.

The man hesitated as if weighing his options. He directed a final, penetrating glance her way before issuing the order.

## 2

JACKSON WOKE to an eerie weightlessness and a massive bang. Then the taxi's front end slammed into the pavement. As if a giant hand had lifted the bumper and then let go. His head jolted forward and then whipped back. A black cloud surrounded the car. Thick smoke poured in. All of this seemed to play out in slow motion.

He coughed and struggled to clear his muddled head. He covered his mouth with his shirt and took stock. Other than ringing ears and smoke-filled lungs, he was unhurt.

"Okay?" he yelled to his driver, who still gripped the wheel with both hands. The driver turned to give him a blank look. Then he opened the door, got out, and disappeared into the billowing smoke.

Jackson climbed out also and slung his duffel over his shoulder. Disoriented, he tried to make sense of the explosion. The traffic jam was gone, as if it had never existed. Turned-over cars had been flung outward from the blast zone. A fiery chunk of mangled metal burned at the center of that soulless place. Several bodies and unidentifiable debris were strewn around the edges.

Then he understood. Not the first time he'd seen the havoc wreaked by a truck bomb. But this was the first time he'd had a front-row seat. A deep chill set in.

He ran like hell and started searching, choking and gagging at what he found. Every body was a corpse or a chunk of one. No wounded here at the center. The bomb had contained nails and various metal objects designed to kill. In the outer circles of the blast zone, people had been maimed.

He found no sign of Rose. He couldn't even find the taxi she'd been in. Increasingly desperate, he widened the search. Maybe her car made it through the roundabout before the bomb went off. But he knew better. Her taxi had to have been up here somewhere, close to the blast.

Other bystanders arrived and grimly joined the hunt. None of the living spoke. No words were adequate. There were many things he didn't know, many things he would never know, but he knew Rose. If she had indeed made it safely through, if she were okay, she'd have gotten out of her taxi and come running back to help. No question in his mind. She'd be here, doing whatever needed to be done.

In the chaos and confusion, he didn't identify the taxi right away. He must have passed it three times before he noticed the furry dice. They lay in the street just past the overturned, burning car. How strange that a meaningless trinket remained intact.

He turned back to the burning car, moving like an old man. He saw it now. He hadn't looked because he hadn't wanted to see. A flipped taxi with a caved-in roof, and all of it fully engulfed. Even if she'd survived the crash, she couldn't have survived the fire.

He landed on his knees alongside the wreck. The smell of burning metal and flesh made him sick. He threw up in the gutter. Flames and heat rose from the wreck and seemed to reach for him. He didn't care. A piece of him— the best part—had been blown away. Leaving nothing but a vast, gaping hole.

Some guy urged him up and steered him to the sidewalk. Jackson could have thrown him off with very little effort but didn't see much point. He sat on the curb with his head in his hands. His chest was lead. He couldn't accept this.

He couldn't. After all this time apart, they'd had one wretched moment in which he was too proud and she was too stubborn to even say *hello*. Their story couldn't end this way. It was too cruel. They'd been so close.

Sirens squealed somewhere nearby and he knew then his hearing, at least, would recover. Right beside him, a thin stream of blood dripped off the curb. He looked around and found the source. A woman sat against a wall—the lady who'd sold him water—with blood gushing from a wound on her thigh. She cradled her crying baby and clutched her empty basket as if it were a lifeline. The kid kept crying and the woman's blood kept flowing. Jackson could see the life draining out of her. At this rate, she wouldn't make it.

He got up, walked over, and spoke matter-of-factly. "I'm going to help you." Obviously in shock, she stared without seeing him. Then he remembered she was Cameroonian and switched to French. "Je vais vous aider."

She blinked and met his eyes.

He grabbed a clean t-shirt from his bag and tied it above the wound. As he worked, he kept talking, asking her name, then her baby's name. Mainly just to keep her awake. She didn't answer right away but her brow furrowed. A good sign.

"Colette," she said finally. "Et Moses."

The bleeding had slowed. Even so, her dark skin became more and more ashen. Emergency responders were arriving but not nearly enough of them. By the time they got to her, it would be too late.

He wasn't going to let this woman die. Not on his watch. He crossed his duffel bag on his back, put Moses in the basket, placed the basket in the woman's arms and picked them up, kit and caboodle. He staggered, re-balanced, and then found his stride.

Several women trotted after him, shouting in English and French. They didn't trust him with their friend. His answers must have satisfied them because soon he was leading a small parade of women and kids away from the roundabout.

For once in his life, he was grateful for his brawn. And for something to do. The physical challenge of carrying his burdens would take everything he had. And these burdens were nothing. Nothing compared to the other, older burdens he fully expected to carry until the day he died. He allowed himself one backward glance at the place where he'd lost a chunk of himself on the burning asphalt, as surely as if he'd lost a limb.

He hesitated. It felt wrong to just leave Rose there. How could he leave her all alone?

The baby started to cry. Jackson suddenly realized that he carried baby Moses in a basket. If God was watching, He had a very dark sense of humor.

They were less than a block away from the roundabout when the second bomb blew. Chunks of concrete and debris landed right behind them. He looked at the women and they looked at him, dumbstruck.

A hush. Then screams. Another cloud billowed and spread, its churning evil headed right for them. They all started to run and didn't look back.

~

Rose didn't know what Raymond said to those scary guys but it had worked. The men lost interest in hassling them further. Not a minute too soon. Sporadic vibrations rattled the windows and buildings they passed. All hell was breaking loose in this city.

After ten minutes at a dead run, the boy pulled her inside a building. The side entrance to a hospital, she guessed, judging by the antiseptic smell. She held her aching sides and leaned against a wall, relieved to catch her breath somewhere cool and safe. An oasis of sanity.

"Are we close to the Continental?" she asked.

Raymond ignored her and peered down the dim corridor.

She tried again, speaking louder, though she couldn't be sure. "Are you ready to go back outside?"

This time he met her eyes and shook his head.

She didn't hesitate. "Yes, you're right, you should stay. Don't worry, I'll wait while you call your mom or dad."

He shook his head again and his lower lip trembled. Poor kid had behaved heroically but it was time for them to go their separate ways.

She went on in what was probably a very loud voice. "We'll ask to use the phone here. Your parents must be very worried about you."

Raymond didn't acknowledge her. Instead, he ran down to a nurse's station and spoke to a woman there. The woman leaned out to stare at her.

Rose assumed the woman understood she didn't require medical attention. After all, she wouldn't be standing here if she did. Even though her clothes were ripped and her face was a mess, nothing was wrong with her that a bath, bandages and a pain reliever—or two—couldn't fix. The trauma was another matter altogether. Only time would heal that. Right now, all she needed was the safety of her hotel room.

She went back to the door and checked outside. The afternoon light had dimmed. No one on the street at all. No vehicle traffic either. If things were dangerous now, they'd be twice as dangerous after dark. Time to get her bearings and get going.

She turned around with a start. Two figures in biohazard suits and masks marched in her direction. They reminded her of aliens. Every square inch of skin was covered. Instead of continuing past, they stopped beside her. One of the aliens bobbed his head and his mask moved at the same time. He was looking right at her so he must have spoken.

She pointed to her ear. "Sorry, I can't hear too well right now. The bombs, you know." She craned her neck to locate Raymond. He'd disappeared and in his place were two women dressed in scrubs and masks, watching her.

That's when the men grabbed her.

~

When she woke in the middle of the night, fluorescent lights from the ward outside her room illuminated a crack in the ceiling right above her. Just a crack. Not shaped like a rabbit. Not like the one above little Madeleine's Paris hospital bed. Yet another example of her selective memory. She remembered details from a children's storybook but not who she was or how she'd landed in this mess. The bigger mess, that is.

Her immediate predicament was marginally less mysterious.

She must have seemed a wild animal to the men in the biohazard suits, screaming questions and unable to hear any answers. They wasted no time moving her to a room marked "Quarantine" and put her in restraints while they drew a blood sample.

Eventually they untied her and left her alone in a small, sterile room furnished with a bed, table and chair and a tiny bathroom. One exterior window let in natural light; it was set too high on the wall to see outside. A door porthole gave her a limited view of a large ward adjacent to her room. As far as she could see, none of the beds were occupied and only one nurse, a gloved and masked woman with a regal bearing came in and out.

After banging on the door and yelling for a while, Rose calmed down enough to see sympathetic distress in the woman's eyes. Rose did her best to convey her bewilderment with hand gestures. Then she mimed writing.

Taking the hint, the nurse wrote out a note and held the paper against the tiny window in the door.

*You may be suffering from a highly contagious virus. We regret the necessity for quarantine. At first opportunity, you will be seen by a doctor who will answer your questions. Unfortunately, all doctors are attending to victims of the bombing earlier today. I will deliver first aid supplies and tomorrow you will be seen by a doctor. Please stay calm and know that we will assist you to the best of our ability.*

When Rose mouthed the words "WHAT VIRUS?" the nurse hesitated and then wrote two words.

*Lassa fever.*

And that was all. Rose had no idea what Lassa fever was but she intended to learn, as soon as she got access to the internet. Raymond must have claimed she had a contagious virus. The deception confused her.

One thing she felt certain of—someone had made a big mistake. The guys in the biohazard suits had taken her temperature and it was normal.

An hour after they locked her in, someone had delivered a tray via a wall cubby that Rose could open only after the other side was locked. They'd given her a simple meal of fried plantains and sweet potatoes covered with an oily sauce. Two paper cups contained pills. By then exhausted and ravenous, Rose ate a few bites of the food but didn't touch the pills. She put the tray back in the compartment and found a hospital gown there, along with a short note that explained the pills were pain medicine and an anti-viral.

Her whole body ached from the residual effects of the explosion. Every time she recalled the things she'd seen today, she wished for oblivion. The blown-up body parts and shocked faces of survivors were etched in her brain. How ironic that these ghastly new memories were stamped into fresh cement. Unless she experienced another bout of amnesia, these new memories would be fixed in her head for the rest of her life.

She stared at the pills for a while and then gulped them all down. Eventually, she stripped off her ripped bloody clothes, showered, and pulled on the hospital gown. She tied every possible ribbon and collapsed on the bed.

She didn't know how long she slept. Maybe a few hours. Now she was wide awake. The ward outside her door had gone dark, with no one in sight. She tossed and turned in her narrow bed, longing for something she couldn't identify and practically choking on fear and loneliness.

At first she thought the aches and pains from her face-plant yesterday might have woken her. Or perhaps anxiety and fear. Then there were the horrific sights that replayed in her mind.

However, none of those things had roused her from a deep, drug-induced slumber. It was a strange low voice in her head. Her own name—*Rose*—whispered again and again. The whisper—a voice she sensed, rather than heard—called her name with an agonized intensity that hurt her in some dark, inexplicable way.

She blinked at the crack in the ceiling. Two possibilities—okay, three—occurred to her.

Possibility one. She was dreaming an especially vivid dream. That seemed unlikely because the whispers were in the same voice she'd heard right before the encounter with the Red Boys. Plus, she wasn't asleep. The scabs on her palms itched—an irritating reminder of her conscious state.

Possibility two. This was an elaborate hallucination, induced by the day's trauma and/or the painkillers. That might explain it.

Possibility three. She had lost her mind. Maybe she really had gone cuckoo. How else could she explain a voice that wasn't a voice at all? It seemed more of an expression of torment. If so, she could not confide in anyone here. She wasn't going to give them another reason to keep her prisoner.

She got up and paced around her room, ready to tear her hair out, loathing the sensation of being trapped and imprisoned. If not out of this room, she needed to get the hell out of her own head. Look forward. Plan her next move.

Moonlight spilled in from the high window above her bed. If she could only see what was going on outside, she'd have a better idea of what to expect in the morning. If there was a coup in progress, she'd see some indication. Lights or smoke. Something.

She started by sliding the table against the wall. Then she placed the chair on top of that and climbed up. Still not high enough. She got down, hauled the table onto the bed, put the chair on top and then stood to test her weight.

Balanced on her tiptoes, she now had a decent view of the moon and a partial view of whatever lay some twenty feet below. Which turned out to be nothing but a walled garden with benches and jungle-like plants. Disappointed, she turned her attention to the horizon. No unusual lights or flares. No hints of any attacks or gun battles raging in the city under the same starry sky.

A flicker of blue light caught her eye and pulled her gaze downward. Someone sat on a bench partially obscured by tree ferns. A broad-shouldered man with his head bent over a device of some sort. A phone probably.

Nice to know she wasn't the only one who couldn't sleep. He got up and began to pace around the walled garden. He was tall and muscle-bound and moved with surprising grace for a large man. His hair was longish, almost to his shoulders.

Strangely, she began to relax. The voice in her head diminished into a low hum. Her spirits lightened. For no logical reason. Except perhaps a sense of kinship and connection to another restless soul. Her fellow traveler prowled around the tiny space like a caged tiger.

The noise in her head stopped. Right when the man halted, pivoted and looked up.

She dropped out of sight. Then felt ridiculous. So she went back up on her tiptoes and lifted her hand in a sheepish salute.

He went very still. After a couple of beats, he rocked back on his heels. A flash of white in the dark. Yep, that was a smile. A broad grin, more like. Her scrapes and bruises must be an interesting sight. In a train wreck sort of way.

She peered into the murky garden, trying to decide why he seemed familiar. Without her glasses, she couldn't be sure. As if reading her mind, he moved into a clear patch of moonlight. She immediately recognized him—the tourist from the embassy. What in the world was he doing down there in the middle of the night? Maybe he had the virus, too. But if that were so, he wouldn't be out there free as a bird, would he?

He stared at her for what seemed like a long time, though probably no more than a minute. She stared back, curious to see what he'd do next and grateful for any human contact. It meant a great deal that someone else knew she was up here, cut off from the world, trapped in quarantine. Her loneliness—as familiar as the anger she'd experienced earlier—lessened somewhat.

Head tipped back, he folded his arms against his chest and watched her. That steadfast gaze suggested patience and intelligence. An observer. A lazy grin came and went but his focus never strayed. The shadows obscured most of his features. His eyes, however, glistened as if wet, a trick of reflected moonlight, she supposed.

The minute wore on. Each waited to see who would blink first. She laughed under her breath, trying not to break eye contact. How crazy was this? Two strangers far from home, playing a kids' game. He laughed too, and she was sorry she couldn't hear him. His laugh would be deep, she thought, a warm rumble emanating from that broad chest.

Her knees trembled from the strain of standing on tiptoe. Determined not to lose the staring game, she rebalanced, forgetting that she teetered on a chair stacked on a table stacked on a bed.

## 3

ROSE WOKE to a series of clicks and scrapes. She immediately identified the sounds as someone unlocking the wall compartment and a tray sliding inside.

Wait, what? She *heard* the tray. Giddy with this discovery, she jumped out of bed and tried the door—still locked—and then checked the porthole window.

The big ward, so dark and empty last night, now buzzed with activity and something of a party atmosphere. Children of various ages bounced on the beds. They were all in street clothes. Two or three older kids wandered about the ward, playing with whatever medical equipment they could reach. None of the children looked sick.

She listened hungrily to their chatter. While not perfect, her hearing had improved enough to distinguish between their muffled voices. Two nurses circulated through the ward, scolding the kids and trying to keep them in line. They wore ordinary scrubs. No biohazard suits, no masks, nothing. So whatever ailed those children, they didn't have Lassa fever.

Which raised the question—why would the staff put the children so close to her if *she* had a highly contagious disease? And why hadn't they done anything more than a blood test last night? No doctor had seen her yet. Of course they would be tending to those wounded in the bombings, but surely today a doctor would make rounds. Now that she could communicate, she'd get some answers.

After a breakfast of a small sticky doughnut-like pastry and coffee, she showered and put the same hospital gown on. She was going to have to do something about clothes. Hers were ruined.

A cursory glance in the mirror confirmed the shallow cuts and scrapes on her nose, mouth and cheeks were crusting over. She applied bandages to the worst patches and changed the ones on her hands and knees. The fresh bruises from her tumble off the bed last night weren't too bad. In short, she was a mess, but things could be worse.

In fact, she felt better than she looked. Even though her memory bank remained stubbornly closed, she now knew a few things about herself. Despite her name, she wasn't a delicate flower, at least not in temperament.

With nothing else to do, she made her bed and re-arranged the furniture she'd trashed. The chair and table weren't broken, just battered. Like her.

A nurse tapped on the window and held up a notepad.

*Doctor will be here soon.*

Rose checked that every ribbon on her hospital gown was tied tightly. She'd get some answers and get herself out of here. The sooner she got back to the embassy, the sooner she'd have a new passport.

A prickling at the base of her skull got her up and pacing. It wouldn't be long now. Sure enough, within fifteen minutes, a deep voice could be heard out in the ward.

She went to the porthole and plastered her face against the glass. Over in the corner, just within her sightline, a man was hunched over a tablet device. A curtain of long, dark hair hid his face but she recognized him right away. Her staring contest buddy. The same guy she'd seen at the embassy and again last night.

She rapped on the window, willing him to look up, to come over and help get her out of here. He lifted his head. When he flicked a glance in her direction, she got her hopes up.

But he didn't get up. He stayed where he was, oblivious to her repeated knocking. Totally absorbed in whatever was on his screen, he ignored her and the kids who pestered him, jumping back and forth over his outstretched legs.

~

Jackson knew exactly when she spotted him, even before he raised his head and before she started knocking to get his attention. This uncanny awareness of her was a weird fucking phenomenon. Last night some impulse had told him to look up at the very window where her bright hair caught and held the moonlight. Even while profound relief flooded him, he had wondered if some part of him had known she wasn't dead. Known right where to find her.

Of course this awareness might be wishful thinking on his part. Their families had often remarked upon their spooky, near-telepathic connection. The standard joke was that he and Rose were joined at the hip. To him, in those early years, their bond had felt like an inexorable magnetic pull. Now, he dismissed the idea that their connection had powered up again. Given their history, it was a dangerous illusion.

He couldn't have been more than five or six when Rose started appearing in his back yard when his parents were brawling. She would simply climb the magnolia and wait for him to come out. Then they'd escape to her house. When his father came looking, they were usually curled up in a bean bag chair asleep or watching cartoons hand in hand.

He'd done the same for her, showing up when her brothers picked on her. When she needed him, he somehow knew it and vice versa. Then she'd moved away and that connection disintegrated. When they'd met again years later as young adults, everything was different. Complicated.

In the cold, clear light of day, he filed last night's moonlight meeting under coincidence. A fluke. They had ended up at the same hospital because they'd both survived a terrorist bombing in a city with very few hospitals. Nothing mysterious about that.

Upon arriving at the hospital, he had taken Colette and her baby inside for treatment. After herding the rest of the gang into the overflow tent, he'd gone out to that courtyard to grieve and decide how and what to tell Rose's family.

Later, after she'd disappeared from the window, he'd chatted up the nurses. When they told him about the American woman with a suspected case of Lassa Fever, he'd known immediately the diagnosis did not compute. First off, there were very few cases in this country at the moment. The dry season was only just beginning and the virus typically didn't peak until spring. Also, if she did have a deadly virus, she wouldn't have been at the embassy yesterday.

Assuming the contagious virus claim was a ploy, Rose had chosen well. A quarantine unit was as safe a place as any. Overnight fighting had ignited a volatile mix of vigilante militias, frightened soldiers, and extremist rebels. This morning the current government was crumbling faster than all his intelligence contacts had forecast and insurgents were gaining the upper hand. From here on in, he intended to trust his own data over that of other sources, including his embassy contacts.

This new information changed everything. Now he expected weeks of bloodshed, if not months. To make matters worse, to the rebels, every Westerner was either a potential spy or a potential hostage. He really had no choice but to extract Rose from this geopolitical quicksand and execute a speedy departure plan.

If her illness wasn't a ruse, he'd simply adjust his plan. Better to send her to a secure location and the closest U.S. military hospital than to let her stay here. He wasn't overly concerned about his own exposure to the virus. Lassa Fever wasn't fatal for most adults.

Busting her out of the quarantine unit wouldn't be a problem. No, what worried him was whether Rose would come willingly. It would be just like her to dig in her heels and refuse to leave her do-gooder life behind.

~

Two clicks announced the arrival of her tray. Expecting more fried bananas, Rose opened the cubby door without enthusiasm and found a tablet computer. She pounced. Onscreen was an article about Lassa fever, its symptoms and treatment.

She looked out the porthole, intending to thank the nurse and saw that the ward had quieted down considerably. Most of the children were gathered around the American to watch him draw on a sketch pad. She couldn't see what it was that had them all so enthralled. He stopped and held the sketch pad up so the kids could see. They erupted in delighted laughter, demanding more. He flipped the page and resumed sketching.

Clearly, she should not expect any help from that quarter. The wordless exchange—those moments that meant so much to her last night—hadn't had much of an impact on him. Or maybe he spied on women through hospital windows all the time.

She sat on the bed and started to read about Lassa Fever.

Five minutes later, she went to the door and started pounding. The kids and the dark-haired man looked in her direction once or twice but did exactly nothing.

Her fist started to hurt so she switched to the tablet, whacking the door repeatedly, not hard enough to break the window but loud enough that they couldn't ignore her. The tall nurse with regal posture appeared outside the porthole. With her hands on her hips and a stern expression, she presented an intimidating figure.

Rose had been through too much to back down now. She called through the glass, "I'm not sick. I don't have a fever. Why am I in here and when do I see a doctor?"

The nurse checked up and down the corridor and then lifted her palm to indicate Rose would have to wait five minutes.

It was closer to ten minutes before the nurse returned. Meanwhile, Rose used the tablet to search for news. She found a bare bones news site from a neighboring country. Two short paragraphs reported the roundabout bombing yesterday and some "civil unrest" overnight. The report stated the suicide bomber was believed to be a rebel insurgent. And that was all. They reported nothing about mobs of gunmen wandering the abandoned city streets or about any attempt to overthrow the government.

She started over, scanning search results for international news sites that featured actual reporting. Over and over, error messages came up. Her internet connection was gone.

A tall figure in a protective suit hovered in the porthole, startling her. Until she recognized the stern nurse. Another woman unlocked the door, waited for her to enter and then quickly locked it again.

The nurse's eyes were calm and watchful behind her goggles.

"Thank you for lending me your tablet," Rose said. "My name is Rose Slater."

"I am Nurse Okeke. I did not provide that. Your friend did."

"I have no friends here."

"Don't you?" The nurse's eyes crinkled with amusement.

"What—you mean that guy out there? It's his? Huh. Interesting. Anyway, I appreciate the care you've taken but I've got to tell you, I don't have this Lassa Fever. Honestly, I'm not sick. This is all a big mistake."

The nurse merely nodded and gestured for Rose to continue.

"I don't have a fever and none of the major—or even minor—signs," Rose said quickly, expecting to be challenged.

Nurse Okeke wagged her finger. "In fact you did. Deafness is a common symptom of Lassa Fever."

"I was deaf because a bomb went off right behind me."

"Ah. You were at the roundabout? The boy did not tell me that."

"I don't belong in quarantine," Rose said.

"I agree," Nurse Okeke said.

Rose did a double take. "You do?"

"We are fortunate to have a rapid diagnostic test for Lassa Fever. I ran it this morning."

"If you already knew I'm not contagious, why bother with all that protective gear you're wearing?"

"To keep you safe for as long as I can."

"From what? I don't understand."

The nurse nodded. "I can see that. I can also see that it will be impossible to protect you from yourself."

Whatever that meant. Rose thanked her unlucky stars she'd kept quiet about her amnesia. Now that the virus misunderstanding was cleared up, she saw no reason to bring it up. All that mattered now was getting to the embassy. "So I can leave?"

"Yes, but you must wait for the doctor to discharge you. After the bombing yesterday, we had many critically wounded admitted. More came in overnight, mostly soldiers. All available doctors must stay in the trauma center until further notice—by health minister's order." Her compressed lips made her opinion of that directive clear.

"*Was* there a coup last night?"

"Perhaps. Many homes and businesses burned. Government soldiers fought insurgents and left their dead bodies in the streets. A curfew goes into effect this evening. After that, all transit is restricted. Everyone but health care workers and police must go home at sunset and stay there."

"All the more reason for me to get over to the embassy as soon as possible and get a new passport."

"Even that might be risky. Have you considered why the boy claimed you had Lassa Fever?"

"Speaking of the boy," Rose said. "His name is Raymond. He was going to call his mom to come get him. Do you know what happened to him?"

"I know his name. You have bigger problems than that child. Although, I must say, it is a strange turn of events that Raymond was the one to bring you here. Miss, we live in difficult times. An extraordinary evil has come into our country. Evil like this requires good people to take extraordinary measures. You have so much to learn."

"Undoubtedly," Rose said, without sarcasm. Far be it from her to argue with this older and wiser lady. Rose was willing to bet all the doctors here were scared of Nurse Okeke. This woman looked like she could kick some serious metaphorical ass. Although upon closer inspection, the nurse wasn't really that old. Her height and bearing simply gave that impression.

The nurse paused to make sure she had Rose's full attention. "Above all, you must learn to forgive yourself. Once you do, you can honor the gifts you will be offered. Love is your best hope."

Rose nodded as if enlightened, mainly to be polite. What love? She'd seen precious little evidence in her hotel room of any close relationships. Certainly nothing among her possessions. Not even a package of condoms. The contents of her suitcase could have belonged to a nun. Her only dress was a black polyester drip-dry number, more practical than sexy.

Nurse Okeke's eyes crinkled up and she studied Rose for a long moment. "I will find some clean clothes for you. Do not share our discussion with anyone else. You understand what I'm saying?"

"Not really," Rose said pleasantly.

The nurse clicked her tongue. "You are lucky someone is watching over you."

Rose let out a long, shaky sigh. While she envied the nurse's spiritual beliefs, she knew better. No one watched over her. Even the aid organization she worked for hadn't checked on her welfare.

"After you are dressed," the nurse said, "you may go outside and join Jackson and the children. Stay close to your mighty friend."

Rose chuckled at her word choice. "He may be mighty but he is not my friend. What is this Jackson guy doing here, anyway? Why is he hanging around the ward? He's not a patient, right?"

"No. He saved fifteen souls from the second bomb yesterday, including my cousin and her son. They would not be alive today if he had not been there to lead them away from danger. When I met him last night and learned he needed shelter, I brought him up to the ward. While you slept, we shared coffee." She looked deep into Rose's eyes and added, "Try to remember that your man does not know his purpose here yet."

*"Her man?"* If anyone other than this dignified woman had phrased it that way, Rose would have cracked up. She settled for a noncommittal "Mmm-hmm."

"The children are playing football outside. Not American football. Real football. You can make yourself useful until it is safe for you to leave."

Rose wasn't about to argue that point, either. Better to go along with her orders for now. The formidable nurse obviously wielded more power than her position would suggest. Flying under the radar must suit her purposes.

"Why are all those children here?" Rose said. "They're not sick, are they?"

"They are orphans whose home was burned and looted last night. Outside these walls, they are in great danger."

"But why them, in particular?"

The nurse regarded her for a moment, as if debating with herself. Beads of sweat and condensation had gathered beneath her goggles and mask. Finally, she said in a low voice, "The insurgents take our children, especially those with no family. The boys are forced to become soldiers; the girls are given to men to be so-called wives. We must protect these children. We are their family now. All of us."

~

Rose dressed in the smallest size scrubs the nurses could find and she still swam in them, even after cinching and rolling fabric and securing the pant legs with rubber bands. The plastic clogs they delivered were a tad too tight but still preferable to her blood-soaked sneakers. There was also a long batik scarf that the younger nurse insisted on threading through her hair.

When she finally stepped out of the quarantined room, it was close to noon. The air outside her room wasn't cool but it was fresh. She inhaled deeply, almost drunk on freedom. The nurses stared at her as if they'd never seen a person smile before. Maybe they didn't get a whole lot of that in their line of work. They unlocked the heavy ward doors to let her out and she practically skipped down the stairs, trying not to notice the pain in her knees.

Things outside these walls could very well be more stable than Nurse Okeke believed. Rose intended to see for herself. If the streets were reasonably safe, she planned to depart. The walk here yesterday had been a long one, but if she caught a ride—any ride—even on one of those three-wheeled tricycle taxis, she'd reach the embassy in a few minutes.

On the way down, she recalled her lost wallet. She'd have to hit up her "friend" for a small loan. She couldn't count on winning him over with her winsome charms, that was for sure. A person would have to be pretty hard-hearted to turn down a fellow countryman in trouble.

She pushed through the stairwell door into the baking mid-day heat, then paused. Her view of the surrounding city was unfortunately hidden by a chain link fence laced with canvas. Inside the enclosure, an open-air pavilion served as a makeshift clinic or possibly a waiting room. A few people milled around under the corrugated iron roof.

Beyond that, a dirt clearing served as a playground. A group of children sat under a tree and another, older group played soccer with an improvised ball made of tightly coiled rags.

And there he was—the American. Jackson, the nurse had called him. He played as a team of one, opposite seven little boys. He'd tied his hair back and the dark ponytail whipped around like a living thing. She watched him dribble around two defenders for a breakaway, surprisingly fast and light on his feet for such a big guy.

One of the older boys managed to catch up with him, shouting, "Jackson, you will go down in defeat."

Jackson dribbled straight at the boy, faked left, then put the ball through the boy's legs, into an invisible net marked by a couple of broken chairs.

As they continued to play, the boy trailed after Jackson and kept up a steady stream of trash talk. "You are bigger than an elephant and slower than a mama."

"Yeah? Well, you're no Cristiano Ronaldo yourself," Jackson called.

Another, smaller boy tried to take him down with an American-style football tackle but Jackson was ready for him. He placed his hand on the little boy's forehead, easily holding him at arm's length while the kid windmilled his arms and ran in place.

The insults continued to fly and Rose marveled at the sheer quantity and creativity. Some of the kids were laughing so hard at their own jokes that they gave up playing altogether to roll around in the dirt, holding their sides. She too was hooting and cheering, so elated to be out of lock-up she couldn't stop smiling. Standing under a broiling sun was way more fun than she would have thought possible, even under these circumstances.

Jackson looked up and noticed her on the sidelines. His face changed in a blink. All the joy and liveliness there vanished and he appeared almost angry. She had the distinct impression he wished her anywhere but here. With an inner shrug, she smiled wider just to spite him. She didn't need him to like her; she only needed him to lend her some cash.

He abruptly quit playing and stood in the middle of the field, ignoring the kids pulling on his sleeve while he checked his phone. What on earth had given her the impression she'd shared a poignant moment with this stranger last night? Must have been the pain pills. Add it to the list: *Weird shit that happened to me in Africa.*

She wandered to the perimeter fence and peeked through a rip in the fabric. What she saw encouraged her. People were going about their business. A woman selling oranges swayed down the street under the weight of a crate. Passing traffic seemed light, although this did appear to be a back street, perhaps a service entrance. The streets appeared safe enough to go ahead and take her chances out there.

A squeal of brakes caught her attention. She pushed the canvas flap wider to see a large truck with an open bed pull up and park with two wheels on the sidewalk. Three men carrying automatic rifles slammed out. Dressed in camouflage fatigues and combat boots, the soldiers were headed for the hospital's main building. She couldn't see their faces; however, their body language spoke volumes. They weren't afraid of anyone or in any particular hurry. If those were government troops, order had been restored and the city was returning to normal. If they were the militant insurgents the nurse had mentioned, the shit had hit the fan.

Concealed by the canvas, Rose followed them, walking parallel, hoping to learn something useful.

"How do you know they are here?" one of them said.

"They ran away last night, quick-quick like little rats," said another. "I am certain this is where they came. They know that old auntie will hide them."

Rose instinctively checked the far side of the clearing. The children stood in the shade, about fifteen boys and girls, laughing and teasing one another.

Jackson—where was Jackson? She needed—

She gasped when someone grabbed her from behind. Hard fingers dug into her upper arms and gave her a bone-jarring shake. She sputtered. "Hey, what are you—"

The hands whirled her around and Jackson loomed over her. His infuriated whisper felt like a roar. "Can't you stay out of trouble for five minutes? What is wrong with you?"

"Let. Go," she said through gritted teeth.

He released her and kept his hands raised, spreading them wide, making some lame-ass point only he understood.

She shook off her irritation. "Whatever your problem is, whatever that was about—I don't care. Just don't do it again."

She shaded her eyes. Something else in his expression—besides the anger—confused her. Whatever it was, they didn't have time for it. She needed an ally and he was her best hope.

"They're here," she said. "And they're coming for those kids."

# 4

JACKSON WANTED TO THROTTLE HER. She was as impulsive and stubborn as ever.

"That was unbelievably stupid," he said. "All they had to do was look over and see your feet trotting along under the canvas. Don't you ever stop to think before you act?"

"Put a cork in it," she said. "You don't even know me." Her gaze was steady and those green eyes were nothing if not calm.

Her patronizing tone caught him off guard. He knew then he had it all wrong. She *had* changed. Because the old Rose would have yelled right back at him. This one kept her cool.

"I've got to get those children inside," she said and broke into an awkward gallop, favoring one of her knees.

He lengthened his stride, keeping up easily. He suspected the injuries she'd sustained yesterday were the least of her problems. Up close she was more of a wreck than he'd guessed. *Look at her.* All scraped up and pathetic. If he hadn't known how beautiful she'd been—if he was meeting her for the first time today—perhaps he wouldn't be so shocked. The pretty red-gold hair he'd loved was a dull mop chopped off above her shoulders. Her formerly lush body now resembled a stick figure, much like the ones he'd drawn for the kids earlier. She'd run herself into the ground well before that bomb had detonated.

She slowed. "I'm Rose, by the way."

"Seriously? You're gonna' keep up this pretense?"

She gave him a sideways glance. Something flickered there in her eyes, like a question she didn't want to ask. Or an answer she didn't want to hear. Whatever lurked beneath the surface—it frightened her. Instinct told him her fear had nothing to do with any immediate threat.

"What pretense?" she asked.

"The one where you play dumb and act as if you don't recognize me."

"Of course I remember you from last night," she said. "And the embassy yesterday. Listen, we've got bigger problems. I heard those men talking. They know our nurse is protecting the children. And for some reason, they're after those kids. This is no joke. It's real."

"I'm glad you understand," he said. "Because the situation has changed, even in the last hour. Since you're apparently not sick after all—and your hearing's improved—how about you drop the act. We need to get our asses in gear." So much for playing it cool and not showing his hand. How did she get under his skin so quickly? He couldn't remember the last time he'd felt this irritated with someone.

Rose spared him an incredulous glance. "Drop what act?" By now they'd reached the mango tree and she began to herd the younger children together.

He kept his temper with an effort. "I guess you wouldn't have heard—the airport's closing in a few hours. Plus, as of five minutes ago, all communications in this city are down—no landlines, no mobile, no wireless, no broadband. It's a bad sign. So we're done farting around, all right? We're getting the hell out."

"First I need to make sure these kids are safe," she said. "And then I'm going to the embassy to throw myself on their mercy. I lost my passport yesterday. Listen, I'll be fine. You can do what you want."

He laughed without humor. "Do what I want? If that was an option, I wouldn't be here at all."

"Jackson, no one's forcing you to stay."

"Ha. You said my name. So you do know me."

"Yes, because the nurse told me your name before I came downstairs."

Seeing her mulish expression, a look he knew too well, he changed tack. "All embassy employees are evacuating. I've already arranged for two seats on the last transport out of the country."

Her eyes widened.

"There's a C-17 coming in from Germany this afternoon," he said, "and believe me, that plane will not wait on the tarmac a minute longer than necessary. These insurgents are just crazy enough to launch a missile strike at such a big, fat target. We need to go straight to the airport in case the departure time gets moved up."

Still eyeing him as if he were a lunatic, she said, "Go on ahead. Suit yourself."

"I'm not leaving without you."

"Then help me with the children," she said sharply, "or get out of my way."

Too pissed off to speak, Jackson stalked over to corral the soccer players and to send one of the older kids ahead to knock on the ward door. He'd noticed last night that the interior door was kept locked. One could exit but not enter. Ostensibly due to the quarantine.

"Why do we have to go inside now?" one of the boys asked. "We want to keep playing. I think you are afraid, Jackson. You know we will beat you bloody."

"Yeah, I'm terrified," Jackson said. "I can't take any more punishment. I'll be crying in a minute."

He scanned the hospital grounds. No sign of soldiers or any unusual activity. In fact, the whole place had quieted down considerably. His height allowed him a view of the adjacent street as well. Traffic was nonexistent, except for a beat-up sedan pulling up outside the fence.

Two unarmed civilians got out, a teenage boy and a younger kid. Although it was unusual to see a boy that age driving a car here, he didn't appear to be a threat.

He looked to see what was keeping Rose. She was still under the mango tree with three little girls, helping the youngest one put on her shoes. He'd met the girls earlier: orphaned sisters who were inseparable. Where one went, the other two followed. They even dressed alike.

When he beckoned, Rose gestured to indicate he should go on without her.

He glanced around. This sudden quiet rang his alarm bells. The most reliable barometer of imminent danger was often the most mundane or minor pattern change. The guy who sold sweets to the hospital staff had disappeared in the last five minutes, as had the groundskeepers. If Jackson had learned anything in his checkered career, it was to watch the locals.

These kids needed cover. Now.

He led the children inside. Nurse Okeke waited at the top of the stairs, already counting heads. She'd posted a handwritten quarantine sign on the door warning of a Lassa fever outbreak.

"Soldiers just arrived," he said in a low aside. "Rose heard them talking. She thinks they're after these kids." The nurse nodded briskly, unsurprised. He added, "You know if those men really want in, that sign won't keep them out."

"I have been expecting this," she said. "I have a plan."

"There's three more kids coming," he said. "Wait, here they are."

Three little girls marched up the stairs. Alone.

Jackson swore and started down, nearly tripping over his own feet as he took the stairs four at a time.

"Hurry," the nurse called after him. "Once this starts, we open the door for no one. Not even you."

He burst outside and the extreme hush of the hospital grounds unnerved him. He didn't see her. Where the hell had she gone?

Movement on the far side of the open-air pavilion answered his question. She had stopped to chat with the two boys he'd seen getting out of the car. Chatting. At a time like this. He wondered how much more he could take. Either he was going to kill her or hog-tie her for her own safety.

Even from this distance he noticed how the older one, a gangly teenager, stood too close to Rose, crowding her. Her head was turned and all her attention was focused on the younger boy. The teenager edged behind her, then hooked his arm around her neck.

Jackson started to run.

~

Rose tugged at the arm pinned across her throat and looked to Raymond for help. His resigned expression made her stomach drop. He'd saved her life yesterday. How could he betray her now?

"Solomon is my brother," Raymond said simply. "He knew I lied about the virus. He always knows."

"But why?" she cried, unable to break the skinny teenager's grip. He was stronger than he looked. She'd been so happy to see Raymond again; she'd walked right into this.

"The general said he'd make him a lieutenant," Raymond said, "when he found the American lady spy."

"I'm not a spy!"

The older boy's voice in her ear confused her. "I won't hurt you if you just go along."

"Like hell I will."

The moment she started to scream, he applied pressure to her windpipe. Then he began dragging her away, out of sight of the main building. There was no one else to help her. Anyone with sense had gone to ground.

Jackson would be upstairs with the kids by now. Or maybe he'd already left for the airport. He would be on that last flight tonight, telling people about the woman who'd missed her chance to escape.

She couldn't speak, couldn't breathe. The corner of her mind that still functioned wondered why this teenager was choking her. He wasn't much older than Raymond. He might not even understand what he was supposed to do with a hostage.

Raymond had not budged. He watched as his brother pulled Rose toward a new gap in the fence. The younger boy didn't flinch at the strangled noises she made. Even if she lived to be one hundred years old, she would never forget the sadness in his eyes.

Her vision became dim and hazy as she fought for oxygen. Close to blacking out, she didn't see the large projectile that smashed into Solomon until it struck. The collision freed her from his grip and sent her airborne.

If this was indeed her time to die, it wasn't too bad, she thought. That impact and subsequent flight—sailing up and away, totally free and clear—didn't hurt at all.

Until it did. She landed hard with her back taking the brunt. Her head smacked the ground and she slipped into darkness.

~

Someone carried her. She didn't know where. The destination seemed unimportant. All she wanted to do was sleep. Warmth touched her cheek. She snuggled against something soft and relaxed for the first time in a long time.

Exhaustion pulled her down into darkness. She didn't have to fight, or struggle, or run.

"It's going to be okay." The deep voice soothed her. She believed him.

She dreamed soldiers in red caps chased her into a McDonald's. The restaurant manager handed her a passport and a broom. She asked the man what she was supposed to do with the broom and he told her she couldn't go home until she swept up her mess. Dream logic being what it was, she dutifully swept the McDonald's kitchen. The manager kept pushing and prodding her to go faster and she kept telling him she was doing her best.

Someone kept telling her to wake up. She grumbled and told him off. This annoying person—whoever he was— would not let her rest. She drifted between sleep and awareness, vaguely irritated.

When she finally woke all the way, she was in a pitch-dark room that smelled of disinfectant and various musty odors. Her head hurt and she was sitting on something lumpy and hard.

She reached up to feel the goose egg on the back of her head. As she shifted position, a gruff voice whispered, "Stop that."

She went very still. Jackson's voice. She was sitting on his lap. That particular hard lump under her bottom was an erection. She scrambled off him awkwardly.

Something metallic clattered on the cement floor.

He restrained her. "Quiet," he said, low and urgent.

A thin rectangle of light shone under the door. As her eyes adjusted, she realized this room was actually a closet, only about twenty square feet. Shelves lined the side walls and a jumble of mops, brooms and buckets took up most of the floor space. She sat against a cinder block wall between stacks of buckets that smelled horrible. So nasty she was on the verge of gagging.

"Where are we?" she managed to whisper.

Jackson pinched her, not hard, but enough that she got the message. *Not now.* He kept a hold on her arm as he listened. And then she too picked up a faint, repetitive echo, like footsteps in a stairwell.

A long minute passed. She began to shiver in reaction. He reached over and pulled her against his side. After an initial hesitation, she relaxed. His body heat helped.

The echoing noise grew fainter and then died away.

Jackson kept his arm around her. She was very aware that his large hand rested heavily on her right shoulder, close to her face. He smelled good, like spicy soap, and better than anything else in here.

When he bent down, his lips tickled her ear, making her shiver again. "We're in a closet on the hospital's ground floor. They came running into the building right after I carried you in here."

"Those soldiers we saw earlier?"

She sensed his nod. "A group went upstairs."

"How do you know it's them?"

"Oh, it's them all right."

"What exactly happened out there? Were you the battering ram that knocked me out?"

"Unintentionally." He didn't sound the least bit apologetic.

"What happened to Raymond?" she asked.

"The little one? He ran off. That was an hour ago, at least. You've been out for a while."

"What about his brother?"

"He ran off, too." Jackson motioned for silence. Once again, he seemed to hear something she did not.

Her legs were cramping. Sitting here waiting—not taking action—had to be worse than facing down the soldiers. Well, probably not worse than that, but it sure seemed like it. She straightened, doing her best not to lean on him. After several strained minutes, she sleepily tipped sideways, so far she nearly fell over.

Jackson pulled her upright and she centered her back against the cinder block. The cycle repeated itself. The next time she slumped, she came perilously close to knocking over some aluminum buckets.

Jackson made a huffing sound of exasperation, hooked her around the waist, and pulled her against his side. She stiffened when she realized she wanted to cuddle up against him. What was wrong with her? She didn't know this man.

"Give me a break," he said. "If you fall over and make a racket, we'll be in deep shit. Is it really so difficult to lean on me?"

Recognizing a rhetorical question when she heard one, she tried to relax. There was nothing remotely personal about this. He certainly wasn't going to tip over if she leaned on him. He felt immovable, sturdy as a giant boulder. Still, the undercurrents of annoyance and resentment that flowed from him made her cautious. She sat carefully for a few minutes until her head felt too heavy to support. Forgetting about her goose egg, she tipped her head against the wall. The sudden pain made her jerk forward.

"Enough," he said testily and yanked her against his shoulder.

She gave in this time and let herself rest. His cotton shirt felt soft. Comforting. On an involuntary sigh, she remembered a fragment from her dreams earlier. Or had that been real?

She must have nodded off because next he was shaking her arm.

"You can't fall asleep. I had enough trouble waking you before." He didn't sound real happy about having to look after her. Not that she blamed him.

She covered a yawn. "I don't hear anything. If the bad guys are upstairs, why don't we make a run for it?"

"We're waiting for our ride to the airport. I don't want you out in the open until he gets here. Let me check the status."

"Why me, in particular?"

He paused in the middle of pulling something out of his pocket. "They've identified you as a kidnapping target." He enunciated slowly, as if she were mentally impaired. "Don't you remember what happened outside?"

"Yes," she said, peeved. "I just don't...accept that I'm in any more danger than you are."

"It could have something to do with your work here—you've been giving vaccinations and stuff like that?"

"Uh, yes." She looked away, unwilling to admit he probably knew more than she did and equally unwilling to tell him about her memory loss. She'd told no one except the hotel manager yesterday morning. Then again, no one really cared.

Mindful of the self-pity creeping in, Rose sat up straighter, disgusted with herself. Nope. Not going there. After all, her memory loss was likely temporary. If not quite a first-world problem, amnesia came close. People here had life and death problems to contend with. In any case, she saw no point in sharing her problems with some cranky guy she'd never see again. That is, if they ever got out of this damn closet.

"Why would they want me?" she asked. "I was in the wrong place, that's all."

He frowned. "That blow to your head must have been worse than I thought. There's a lot of suspicion and mistrust towards aid workers in this part of the world. Conspiracy theories abound." He pulled a device from his pocket and started typing, his thumbs a blur of motion.

"Is Raymond's brother one of the insurgents?" she asked.

He spoke absently as he typed. "That teenager who grabbed you? Not necessarily. He could be with a rebel group. Or local vigilantes with no allegiance to anyone. Take your pick. Whoever he is, he obviously doesn't know the American government refuses to pay ransom demands for its citizens. As a policy. Other countries pay, but not ours. If it's money they're after—and it usually is—the kidnappers are shit out of luck."

"As is the hostage," she concluded.

He looked up. "Our ride should be here within ten minutes, barring complications."

She inspected his phone. "How did you organize that already? I thought you said there was no phone service at all. Is it a satellite phone?"

"Among other things."

"But there's no sight line. We're inside."

"I installed an external antenna," he said, studying her. "Last night." He turned back to his device and opened an app of some sort. A colorful grid appeared.

"What is that?" she asked.

"Another view of this building."

Her chin rested on his shoulder while she watched bright orange blobs darting around the grid. The display's 3D rendering included GPS coordinates and other sets of numbers. One could see a blob's location within the building, even its elevation.

"Oh, I see," she said. "Infrared sensor. Those are heat signatures."

He lifted his head as if she'd said something unexpected. Reflected light from his screen danced across the planes of his face. His features were sculpted and...different. Interesting. She hadn't noticed this until now. Even with that fringe on his chin, he was compelling.

Now that he was only inches away, she couldn't help noticing other things about him. His lips were full, in contrast to the hard angles of his cheekbones. His hair was straight and silky, and so long that a lock of it brushed her ear.

Even before he glanced sideways, those sensual lips quirked with amusement while she scrutinized him. Screen forgotten, he turned to look her full in the face. His expression softened.

A sudden flash of yearning sparked between them. A tentative, unformed longing that felt physical, like an ache. He moved closer. For a fraught instant, she thought he might kiss her. He felt this too, she was almost sure of it.

He searched her face. More questions. He tilted his head. A flicker of disappointment followed. The light in his eyes faded.

The moment went by so quickly she might have imagined it. She hadn't, though. Whatever test he'd just applied, she was a "fail." His final verdict could not have been more obvious if he'd shouted the word.

## 5

MESSAGE RECEIVED. They were, after all, squeezed into a tiny, dark room, a circumstance that created false intimacy. Unfortunately, Rose knew she would have kissed him back. A man she barely knew. With armed men searching the building.

Acknowledging that, even to herself, was both painful and humbling. What kind of person was she? Was this normal for her? She retreated a few inches to give him space and he went back to his device. The odd, disorienting exchange had been a conversation, though neither had said a word.

Jackson reminded her of a still, deep pool with powerful hidden currents. A warning floated into her head. *Swim at your own risk.* She would have to be more careful. She had almost jumped into that deep pool. Recklessly. Willingly.

"How do you know about heat signatures?" he asked.

"Beats me," she said, feigning an upbeat tone.

"Turns out not everyone is upstairs. At least one person is on this level with us, about twenty meters away. He—or she—isn't moving around at all but it's smarter to be cautious and stay quiet."

He put the device down, unfolded his legs and changed position. She expected an awkward grunt or two but he moved fluidly. This was a man who knew his body well. Like a dancer, she thought, as unlikely as that seemed.

She stretched her legs too, carefully navigating her feet between the brooms and mops. The pain in her head had diminished. She touched the goose egg and rubbed her fingers together. No blood. She wasn't nauseous, another good indicator. Clearly, she had a hard head.

"I could have told you that," Jackson said.

She jerked in surprise and bumped her head on the wall again.

He laughed softly. "That answers one question." When she just stared at him open-mouthed, he added, "You couldn't have forgotten. This used to happen to us all the time."

She rubbed the back of her head. "What did?"

"Come on," he said. "You know exactly what I'm talking about." His fingers were gentle as he searched her scalp. "You never doubted it before, not even after...everything happened."

"After what happened? Wait, you mean we actually *do* know each other? Why didn't you say so?"

He shushed her.

Frustrated beyond words, she wanted to punch him in the arm. Then she heard what he heard. More footsteps somewhere on this level. Doors opened and shut repeatedly. The sounds of a systematic search.

She held her breath until the noises receded. The searchers were still out there, but it sounded like they'd continued on to a distant hallway, skipping this one.

Jackson got up, unlocked the door and returned to crouch next to her. He'd done it silently, in three seconds flat. How did he do that? She would have knocked over half the contents of this closet. Any normal person would have. Though he looked like a linebacker, he moved like a ninja.

He hunkered in front of her, so close she saw the slow beat of his pulse in his neck. He showed no sign of fear. Certainly not panic.

"Why did you *unlock* it?" she whispered.

"Gives me the advantage. They won't have their guard up."

"But—"

He cut her off. "Believe it or not, I know what I'm doing. Nothing will happen to you—not on my watch."

A burst of raucous laughter directly above them made her jump. He slid his right palm between her shoulders blades and kept it there, solid and warm. She exhaled shakily. He held one finger to his lips and steadied her.

Who was he? His intensity when he spoke to her indicated they'd been close at one time. She'd have to explain why she didn't remember him. Just as well he wasn't the warm and fuzzy type. His chilly attitude would spare her any sympathetic questions about the bombing yesterday or the nightmare of losing her memory. Indifference would be easier to cope with than sympathy.

Doors slammed over and over as the soldiers searched the first floor. She felt the increased tension in Jackson's body though his breathing stayed slow and even. Her own breath came in shallow pants she tried to muffle with her fist.

A new commotion down the hall—soldiers shouting furiously—didn't help. Jackson leaned in close. Even in this light, she saw his grim determination.

"Listen," he said. "I won't let them take you. As long as you keep still, you'll be safe. But you can't argue with my methods. We're doing this my way. Are you with me?"

She wanted to ask why he thought she'd argue and then thought better of it. After all, he knew her. She nodded her agreement.

"No matter what happens," he said, "stay where you are until I'm done with them. As soon as it's quiet again, make a run for it. Turn left into the hallway and go straight to the back door. You might see...things along the way. Don't stop for anything or anyone. Keep your eyes on the goal. Don't wait for me. Head directly for the sliding door exit straight ahead. You can't miss it. Oh, one more thing."

She felt his fingers in her hair as he removed the batik scarf. "I'll need this." He made her repeat his instructions before adding, "Your ride to the airport is an ambulance. They're expecting you."

"But not you?"

"Don't worry about me. If I miss it, I'll get the next one."

She didn't believe that for a second.

~

Jackson cradled her against his chest to balance her weight and prepared to hoist her to the top shelf. She didn't protest. So far, so good.

Then she glanced at him, and what he saw shook him. Her wide-open gaze revealed a trust he hadn't seen in a long, long time. Not since they were kids. She was apprehensive, sure, but nothing fraught. No guilt. No blame. Just faith that he knew what he was doing, along with that same self-possession she'd always shown under pressure.

Relief flooded him like a balm that soothed old wounds. A gift from the universe, as his new friend the nurse would put it. No matter what happened next, Rose trusted him. That meant a great deal. He wasn't sure why it should, but he would take it.

He got on with the business of concealing her. It wasn't difficult to hide her like a pancake in a stack of heavy sheets. As he pushed and rearranged the fabric around her arms, he tried not to notice that her skin had the same baby-soft texture he remembered. Then he accidentally touched the soft curve of her ass through the baggy scrubs. She wasn't wearing underwear.

Other than a quick intake of breath, she stayed quiet.

"Sorry," he muttered and quickly moved to tuck her long legs out of sight. He didn't want to remember the satiny length of her inner thighs or the way he used to slide his hands up and down them every chance he got. Back when he was a hungry nineteen-year-old and never satisfied.

She didn't make a peep while he got busy with his preparations. He could almost hear her thinking, trying to identify what he was doing and connect the dots. *Yeah, good luck with that.*

She began to pant. He paused. Even now, despite knowing she was only hyperventilating, he got hard just listening to her. Mental images appeared—how she'd look in his bed, flushed and yearning—her knees spread to accommodate him while he kissed his way up those long and lovely legs. But any distraction put both their lives in danger.

"For fuck's sake, don't pass out," he said.

She stifled her breathy gasps with only partial success, sounding remarkably like a porn star faking an orgasm.

He repressed a snort. Why this seemed funny he didn't know, nor did he care. Dark humor had helped him keep his sanity so many times he wasn't likely to question the habit now. If he failed today and ended up departing this country in a body bag, he fully expected his warped sense of humor to be in there with him, keeping him company in the afterlife.

As little kids, he and Rose used to laugh so hard she routinely wet her pants and would have to run home to change. Then they'd laugh about that, too. They'd laughed all the time. More accurately, Rose laughed a lot. Him, not so much. Later, after her family moved away, he laughed even less.

Years later, once they'd grown up and met again as young adults, their childhood rapport was effectively gone. She'd stopped laughing at his jokes. Or telling him her secrets. At first he'd been sorry they'd lost the strong link they'd forged as kids. Soon they were too busy finding delight in each other's bodies to do much talking. Or laughing. At the time, he'd accepted the trade-off with every lusty fiber of his being. He'd been too young, horny and self-involved to think deeply about what they'd lost. In the end, sexual infatuation hadn't been enough to sustain them.

The devastating aftermath of her family's tragedy had proven that. She had drop-kicked him out of her life. And never looked back.

And now? Who knew? He didn't understand her games or this business of pretending not to know him, nor did he particularly *want* to understand. With luck, there'd be time later to hash this out. If he survived. The escape window would be a narrow one. He'd get her out safely and if he didn't make it, so be it. He could live with that. Or die.

He moved into position, got his weapon ready, and shut her out of his mind. Since the door opened outward, the soldiers would see him almost right away. The trick would be a distraction—however brief—before the door had opened fully. He tied her scarf to a mop handle.

The searchers were now only three or four doors down, cocky and careless as they slammed in and out of rooms.

Jackson checked his device again. Their ride would be here in five minutes. Other than the two searchers, one heat signature remained downstairs, static, same as before. He assumed that must be a petrified hospital worker. Probably not a threat. The rest of the soldiers were upstairs, hovering too close to the stairwell for his peace of mind.

He could no longer pinpoint the whereabouts of Beatrice Okeke and her charges. He'd identified them earlier as a cluster of blue and orange, huddled in the ward almost directly above them. Now the nurse and the children had disappeared from his screen. Just like that.

~

In the endless seconds while she waited for the door to swing open, Rose stayed flat on her back, fists clenched, with her eyes squeezed shut. When Jackson rebuked her for hyperventilating, she hardly noticed. Every ounce of her concentration went to controlling her body, inhaling and exhaling through pursed lips. Impossible to know if this was her typical reaction to extreme stress. Was she a big baby or a tough cookie? Would knowing make any difference?

The door flew open.

A man's voice at the threshold. Asking a question in words she didn't understand. She heard a quick gasp, followed by a muffled impact. Then a rapid succession of gruesome sound effects. A sickening thump, soft and ripe like a watermelon splitting. A thud when something heavy hit the floor. Another thud.

A man gurgled horribly, just below her. Choking on his own blood. That went on for an endless, ghastly minute. And then he stopped.

There'd been no shouts. No gunshots either. No disturbance loud enough to be heard beyond the closet. The room stayed quiet. She waited a couple of seconds. Was Jackson dead?

A powerful smell—caustic fumes—wafted up to her level. When strong hands lifted her, she released a pent-up breath, recognizing his touch even before she opened her eyes.

"Thank God," she said. The room whirled when he swung her down. Her foot landed on an object that gave way. That wasn't the floor. She looked, recoiled, and tried to jump away. But there was nowhere else to go. Two soldiers lay in a crumpled heap at her feet, surrounded by pooled blood and gore.

She stared. Jackson pressed a damp towel over her nose and mouth. Reacting instinctively, she gasped and fought him.

"No, hold that rag over your face," he said. "I'll come back for you."

He went into the hallway. Rose held her breath, hearing only her own blood pulsing in her ears. Her eyes stung from the noxious fumes and she wanted to throw up. She looked down again and wished she hadn't. A sob escaped her throat.

The men's eyes were still open. One had been impaled by a mop, straight through his throat. The other had a towel crammed into his mouth. Asphyxiated by chemicals, presumably. Her stomach heaved when she saw the scarf she'd been wearing attached to the mop.

Who was Jackson? *What* was he? She'd completely underestimated him. An understatement so colossal she wanted to laugh. He'd killed two men using his bare hands and sundry items from a janitor's closet. With a minimum of fuss.

She stared at the ceiling. As horrifying as this was, she wasn't sorry they were dead. Not at all. These were the same men she'd eavesdropped on earlier. They wouldn't be taking any children anywhere.

When Jackson returned, she practically leaped into his arms. He lifted her over the carnage, set her down, then grabbed her hand. Together they raced down the empty corridor and into the abandoned Emergency Room. An ambulance, presumably the ride Jackson had arranged, was just now reversing into the unloading area outside the sliding glass doors.

A movement on her right had caught her attention. She missed a step and let go of Jackson's hand. Someone was hiding behind the nurses' station.

Raymond stood up slowly and lifted one hand in a small heartbreaking wave. One of his eyes was swollen shut.

Jackson backtracked. "What are you doing Rose? He's fine. Let's go."

She glared at him. "Did you give him this black eye?"

"That wasn't me." He tugged at her elbow.

She dug in her heels. The boy had no expectations; she saw it in his face. Bleak acceptance marked him as unmistakably as those purple bruises.

"We can't leave him here," she said.

Jackson scoffed. "We sure as hell can. He almost got you kidnapped. And you *would* have been taken if I hadn't knocked the crap out of his brother."

"That wasn't Raymond's fault. He saved my life yesterday. I wouldn't have survived that second bomb if he hadn't made me leave the roundabout." She extended her hand to the boy. "You want to come with us?"

Raymond stayed where he was. His eyes were on Jackson.

Just outside, the ambulance driver shouted at them to hurry-up.

Jackson's voice hardened. "We're out of time. Even if we take him along to the airport, what are you going to do with him once we get there? They won't let him board that plane. So you're just delaying the inevitable. It will be that much harder to leave him. Say your goodbyes."

Even as he said it, men's voices echoed from the far stairwell. Only a matter of minutes now before those soldiers discovered the bodies in the closet.

"Come with us," she urged Raymond. "We can take you to a safer place."

He came around the desk and darted to her side.

"It's all settled then," she said and rested her hand on his shoulder.

"Fine," Jackson said in an aggravated tone. "Whatever it takes to get you moving." He herded them towards the bay where the ambulance driver waited to whisk them away.

They were almost at the door when a high whining noise sounded above them.

For a fraction of a second, she and Jackson exchanged an arrested glance. *Incoming.* The sorrow and regret in his eyes made her blood run cold.

# 6

JACKSON PUSHED her flat just as a huge bang rocked the entire building. He lay spread-eagle over her and Raymond, sheltering them from falling debris.

"Missile strike," Raymond said matter-of-factly, in a polite schoolboy voice while rubble plunked around them.

Something hit her elbow and she gasped. Jackson tucked her arm under his. Then he let out an "oof" and a long sigh.

None of them moved for a minute. Dust filtered from the ceiling. Squashed at the bottom of the pile, Rose could hardly breathe.

She nudged Jackson. "Is it safe to move now?"

He didn't answer. He was a dead weight. Suddenly afraid, she yelled his name several times. Still no answer.

Raymond managed to crawl out and then dragged her out, too.

"Are you okay?" she asked. The boy nodded, freakishly calm. He was unscathed. As was she.

Jackson, however, was slumped facedown. She quickly checked him over and found no visible trauma. Raymond pointed out a baseball-sized chunk of cinder block a few feet away. She ran her fingers over Jackson. Sure enough, a bump had formed on the crown of his head.

She felt his neck. And there it was—a slow and steady pulse. "Thank goodness." She touched his mouth and felt his breath on her fingers. Her own came out in a long whoosh. She sat beside him cross-legged, brushing debris from his nose and mouth.

He muttered something. She leaned in. The second time left no room for doubt. He'd said her name. He didn't wake up, but his chest rose and fell in a reassuring rhythm.

Raymond went outside. Rose heard people shouting but she had no interest in anything other than staying with Jackson until he came to. She kept her hand on his jaw. He'd become important to her very quickly. Of course, he *had* saved her from a kidnapping and protected her. But those weren't the only reasons. Perhaps she did remember him, deep down. That would explain that yearning moment they'd shared and why she'd been so ready to kiss him.

Their history, whatever it was, didn't change the fact that this nightmare wasn't over. They still had to get to the airport. And then there were those soldiers, who may have been distracted by that missile strike, but for how long?

Jackson's eyelids fluttered. Worried that the plaster dust would hurt his eyes, she leaned in and gently blew the particles away. He blinked and waved as if she were a mosquito.

Exhaling in relief, she ordered, "Keep them closed. Almost done." She blew the last bits away from his long eyelashes. "Okay. Now."

His eyes flew open. "What spiked me?"

"A chunk of the ceiling. And guess what? Now we've got matching goose eggs."

He stared at her as if he'd received an unexpected gift and she was pretty sure it wasn't the goose egg. She spotted more plaster in his dark hair. Nicer than hers, she thought, apropos of nothing. She plucked out the pieces. His expression of perplexed gratitude gave her pause. He kept looking at her like she was his long-lost best friend. Like this, he was a different man.

She brushed a few last strands of dusty hair away. He closed his eyes and a sigh escaped him. He turned slightly so that her hand rested on his forehead.

Raymond stepped through a gaping hole where the door had been. "The second floor got hit."

Her heart jumped to her throat. "Did you see anyone? Kids? Nurses?"

"I'll look again," Raymond said.

Rose closed her eyes. "Who shoots fucking missiles at a fucking hospital? Assholes."

Jackson grabbed her hand and squeezed it. He was watching her. Following her instincts, she put her other hand over his and held on. Something powerful— something she couldn't quite identify—linked them as surely as their hands did. Just as it had earlier. Then it was gone and she realized she was trembling. She took her hands back.

Raymond appeared again. "Some walls fell down. I saw two dead soldiers, that's all. More Red Boys just got here. They are taking supplies from the other building."

"Now?" Rose exclaimed.

The boy shrugged.

"What time is it?" Jackson asked.

Rose spotted a wall clock behind the nurse's station. "The clock stopped at three o'clock."

Jackson propped himself up on one elbow. "We've got only about two hours till sunset. We have to go. The driver's waiting."

"No he isn't," Raymond said. "The motor is running. But so is the driver. Down the street as fast as his pudgy legs will take him. Mr. Jackson, if we don't take that van, someone else will."

Rose pushed Jackson down. "Not yet. How many fingers am I holding up?"

"One."

"Good," she said. His color was better already. "Wait here."

She stepped outside. The ambulance waited, untouched by the blast, with its back doors open and motor running, just as Raymond said. Most of the hospital building was intact, except for the second floor. Exterior walls had collapsed, exposing interior rooms. Small fires burned here and there. If the stairwell was intact, maybe the nurse and the kids had indeed gotten away.

At the far side of the parking lot, half a dozen men in red berets were loading boxes into a truck. They had a Westerner, a blond man, with them. At gunpoint.

The blond man looked over, saw her and called out, "Rose!"

She froze, as did the soldiers. The blond man gestured at her. Obviously he knew her, but why would he call their attention to her like that? The soldiers conferred with one another. One of them spoke on a phone while staring right at her. Then the soldiers pushed the man into the truck and drove away.

She took a few steps to see which direction they'd gone.

Jackson's voice sounded behind her. "Don't even think about it. We're getting out of here."

She turned to see him swaying like a redwood tree in a windstorm. A watchful Raymond followed at a safe distance, ready to jump out of the way of the falling giant.

She ran to duck under Jackson's shoulder. He was almost a foot taller than her but she managed to keep him upright. Together, they hobbled to the ambulance.

"A guy just called my name," she said.

"I heard. Who was he?"

"I don't know but some soldiers had him at gunpoint."

Jackson regarded her skeptically. "Is that right. Well, whoever he is, we can't help him now."

Rose glanced at the smoking second level, still heartsick at the thought of the children who'd been up in that ward. "I don't understand how this could happen. These insurgents have missiles? And they're so incompetent that they hit a hospital?"

"It was a rocket-propelled grenade and no accident," Jackson said. "Anyway, insurgents might not be the ones responsible. It's equally possible the government did that. Haven't you been paying attention to politics in this country? *How* many months have you been here?"

Rose let that pass, reminding herself he didn't know her situation. The faint disgust in his tone bothered her more than it ought to. His sweet mood sure hadn't lasted long.

"Were those soldiers actually insurgents?" she asked.

"Or their allies."

She wondered how he knew all this. "You're saying the soldiers were the target and the government doesn't care that this is a hospital?"

He nodded as if talking took too much effort. His skin was sallow.

She lowered him so he sat just inside the ambulance door.

"Can you drive this thing?" he said faintly.

"Of course," she lied.

She swung his legs up and then pushed him all the way inside. Raymond helped her secure the doors and ran around to ride shotgun.

As soon as she got in the driver's seat, Rose raised her hands slightly, trying to psych herself up for this. She had no idea if she could drive an ambulance. But she'd seen a California driver's license in her wallet. She fumbled for a seatbelt and found none. Screw it. A missing seatbelt was the least of her worries.

Retching noises came from the back of the van. Jackson needed a doctor. And here she was, driving him *away* from a hospital. Not that she'd ever seen any doctors. They'd been busy elsewhere. Still, nurse Okeke would have known what to do for him.

"Should we be taking this ambulance?" she wondered aloud. "I hardly saw any yesterday. They'll need this. Maybe we should find a different vehicle."

"No, no," Raymond. "We need to go."

Rose couldn't stop thinking about the children who'd been hiding upstairs. She put the van in gear and slowly accelerated away from the emergency room. Civilians—presumably hospital employees and ambulatory patients—milled about near the hospital's main entrance. A few soldiers faced the street waving their arms overhead. She couldn't tell who or what they were signaling.

She paused to idle near the stairwell she'd used earlier. There wasn't any movement or sign of life at this end of the building. Only some parts of the second floor were ruined. "We should make sure the kids aren't trapped."

Jackson roared from the back, "Go."

"I just want to see—"

Jackson and Raymond both yelled "Go!"

"Not that way, the other way," Raymond instructed her.

Rattled, she turned the ambulance in a wide circle and set her sights on a service driveway at the other end of the complex.

Just as she completed the turn, a jeep came from out of nowhere and zoomed up behind her.

She checked the side-view mirror. Two men. Both wore red berets. She breathed a little easier when she recognized the passenger. He was the round-faced leader she'd met yesterday. He'd been kind and friendly, the only nice one of those Red Boys.

Raymond looked back, then slid lower in his seat. "It's General Mutan."

"Mutton? As in lamb?"

"No, Mutan," he said, pronouncing it for her. "He is the head of the Red Boys."

"What's happening here?" she said. "What's this guy up to?"

"My brother said the hospital is the Red Boys' new headquarters," Raymond said and slid all the way to the floor.

Everything in this country was upside down and inside out. Soldiers in uniform stole children from orphanages. The government fired on its own people. What if these Red Boys were here to fight the good fight against a rotten regime? She eased up on the accelerator.

The jeep drew abreast on her left. The general made eye contact and signaled for her to stop. She smiled in return, stalling for time. Maybe Raymond's brother was a loose cannon out to prove himself—maybe the kidnapping had been his own dumb idea.

"This general might help us," she said. "Maybe we can get a ride and give them this ambulance. Look, he's friendly. He might be a good guy. After all, those soldiers were—"

Raymond settled the question when he reached over, grabbed her foot, and slammed it down on the gas pedal. She yelped and the ambulance leapt forward. Equipment banged against the van walls and a few thuds followed— Jackson getting tossed around.

"So. We're doing this," she said, trying to convince herself. She headed for the exit holding the wheel in a death grip. No way would she be able to outrun the jeep. This ambulance, however, did have considerably more mass. In a collision, it would crush that jeep into a tin can.

Raymond crawled back onto his seat. "Get your seat belt on," she said and then called over her shoulder. "Okay back there?"

Jackson didn't respond. She didn't have time to ask again. The jeep was about to overtake them. She looked ahead. A tank was just now lumbering into the service driveway, blocking their only exit. This was just like one of those ridiculous scenes in an action movie.

"If you stop now," Raymond said, "they won't let us go."

She was inclined to agree. Which left only one option. "Hang on."

She stood on the gas pedal and steered left, straight at the canvas-lined fence, praying Jackson heard her warning. They blasted through the fence and took a section with them.

Metal posts bounced off the ambulance hood and sailed over. A swath of chain-linked mesh and canvas caught and flapped on their front bumper. Then that flew off, too.

She flicked a quick glimpse at the mirror and saw the fence hit the jeep. Wire and canvas tangled together and trapped the two men. The jeep screeched to a halt.

Rose bumped through an adjacent vacant lot at full speed. Within seconds, the ambulance dropped over a curb and landed hard in the street behind the hospital.

She checked the mirror again. No one pursued them. They were free and clear. "Like a hot knife through butter," she crowed.

Though traffic was nonexistent, four or five untended goats wandered in the street ahead. In a moment of inspiration, she found the siren switch and let it rip. The goats scattered and she roared on.

"I don't suppose you know how to get to the airport," she said to Raymond, shouting to be heard over the siren.

Raymond shook his head. They passed a commercial strip. Men were running out of shops carrying stuff. Big stuff like TVs and computers.

"Okay," she went on, "can you show me how to get to the roundabout where you met me?"

He gave directions and she took several screaming turns with the siren blaring. The few people who were out on the street did a double take when they saw her behind the wheel. She blasted past before they could do more than look surprised.

In less than a minute, the ambulance barreled onto the main boulevard, one intersection past the roundabout. Thankfully. She didn't want to ever see that place again. With any luck, she wouldn't have to. They'd get out to the airport and be out of this insane country by sundown.

Jackson's continued silence worried her. The siren made such a racket she couldn't hear a thing. She flipped it off. They no longer needed it. Traffic was so light on this boulevard she was beginning to worry about that, too. Why weren't there more cars on the road? She saw a sign for the airport and made the turn.

"Go check on Jackson," she said to Raymond.

A large open-bed truck filled with men in camouflage approached from the opposite direction. She ducked her head as they passed and wondered which warring faction that group represented.

"It doesn't matter," Jackson said in her ear.

She jumped and the van swerved. His lips had touched her ear lobe, sending shivers up her spine. Irritated and flustered, she steadied the wheel.

He climbed through the gap and settled into the passenger seat, taking up quite a bit more space than Raymond, who now perched behind them.

"How do you do it—read my mind like that?" she said. "*Stop*."

"I would if I could. Believe me, I've tried."

The low winter light illuminated the lean planes of his face. He had tied his hair back with a length of gauze bandage, accentuating his slightly exotic features. She wondered again about the ethnic mix in his family tree. A wandering Viking must have visited one of those branches.

"It's not mind-reading, you know," he said. "It's more like…we're tuned to the same frequency. At least that's the way it used to be. The way we used to be."

She'd have to explain about her memory loss. Soon. But what was he up to—why mess with her head like this?

"Know what I think?" she said. "I think you're tuned to the full-of-shit frequency."

His laugh was rich and deep. A quick glance told her his color had returned. When he grinned, a dimple appeared near his mouth. A dimple, for God's sake.

She found herself grinning with him. "You're making this up as you go along. Aren't you?"

"I wish I were." His dimple vanished.

"So what's your story?" she asked. "Most people wouldn't be laughing right now. Are you some kind of adrenaline junkie?"

"I used to be," he said shortly.

His shoulders were so wide that when she looked back at Raymond, her jaw brushed against him. A wave of shivery longing hit her. This crazy house-on-fire attraction supported the ex-lover theory. Her body seemed to recognize him, even if her mind did not. Still, she couldn't imagine sharing anything more than a few nights of hot sex with this one. He was too—something. She didn't understand what or who he was, really, other than cranky and dangerous and—different.

She edged away and kept her eyes on the road ahead. "I see you're feeling much better."

"Now you're reading *my* mind."

"Not at all. You're upright and you aren't retching anymore. Still, you should be careful after a head injury. I wonder if we shouldn't go back to the embassy. Some staff must still be there."

"There's a mob forming in the streets around the compound. Doesn't matter whether they're hired goons or local protestors, it's too dangerous for you."

"How do you know all this?"

"I just looked at my device. Plus, I got a message."

"From whom?"

She felt him studying her. "You don't need to know," he said finally.

"Thanks for the vote of confidence. You forget, I saw how you killed those two men. With a mop and a rag, for Christ's sake. So the cat's out of the bag, so to speak. You might as well tell me who and what you are."

"I'd remind you we're not alone."

She nodded grudgingly. Could he be some sort of special ops guy, or a CIA agent? "Back to the business at hand. It seems unlikely we'll make it to the airport without getting stopped."

"First things first. We need to drop off your little friend. Here is as good a place as any. Kid, can you find your way from here?"

A small "yes, sir" came from the back of the van.

"Hold it," Rose said. "I'm not so sure about this." She pulled to the curb and turned to see Raymond already opening the van's back doors. "How far is your home?"

"Not far," Raymond said. "I know the way."

He hopped out and regarded her solemnly from his good eye, the one that wasn't swollen shut. His brother must have been the one who'd given him that black eye. And she couldn't do a thing about it.

"Will your mother be there?" she asked.

The boy shook his head. "The virus took her last year."

"Your father?"

"He is...working."

Rose turned to Jackson. "We can't let him go by himself."

"He'll be safer at home than he is with us."

She was about to argue that point when Raymond called, "Be careful, Miss." He slammed the door before she had a chance to say goodbye. She craned her neck to watch him go, but he'd already dashed down a narrow alley.

She drove on. "Which way?"

"Just keep going straight."

She kept her face averted so Jackson wouldn't see her fury and held herself rigid to keep from pounding the steering wheel. She was sick of seeing children with the eyes of bitter old men. Sick of seeing human beings treated as disposable items.

"You can't save everyone," he said. "You ought to know that by now."

These memories extended back only thirty-six hours. A lifetime of such experiences seemed unthinkable. She wanted no part of a world like this.

She set her jaw and swiped at her eyes. "Should I?"

"We're going to a rendezvous point," he added, more gently. "We need to ditch this ambulance and take cover for a while."

"You seem to know your way around here pretty well."

"I've been in this country several times before."

"What for?"

"Another time," he said. "Next left. Turn in that driveway."

She pulled into an abandoned gas station. This part of the city was a ghost town. "Where is everyone? What do they know that we don't?" She shut off the ignition. "Now what?"

"We hide." He indicated with his head. "Over there by that restaurant. Quickly now." He jumped out of the ambulance and when she joined him, hooked her elbow and pulled her across the street.

She jogged to keep up. Then skidded to a halt. "In that thing? You're kidding me."

"Nope," he said, sounding almost cheerful.

## 7

SHE FACED A SQUAT, filthy dumpster. The odor of rotting food rose to meet her.

"Ladies first," he said with a wave.

"Oh no. No, no, no."

"We're sitting ducks out here."

She glanced around. A deep rumble could be heard in the distance. "What is that?"

"A military convoy coming in."

Diesel engines. Lots of them and coming closer.

"You have a better idea?" he asked. His dimple reappeared.

"You don't have to look so pleased about it." She climbed up and in, unsteady and unsure where to put her hands, cringing the whole way. "Eww. Eww." She lowered her butt onto the least disgusting surface she could find, a slimy cardboard box, and closed her eyes tight. "What is it with you and stinky places?"

"You're alive, aren't you? Stop complaining." With a gusty sigh, he settled in as if he were easing into a Lazy-Boy recliner. "Keep your head down."

She opened her eyes warily. "Ugh, there are maggots all over the place. My shoes are just plastic clogs. They'll crawl right in."

"You'll survive."

She curled inward and held her elbows. "Now what?"

"Now we wait."

"For what?"

"For my colleague to make contact."

She lifted her head. "You have a colleague? How will he know where we are?"

He pushed her head down and she got a whiff of something in the bottom of the dumpster that smelled very much like vomit. She gagged.

"We'll be easy to find," he said. "This hiding place is perfect."

Perfect? She stopped mid-gag to scowl at her knees, thinking how much she hated him right now.

He searched his backpack for something. When he stood briefly, the slimy cardboard box she sat on shifted, forcing her to re-balance in the garbage heap and brace her foot in a pile of maggoty food.

"What are you doing up there?" she griped.

"Getting us out of here."

She started to ask for an explanation when the trucks started to rumble through, passing very close to the dumpster. The noise was deafening.

He pressed her down again. His palm was so big it spanned her whole head, ear to ear. She kept wondering about the various disgusting things he might have touched before he planted his hand in her hair. Different parts of the dumpster were disgusting in different ways. One corner smelled like poop. Another like rotten meat. She was convinced she'd never get the stink out of her nostrils. Or her hair.

"These are personnel carriers," he said, raising his voice over the roar. "Coming in from outer provinces. Probably some supplies and weapons. But mostly troops. One helluva lot of soldiers pouring into this city."

Distracted from her misery, she said, "How do you know that?"

"I'm a data geek. Data always tells a story. You just have to know how to interpret it."

She didn't ask what he meant; she couldn't think about anything other than escaping what had become her own personal hell. Maggots were now crawling over her feet.

The convoy of passing trucks went on and on with an incessant, vibrating hum. Jackson kept his hand on her head. The funny thing was, now she wanted it there. The weight of his palm kept her centered and, if not calm, less likely to climb out and run howling into the street, convoy or no convoy.

Her memory loss had been terrifying enough. Throw in the violence and death she'd witnessed and now this, having to hide in a pile of garbage—it was simply too much to bear. She felt like she was being swept down a swift river, closer and closer to a waterfall. The current was too strong. How was she supposed to fight her way out of this?

"The afternoon's almost gone." She heard her voice cracking and was past caring. "Do we have any prayer of making it to the airport? The truth, please."

After a long pause in which he seemed to be taking her measure, he slowly lowered his palm to the center of her back and kept it there. Brown eyes met hers and he inclined his head in the barest nod. "Maybe. We have one more shot."

"Which is?"

"My colleague. If there's a way, he'll find it."

"If he's anything like that ambulance driver, we're screwed."

"No, I've known Markus for years. He won't let us down."

"When we get out of here," she said to her knees, "I'm going to take the world's longest shower. And use an entire bottle of shampoo. I'm going to gargle with it."

"That shower will have to wait until we get to Germany. We're not going to be the most popular passengers on that airplane."

She groaned. "Shoot me now."

"Think about something else," he said. "Go to your happy place."

"I don't know my happy place. I don't know shit. Except that I'm sitting in it."

"No, you're not. You're on a beach."

"I am? Where?"

"We're in Fiji. The sand is crystal white. The water is turquoise."

"Oh, you're there, too?"

"Of course. You're wearing a red bikini. You look great."

She smiled to herself. As fantasies went, it wasn't bad. "Do I really?"

"You're taking care of yourself for a change. You've been eating grilled fish and vegetables every night. And you're getting lots of sleep."

"I am?"

"Yep. You run on the beach every morning. You're in the best shape of your life. There's a waiter coming over. Pina colada?"

"I hate pina coladas."

"A margarita, then. Frozen?"

"On the rocks. No salt."

Maggots crawled between her toes. She went rigid. This wasn't a tropical paradise. Not even close. No way could she sit in here a minute longer.

He whipped her shoes off, flicked the worms away and then held her feet in the air. "Do you want a paper parasol in your drink?"

"Damn straight." She exhaled. She didn't hate him anymore.

The last truck in the convoy passed. Everything went quiet. In the fresh silence, a new sound caught her attention. A whirring noise above them. Not close, but not far. She looked at the sky. "What is that sound?"

"What sound?"

"That buzzing. Like a loud mosquito. Except mechanical."

"Couldn't tell you," he said, intent on what he was texting though he still held her bare left foot in his other hand.

The buzzing faded away and when he squeezed her foot, she started in surprise and tried to pull it back. He held on to it and sent her a brief, smoldering glance she could not interpret. He looked almost angry.

"Who are you talking to?" she asked.

"Markus. He's on his way."

"Yay. Can we get out of here now?"

"Not yet. There are two more trucks lagging behind the rest—not too far away. Ten more minutes max."

No, he wasn't angry. He was distracted. Probably not even aware his thumb massaged the ball of her left foot in slow, deep circles. The sensations he created were delicious. A ripple of pure pleasure spread through her body, striking a chord that vibrated between her legs.

She suppressed a sigh and started talking in the hope that he wouldn't notice her blush. "Ten more minutes is enough time for you to tell me what you do for a living."

"Yeah, no, can't tell you that."

"You can't or you won't?"

Silence. She twitched. If he could make her feel like this using only his thumb, what else could he do?

"Okay," she said swiftly, "let's try this another way. What brought you to this country?"

His thumb stopped circling and he looked at her askance. "Don't be coy, Rose. It doesn't suit you."

The time had come. She couldn't put it off any longer. "I'm not being coy. Here's the truth. I really *don't* know. I have no idea who you are. As in, no memory of you whatsoever."

He scoffed and pushed her feet back into the clogs. "Not that again. Don't be so melodramatic. Can I just point out—you're not the same either. That's not a compliment by the way."

"Fair enough. Please, just listen for a second. I should apologize and explain why—"

"The girl I used to know wouldn't have done what you did at the embassy yesterday. That behavior was petty and, frankly, beneath you. Giving me the brush-off the way you did? An old friend you haven't seen in ten years. Eight thousand miles from home."

She leaned closer and willed him to believe her. "*I don't remember you.* I woke up yesterday with no memories. None. I didn't recognize you at the embassy and even now, all I know is your first name and the precious little you've told me about yourself. I gather you came here to see me?"

She paused, expecting him to reply. When he didn't, she added, "It's been ten years, you said. We haven't seen each other since I was, what, eighteen?"

"Seventeen," he corrected, searching her face. Whatever he saw made him shake his head. "It was summer. Your birthday's in October so you weren't eighteen yet."

"How old were you then?"

"I was nineteen. As you damn well know."

This past he spoke of seemed mythical. But at least now she knew their relationship could not have been serious. They'd been teenagers. So why were his boxers in a bunch?

"I'm sorry you don't believe me," she said evenly. "Bizarre as it sounds, I'm telling you the truth."

"Sure you are. You always did like telenovelas."

"What?"

"Never mind," he said. "You seem to be functioning pretty well for someone with no memory."

"My short-term memory is fine. I remember everything that's happened since I woke up yesterday. But nothing before that. I think this is called retrograde amnesia. From what I read, it's not uncommon for people with this type of amnesia to retain everyday knowledge, even technical skills—"

He cut her off. "Seeing as your medical degree comes from the University of Wikipedia, why don't you hold off on the self-diagnosis? I'll say this, you're certainly acting like yourself."

"Which is what, exactly?"

"Stubborn and opinionated."

She nodded, unoffended. Sounded plausible enough. She *felt* stubborn and opinionated.

"Tell me," he said, looking askance at her, "what caused this mysterious amnesia?"

She lifted her shoulders. "From what I read online this morning, there's a long list of potential causes for my memory loss. Lassa Fever is not one of them."

"Why did they think you had Lassa Fever?"

"Raymond's idea. He lied so that the guys we encountered on the street after the bombing wouldn't go near me. It just so happens that some people with Lassa Fever lose their hearing. Clever, right?"

He nodded slowly. "You're sure you're not sick?"

So he believed her. Finally. "How long have we known each other?"

He opened his mouth, hesitated, then closed it.

"Hey, I'm the one with amnesia. That wasn't a difficult question. How long?"

"Have we known each other?" He made a show of checking his device.

What was he hiding?

"Forever," he said finally. "I don't remember *not* knowing you."

"Did we live in the same neighborhood?"

"Around the corner—the first seven years."

"We were friends for a long time, then. Why the ten-year gap? When did we become enemies?"

~

*Careful now.* He was picking his way through a minefield. What she'd said had the ring of truth and he was inclined to believe her. This certainly explained her behavior over the last two days. With all her faults, Rose had never been devious. Or a liar.

The most expedient thing, he decided, would be to frame their past as an uncomplicated one. Boring even. He'd get her cooperation and they'd proceed on as acquaintances, if not friends. He wasn't so starry-eyed as to think they could ever go back. By the time she regained her memory, he'd be long gone.

"We're not enemies."

"Hmm," she said, not completely buying that, he thought. "Do you mind if I ask about your heritage? Not that it matters, but it's a little unusual, isn't it?"

"People never know what I am. I'm hapa."

"Come again?"

"Half-anglo, half-Asian. My father is Korean-American. My mom was French."

"An interesting mix."

"One way to put it. They met and married in graduate school. She wanted a green card. Who knows what he wanted? Other than the obvious."

"You said your mother *was* French. Did she pass away?"

He didn't trust himself to do more than nod. Even after all these years.

"I'm sorry."

"So am I."

"An illness?" When he didn't answer right away, she prompted, "An accident?"

"Yes." He'd been seven. His father had picked him up from school one day and informed him that his mother had died in an accident. Many years later he'd learned—from Rose's mother—*accident* was a euphemism for swallowing enough sedatives to kill an elephant. To this day, Oswald refused to say his wife's name, much less discuss her death.

"I don't even know your last name," she said.

"Lee."

"So what's our deal? What's our story?"

"We were friends as kids. Then your family moved away to southern California. You were seven I think."

"Then how did we…"

"Ten years later, I spent the summer with my aunt and uncle, not far from your family. I was going into my second year at Cal. You were about to start at Santa Barbara. We had a summer fling. When that summer ended, we went our separate ways."

The first of the trucks rolled past. He checked his screen. "That was longer than ten minutes. One down. One to go."

"You came all the way to Africa to visit me? Why?"

"Your mother called me. When she heard I was travelling to Senegal on business, she asked me to stop here on the way. She's worried. You weren't responding to her emails or phone calls."

Rose looked stricken. "I don't remember my mom. Not her voice. Not even her face."

"She's a nice lady. You're lucky. Why would you worry her like that?"

"Maybe I'm not thoughtful," she said tartly. "I have no idea, remember? This is absurd. We're right back where we started."

The second truck lumbered past and then the street became quiet again.

"Not quite," he said. "Now we know what we don't know."

Rose glanced up at him through her lashes, obviously unconvinced. Then she elbowed him and a laugh came out her nose. "Like that makes any sense. You're still tuned to the full-of-shit frequency."

It was enough to make him believe in time travel. Even sitting in a pile of garbage, she found a reason to laugh. Like the old days.

That last summer together, they'd spent most of their time at the beach. They used to lay on a towel sharing salty kisses and making each other so hot they could barely stand it. They had sand in their hair, sand in their swimsuits and all the time in the world to play, to explore, and learn to love. Back then he'd believed that life would always be that good. That easy.

This was the girl he used to know, the one who would start to tell a story and then laugh so hard she couldn't finish. The one who could make him forget how screwed up the world was. She might have lost her memory; she hadn't lost herself. He envied that, even if it proved to be temporary.

Unfortunately, he couldn't forget so easily. The kid he'd been—the one who'd laughed with her—was gone forever and he wasn't coming back. Too much water under the bridge. Too many disappointments. Too many women that weren't her.

Strange how things played out. If she hadn't lost her memory, he wouldn't have had this fleeting glimpse into the past. Or a visit with a girl who may as well have

vanished ten years ago, the day her sister died. The .
had changed everything. But he harbored no illusio.
hopes. He had outgrown his adolescent dreams.

His device chimed, returning his attention to the
present and Markus's imminent arrival. "Let's get out of
here."

Rose took his proffered hand and sprang to her feet,
only to sway in place. She was running on empty. She
hadn't complained but he remembered seeing a breakfast
tray that contained only a pastry and a cup of weak coffee.

He was in better shape by far, even after getting bonked
with a chunk of concrete. He'd eaten more, for one thing,
having polished off the two substantial breakfast trays the
nurses brought him. Plus, he'd guzzled about a liter of
water during the soccer game. She hadn't had any water all
day. He lifted her out of the dumpster and set her on her
feet.

He vaulted out himself just as a battered Toyota
compact pulled up with Markus at the wheel sporting
newly white-blond hair that clashed with his brown skin.
Markus's heritage was even more of a hodgepodge than his
own: Dutch, Thai, Japanese, and possibly a dash of Pacific
Islander.

Markus revved the engine and called in his Australian
drawl, "If you want to get to the airport, you better hurry
the fuck up."

Jackson helped Rose into the back seat and then slid in.
"Nice to see you too, buddy. Did you retrieve it?"

"Of course I retrieved it. You didn't give me much
choice now, didja?"

"I almost didn't recognize you." In an aside to Rose,
Jackson explained, "Markus changes his appearance the
way others change their clothes. Some disguises work
better than others." To Markus, he said, "You know you
look ridiculous with that bleached hair, right?"

"Yeah? That stupid fringe on your chin makes you look like Charlie Chan."

"Who?" Rose said.

"A character from an old movie. I'm part Korean, not Chinese, you racist bastard."

Markus hooted. "Fuck you too, mate and the horse you rode in on." He took off like a shot and soon they hurtled down a series of side streets and alleyways. He said over his shoulder, "You two smell worse than a bucket of prawns in the midday sun."

Jackson reached over and buckled Rose in. She blinked at him, somewhat dazed. She was wondering how she'd forgotten to buckle her own seat belt. Her stress level was through the roof.

"What about yours?" she said.

He clicked himself in and then had a thought. Was she talking about his seat belt or his stress level? This non-verbal communication still mystified him. If he hadn't experienced the phenomenon firsthand, he wouldn't believe it.

When the car careened into the next turn, she fell against him. To his surprise, she didn't scoot away. She stayed with him, hip to hip.

"I'm Rose," she said, raising her voice for Markus's benefit. "Do you have a first name?"

"Markus goes by one name," Jackson said.

"You can skip the pleasantries, princess," Markus said. "This ain't no embassy cocktail party." He sped up while simultaneously checking his phone. "We're on the wrong side of about seven roadblocks. I can get you around six of them, but not the last. It's right before the airport and it's the only way in. You might not make that flight."

"We have to try," Jackson said and rolled up his window. The wind had picked up, creating billowing dust clouds that blew out from the continent's vast interior.

Once darkness came, this night would be cold and dangerous in more ways than one. Anyone caught after curfew risked capture. Or worse.

Markus called out, "What were you thinking, mate? You know the rules. Hell, you're the one who drilled them into my head. We're Switzerland. We don't take sides. No politics. No religion. No personal agenda."

"We're Switzerland with a conscience," Jackson said. "Think of it as beta testing the software. The boss doesn't have to know."

Markus made a sharp turn onto a two-lane highway, a straightaway with swampy ditches on either side. "He already does. He uses geofencing to monitor us in the field. He knew the moment you deviated from the plan. I've never heard him so ticked off. He mentioned cancelling the Senegal project."

"The whole project?" That wasn't good. Not good at all. A lot of people were depending upon the project's success. It mattered.

"He wants you out of this country, this continent, this whole goddamn hemisphere. He's right, you know. Things have gone from bad to worse. First the roundabout bombing. Then the missile strikes on that hospital. I just learned three aid workers disappeared yesterday from the Old Quarter. Hey princess," Markus said in a cooler voice, "two of those people were nurses from your NGO. One was a doctor. You wouldn't happen to know anything about that?"

Rose stared at the back of Markus's head. "How do you know which NGO I work for?"

"The ex-pat world is a small one, sister. I know who you are."

"Then maybe I should pick your brain," she muttered.

Markus addressed Jackson in the rear-view mirror. "Why didn't you get out when the getting was good? I could have picked you up from that hospital early this morning, long before all hell broke loose."

"I had my reasons."

Markus snorted. "Who are you kidding? You had *a* reason. Singular. It's sitting right next to you. You ruined months of ground work, valuable assets, and risked your job—all for some pussy."

Jackson felt Rose flinch and waited a beat, figuring she would want first crack. The girl he used to know would have ripped into Markus and told him off. But the new Rose just rolled her eyes and ignored the crass remark altogether.

"Markus," Jackson said sharply, "try not to be such a dickwad. She's been through shit you know nothing about."

"If you say so," Markus said. "But we both know you'll be the one to pay. Don't be surprised if Holloway fires your ass."

"Shut up, Markus. I'll deal with the fall-out." Rose didn't need to hear this. The choice to stay had been his, not hers.

The truth was, getting fired would be a bitter blow. The job was the best one he'd ever had. Will Holloway had unmatched resources and a reputation for getting things done without any bullshit. There were no endless meetings or dumb-ass decisions made by committee. Holloway didn't let much get in his way. Which also meant he wouldn't tolerate a loose-cannon employee who jeopardized their operation.

Rose kept giving him worried looks. She said nothing; however, he wasn't fooled. She was saving the third degree for later.

A roadblock appeared about half a kilometer ahead, complete with two tanks and armed men flanking both sides of the road. They joined a long line, about forty vehicles deep. The soldiers were letting cars through one at a time.

"Are they checking passports?" Rose asked.

"If that's what you want to call it," Markus said. "It's mainly for collecting 'courtesy donations.' A U.S. twenty folded inside each passport should do the trick."

"I lost my passport," Rose said.

"Whatever," Markus said. "Hide and keep your mouth shut." He tossed a dirty blanket into the back seat.

Jackson caught it before it hit Rose in the face, then waited for her to get settled on the floor. Her silence troubled him. If they'd just met, he would have described her as fearless. But he knew better. Her lips trembled with repressed fury and a distress she would never, ever cop to.

He plucked a strand of hair away from her mouth and rested his hand briefly on the back of her neck. She lifted a suspicious eyebrow before curling into the fetal position.

He covered her with the blanket. "Try to relax."

Her laugh could have been a sob. "Yeah, right."

## 8

ROSE CROUCHED on the floor of the car. The wait to get through the roadblock seemed endless. This had been the longest day of her life. Except—she couldn't even make that claim. Maybe it was. Maybe it wasn't.

She wanted a bottle of water, a shower and a bed, in that order.

Jackson lifted a corner of the blanket. "I'm going to stretch my legs over you so you're less conspicuous. I'll try to keep the weight off you. Sorry babe."

"*Babe?*" she repeated.

Markus chortled.

She felt a twinge of guilt. Jackson could have left the hospital this morning, but he'd stayed. If he hadn't tackled Raymond's brother, she would have been taken. She didn't want to think about what would have happened if Jackson hadn't been there. Then he'd risked his job to get them rescued. She wasn't exactly sure what rule he'd broken to incur his boss's wrath but the fact was, he had done it to save their butts.

The presence of that jerk Markus kept her silent. She'd thank him later, once they were safely at the airport. "How close are we now?" she asked.

"We're about ten cars back from the checkpoint." Jackson rested his feet on her rear-end. True to his word, he didn't get too comfortable. Good thing. She'd noticed his feet. They had to be a size fourteen, triple-wide.

He and Markus exchanged observations about the soldiers and civilians who loitered around the roadblock. They spoke in a staccato shorthand she didn't understand. Was this spy jargon? Nothing would surprise her. These two had referred to a boss, but everyone had a boss. Even masters of espionage and criminals. That whole business about technology and staying neutral from politics—well, that could apply to all manner of enterprise. They could be arms dealers. After all, arms dealers weren't political either; they just sold to the highest bidder. Period.

"Three cars to go, Rose," Jackson said quietly. "Stay right where you are and let us handle this." Then his tone altered. "Markus, do you see that girl over there?"

"Which one?"

"On the other side of the barrier."

"Yeah mate, I see her."

"What is it?" Rose asked from under the blanket.

"There's a girl in a long dress," Jackson said. "Something's not right about her."

Markus said, "I agree she's out of place. 'Course she could be waiting for her husband to get off-duty."

"She can't be more than fourteen. Look at her waist."

"A pregnant teenage bride," Markus said. "Not uncommon."

"I'm not convinced she's pregnant," Jackson said. "She looks spacey. And her hair is pulled way back from her face."

"I don't see what—"

"Get us out of here," Jackson said urgently.

"You'll lose your place in line. If you're wrong—"

"Do it!"

Rose felt the car lurch into reverse and then go forward in sets of short jerky movements. They were doing it. Turning out of the line. Now they'd never make it to the airport in time.

"What's happening?" She twitched the blanket aside, only to see a ferocious look on Jackson's face.

He bellowed "Get down" and threw himself on top of her.

She had time for one thought. *Again?*

A huge bang came next and an impact that rocked the car. Metal struck metal and objects rained down, hitting the hood, the roof and the windshield.

That same acrid smell. The same horrible silence.

"Are you all right?" Jackson said. He might have shouted this. She couldn't be sure. He sounded far away. That, too, was the same. The same soul-crushing, earsplitting horror.

He pulled her off the floor saying, "Don't look."

Smoke swirled around the car like a dense fog. Outside, people moved around and shouted in disjointed bursts. It didn't seem real. But of course this was all too real.

Jackson held her head between his hands. "*Look at me. Only me.*"

His eyes were fierce, compelling her to do exactly as he said. Had he said those words aloud or just *thought* them? She didn't know. Chills racked her body.

Jackson pulled the blanket up and around her, then kept her in a tight bear hug while he spoke to Markus. Being inside the car had protected the three of them from whatever—whomever—had blown up.

Jackson cupped her chin and asked her a question that she didn't quite comprehend. Though she could hear him reasonably well, she felt removed from this unspeakable thing. She didn't quite believe that it *had* happened. It was all a mistake. A hoax.

He repeated the question until she finally understood he was asking if she would be all right in the car by herself.

She nodded mutely. Of course she would. She wasn't the one who'd been blown to pieces.

The two men got out of the car. Though she tried not to look, tried not to see, her peripheral vision registered blood spattered on the window. The setting sun lit up the jagged red streaks like an abstract painting.

She hugged her arms and waited in the car, ashamed of her own weakness. Even that Markus guy had stepped up. If this incident were a test of character, she had failed.

A few minutes later, Markus got back behind the wheel. "We're done here. No one's getting through. Even if we did get through, the airport is locked down tight now."

She forced herself to ask, "How many people were killed?"

"Just one. Just the girl. Nothing short of a miracle that no one else bought it."

Jackson returned to the back seat and stared straight ahead, clenching and unclenching his hands. Markus started the car and drove them back towards the city. A grim silence fell. Their chances of escaping the country tonight had dropped to nil and they all knew it.

Jackson's white-faced silence finally penetrated Rose's shock. He had faced what she could not. She slid over and touched his arm, wanting to offer comfort, though unsure how best to do so.

"How did you know?" she asked.

"There was something off about her," Jackson said. "She looked other-worldly. Happy too, like she was already seeing the other side. And glad to be going. That's how I knew. All at once, I could see it coming and there wasn't anything I could do to stop her."

"Why would she look happy?"

"Brainwashed, maybe. Or so fucking miserable that death was a welcome alternative."

"What was it about her hair that clued you in?"

"That hairstyle is a funeral ritual in some places." His expression was both furious and disbelieving. "Did you see what she did? No, that's right, you were on the floor. At the last second, right before detonating, she bolted off in another direction. A final act of free will that ensured she didn't kill anyone else. That was one of the bravest things I've ever seen. She defied whatever monster forced her to wear that belt." His throat worked. "Who and what is so fucked up that they make a young girl kill herself for a cause?"

Rose wished she could erase the memory for him. Wave a magic wand and give him amnesia, too. Amnesia would be a blessing after what he'd just witnessed. The horror would be in his head forever.

He looked down at their clasped hands and squeezed hers so hard her bones hurt. She didn't pull away. He hung on and they stayed like that all the way back to town, physically close but otherwise miles apart.

Not one of them spoke for the next fifteen minutes. The wind had picked up and buffeted the car with grit that caked the blood-smeared windows. They exited the highway and proceeded into a quiet residential area. There were no soldiers or signs of conflict here. You'd never know a civil war raged nearby, except for the total absence of people outdoors.

"We need to get off the streets," Markus said. "The curfew goes into effect soon. I'm dropping you at the safe house."

"Since when do we have a safe house?" Jackson said.

"Since I rented it two months ago," Markus said, "for just such an occasion. It's ready and stocked with a few basics and one luxury. I'm not staying. I've got other plans. We'll talk in the morning. In the meantime, you better decide what you're going to do with her."

Markus spoke as if she wasn't there. Rose felt too desolate to care.

He deposited them in front of a non-descript cinderblock house with a dusty front yard. Although the fighting hadn't touched this area, residents weren't taking any chances. No one was out and about. Markus peeled off the moment Jackson helped her out of the car.

They were halfway to the front door when the sky thundered overhead.

Rose looked up to see a gray whale of an airplane with a U.S. Air Force emblem on its wing. She watched it climb and disappear into the dusky clouds.

The last flight out of this country had just taken off. Without them.

~

The house was small but clean and furnished with the bare minimum, a few chairs and tables, and hopefully a bed or two somewhere.

Jackson steered her into a new bathroom with sleek, modern fixtures. Thick towels and an array of hotel toiletries were stacked on a shelf.

"Is that a hot water tank?" She turned and impulsively kissed his cheek. "Thank you."

He backed up a step. "You can thank Markus next time you see him."

"I'd rather thank you." She caught a glimpse of herself in the mirror and leaned closer. "Holy mother of God."

Her hair was so dirty it had turned a grayish-pink. Dust and grime had settled into every exposed crease and crevice on her body. The shallow scrapes and cuts she'd received yesterday were coated, too. No wonder Jackson had backed away when she kissed him.

He however, looked just as bad. Even his dimple had its own little patch of dirt. Despite the horrors they'd seen—or because of them—she started to laugh.

He stared at her like she had lost her mind. She slid down the wall and collapsed in a boneless heap. When he tried to raise her up, she waved him off.

He wiped up some of the dirt she'd tracked in and left the bathroom.

Maybe he had gone to find a mop. That set her off again. Tears ran down her face. She'd nearly forgotten about his ninja alter ego. Secret-agent man. Data geek. A man for all seasons.

She lowered her forehead to her knees and took a few deep breaths. Her emotions were as much of a mess as she was. Hiccuping, she pulled herself up to the sink, grabbed some toilet paper and blew her nose. Her face was mottled and streaked with dirt and who knows what else. She splashed the worst of it off. The towel she used to dry off turned filthy.

Jackson came back with a bottle of water and a cold beer in his other hand.

She downed the water in one long gulp and wiped her mouth. "Sorry to hog the bathroom. If you want to take the first shower, I can leave." Then she helped herself to a sip of his beer.

He took the bottle back and watched her for a few seconds. "I'll wait. You look like you need a hand."

He was seeing her at her absolute worst. This struck her as unfair. "If there was any justice in this world," Rose said, "people who've been through hell should then become wildly attractive. You know, automatically. Don't you think? Wouldn't that be awesome?"

"Sure," he said, "because that's what's truly important. Your southern California roots are showing."

She fluffed her hair in mock indignation. "Are you implying this is not my natural color?"

"No, I was talking about your values."

She said quietly, "I know what you meant, Jackson." So he thought her shallow? She filed that information away to think about later.

He fiddled with the shower controls and turned the water on full blast. "Come on. You can be hysterical in the shower."

"I knew you were going to use that word," she said. "I knew it. Hey, I was being silly, that's all. Just joking."

"What do you have to joke about?"

"Nothing. Everything."

"Enough." He lifted the hem of her top.

She swatted him away. "I got this."

After a final assessing look, he departed, shutting the door behind him.

Rose stepped out of her filthy clothes and into the shower. She scrubbed from head to toe. When she spotted dead maggots circling the drain, she shuddered and started all over again. After washing her hair twice for good measure, she dried off and wrapped herself in a towel. Her skin glowed and apart from yesterday's scrapes, no one would guess what she'd been through in the last 36 hours.

She walked through the kitchen where Jackson stood with his hands planted on the counter. His head was bowed and his eyes were closed.

"All done," she said lightly.

He looked up with a start and quickly masked his expression.

"I feel human again. Your turn," she added.

As he passed her, his gaze dropped to where her breasts swelled above the knotted towel. The mix of hunger and despair in his glance confused her.

He paused. "There's clean clothes in the bedroom. See what you can find."

She found a stack of t-shirts and jeans, in men's sizes. She pulled on one of the t-shirts and tugged it down over

Unfortunately, the doctor wouldn't tell her anything because of privacy. So that's when she called me."

"I'm fine—other than the memory loss. So you still talk to my mother but not me anymore? That's…unusual. Isn't it?"

"She stayed in touch over the years. Birthdays and holidays, that sort of thing."

There had to be more to this story. He didn't seem inclined to tell her so she left it for now. "If the airport isn't open tomorrow, what are our options?"

"Depends. It's too soon to know. I'll find out what I can and we'll figure something out. For now, the city might be the safest place for us, as long as we keep a low profile. That's kind of hard to do since we obviously aren't locals and most ex-pats are gone. Anyone who is still here is going to be the object of scrutiny, at the very least. You'll need to stay out of sight."

"You don't exactly blend in, either."

"People notice me, but they'll notice you more."

"What does that mean?"

"Don't fish for compliments."

She crossed her arms and sat back to watch him. There was definitely a lot going on under the surface with him, most of which she didn't understand. He lifted a slice of bread to inspect it. It must have passed because he consumed it in about two bites.

She'd been so hungry a few minutes ago; now her stomach hurt.

"Well, that's normal when you haven't been eating properly," he said. He pointed to the bread she'd left behind. "If you're not going to finish that—"

"This mind-reading thing is getting on my nerves." She pushed her plate over. "Go right ahead."

In between bites, he said, "By the looks of you, I'd say you haven't been eating right for weeks, if not months. Just because you're in a third-world country doesn't mean you have to starve yourself out of solidarity. It's not a good look for you."

"I don't recall asking for your opinion. Maybe I've been working too hard."

"Maybe. I'll say this, you're even more of a bleeding heart than you used to be."

She studied him, still more puzzled than offended. They had survived several intense experiences together. Finally, they were safe and after some rest, would live to fight another day. And yet here he sat, scowling at the crumbs on his plate and doing his best to pick a fight.

She was a big girl. What did she have to lose? "Jackson, what's your problem with me? After everything we've been through, you're—"

He cut in. "Everything we've been through?" He watched her through half-closed eyes. "Whatever happened to not remembering anything about your past?"

"Are you playing a game here?" she said, trying to stay calm. "If so, it's one-sided. I've already forfeited. I've been completely honest with you. But for some reason, you keep on playing."

His lips twisted, but it wasn't a smile. "Our game ended a long time ago."

She spread her hands. "Okay. Enlighten me. Who won?"

He refused to answer. When he did finally raise his eyes, fresh antagonism there took her aback. She'd gotten mixed messages from him all day, but this crossed a line. Plus, it didn't add up. If their relationship hadn't been serious, why did he resent her?

Then she recalled how troubled and defeated he'd been earlier and his deep anguish after the suicide bombing. Of course most people would be horrified after witnessing something so grisly. But Jackson wasn't most people. Even though he'd killed two men this morning, that girl's suicide had shaken him.

She put her irritation aside. "Never mind. You know, I haven't thanked you for everything you've done. I've been meaning to tell you that." She wanted to express her gratitude for the way he'd shielded her from seeing the carnage. He'd instinctively protected her from the worst sight imaginable. She wanted to tell him how deeply his selflessness had touched her, but the way he regarded her now, with something approaching bitterness, stopped her.

He shrugged as if she bored him, as if the whole topic bored him.

She leaned over and touched his wrist. "Don't you think it's time to tell me?"

"Tell you what?"

"What happened to us? What in the world did I do to make you dislike me so much?"

## 9

"IT'S ancient history and completely irrelevant," he said, going on the offense to buy time. "This isn't about you or a trip down memory lane."

The fact that she sat here right across from him tonight, glowing from her shower, seemed as miraculous as it was painful. The girl he'd known was long gone, but the woman surpassed all expectations. Despite what he'd told her, she was more beautiful than ever. Even now—underfed, traumatized and battered—she seemed lit by an inner spark. She'd been brave today, handling herself well. When that C-17 departed, she'd accepted the setback without complaint. He didn't know many people who could accept a calamitous event as gracefully as she had.

"Humor me," she said. "I don't even *have* a memory lane. What's the harm in a short stroll?"

"Let it go, Rose." He'd rather think about the sweet curve of her breasts beneath that thin white cotton. He remembered them. Peachy, ripe, and perfectly shaped. They had tasted of summer.

For years he'd assumed his perceptions of her were, if not false, then heavily biased by nostalgia. Turns out, he hadn't imagined any of it. She sat there, as delectable as he'd always thought. He resented craving her. He resented her clean slate of memories. Unfair, but there it was.

"You're not ready to talk?" She slapped the table and got up. "Fine. Until you are, drop the attitude."

...s she walked away. Why was it she pissed ...e no one else could? He couldn't even ignore her ...ause he couldn't keep his eyes off her for more than ten seconds.

"Giving me orders now?" he said, scornfully, desperate to cover how turned on he was.

Now that she was standing, he had an even finer view of her long legs. The t-shirt only reached her upper thighs. *Shit*. He gave himself a mental thump upside the head. This was their old pattern and he had fallen right back into it. She'd kept him in a perpetual state of arousal the summer they'd become lovers. Their strong physical attraction had pushed everything else aside.

She turned in the doorway. "Maybe that's what...never mind."

"Why not just say it—you think *I* need to be ordered around."

She smirked and stuck out her tongue. "Maybe you do."

Damned if that wasn't exactly what she would have said and done twenty years ago, back when they were everything to each other. He corrected himself. Back when she was everything to *him*. Before they'd grown up and become lovers.

Longing for that old closeness welled up and his anger evaporated. He had truly believed his feelings for her had died a natural death. In those years apart, long stretches had passed when he managed to forget her, his oldest friend and first lover. He hadn't forgotten her at all. He may as well have swallowed a rock ten years ago and carried it around this whole time.

Tomorrow he would find somewhere else for her to wait out the coup. If the embassy wasn't an option, he'd find someone willing to house her until the airport re-opened. Then put as many miles between them as he could.

He pushed his stool back and stood up. "We're all done here. Why don't you just go to bed." The moment he said it, he knew he'd made a mistake. She'd take it as a challenge.

Sure enough, she came right back and met him toe to toe. "You really make me mad, you know that? I've just survived the worst two days of my life. You did too, even though you won't acknowledge it. Can't you just—" Her voice broke. "Just talk to me. We'll get through this together. No matter what happened in our past, we should be able to treat each other with decency and kindness. That's all. I'm not asking for anything more."

She thought she wasn't asking too much. Wrong. Even this, standing so close without taking her in his arms, was asking too much.

Her voice thickened. "You wish I'd just shut up, don't you? You wish you were anywhere but here. And no, I'm not reading your goddamn mind. I'm empathizing with a fellow human being. Nothing mystical about that."

"Stop it."

"What did I do to you?" she asked. "It must have been awful. And don't give me that line that we were just friends or that it was all very ordinary. That isn't true. I can see it in your face every time you look at me. I caused you pain, didn't I?"

"You're making way too much of this."

"Well? Did I dump you? Or cheat on you? Tell me what happened. Who knows? It might be therapeutic for us both."

"No it wouldn't. There's nothing to tell." The truth wouldn't set Rose free. That was something some moron made up. Someone who had never survived a traumatic experience. The truth would cause more suffering.

He didn't want to lie anymore. And he was sick of censoring himself, picking and choosing words every time he opened his mouth. That left him with one alternative. Say nothing at all.

"Are you sure?"

That tiny catch in her voice did him in. He hated it when she cried. With a resigned sigh, he reached for her, prepared to keep her at arm's length while administering brotherly pats on the back. He waited for her to weep or vent, but she didn't.

Dry-eyed, she braced her hands on his chest and searched his face. Her shattered expression didn't really have anything to do with him. How could it? By her own admission, she didn't know him. No, this would be exhaustion, pure and simple.

"I think I *will* go to bed," she said. "Speaking of which…"

"There's two pallets in there. If you want privacy, I can drag mine out here."

"Don't bother," she said briskly. "It'll be fine. What are my chances of finding a toothbrush in the bathroom?"

"Excellent."

He watched her go. Her shoulders were rigid with tension and if she held her chin up any higher, she might just miss that doorway and hit the wall instead.

While she was in the bathroom, he checked his messages. One from his boss, asking for a status report. He stared at his phone for a while and then put it away. If Holloway was going to fire him, a delay wouldn't make much difference.

According to Markus, all borders were closed. That meant nothing. Borders were so porous here, the announcement was merely symbolic. There was always a way. He'd find one. Tomorrow he'd be able to truthfully report that he had left the country. As to whether he still had a job…he'd face that hurdle later.

He got the beds ready and washed the dishes. It sounded like Rose had gotten in the shower again. Talk about overkill.

After a few minutes passed, he went to the door and listened. Underneath the running water, other sounds came through at irregular intervals. Soft echoes that sounded suspiciously like fitful gasps and sobs.

He put his forehead on the door and fought the urge to go in. She needed him. But what would going in there accomplish? Other than making him feel less like an asshole. The only way to get through this was to be brutally honest with himself. He wanted to kiss her until she forgot what she had asked him.

He remembered quite well how good they had been together. They'd been passionate lovers, even when they had no idea what they were doing. Not that he hadn't enjoyed the other women he'd been with in the years since. Of course he had. Still, nothing and no one had ever given him the same intense pleasure as learning her body over that one golden summer. Every bumbling move he'd made had been joyful. Right up until the end.

Making love to her now, when he knew exactly what to do and how to please a woman? Oh, yeah. In the short term, it would be very, very good. In the long term? Not so much. Once she recovered her memory, he'd be the one left behind. Again.

The shower cut off with a thump. Relieved to have the decision made for him, he straightened and started to walk away. He didn't want her to find him hovering out here like a lovesick fool.

A loud echoing smack came from inside the bathroom, like something hitting the floor. He burst in the door. And there she lay, half-sprawled and down on one knee.

He pushed his way in to the shower.

She scrambled to her feet. "I slipped, that's all. I'm okay."

He grabbed a dry towel and folded her into it. She was shivering and her face was whitish-blue. He felt her cheek. "You're not okay. You're freezing."

She wouldn't meet his eyes. "We used up all the hot water."

"Damn it, Rose." He wrapped her in his arms to share his heat. Her shoulders felt small and fragile. "Then why take another shower?"

"I forgot to gargle with shampoo. Remember what I promised myself in the dumpster?"

"You didn't have to come in here to cry. Don't hide from me."

"I wasn't crying," she maintained. "I was gargling."

He tucked her head under his chin and his pent-up frustration made him sound angrier than he intended. "Bullshit. If you need to cry, you cry with me. Understand?"

She pulled out of his arms and limped toward the door. "No thanks."

"I don't care if you cry," he said, even more infuriated though he couldn't have said exactly why.

"I don't suppose you do."

"Hold it." He pulled the towel around her more securely, grabbed another for her hair, and forced her to sit on the toilet seat. "What did you do to yourself?"

"I banged my knee again," she said in a flat tone. "The same one I hurt when the bomb went off yesterday. God, was that only yesterday?"

Her right knee was bleeding and newly swollen. He gently explored the bump and bandaged her knee. With that done, there wasn't much more to do except get her off her feet. What worried him was she didn't protest when he picked her up. She went along without a single word.

He carried her into the bedroom and set her on one of the beds. Still too pale and quiet, she stared unblinking at the ceiling. All her feistiness was gone. Seeing her like this disturbed him. He'd always considered her unusually resilient. Every time she got knocked down, she got up. Until now.

He frowned. "You're a wreck, girl. You need to sleep."

"Yep," she said with a faraway look. Her teeth were chattering.

She needed him. Tomorrow they'd start over. Tonight she needed him.

Once he accepted that, his decision was easy. Every rationalization, rule and restriction he'd imposed on himself went right out the window. There was no room for guilt, shame, or second-guessing. He would stay with her. Keep her safe while she slept. They'd get through the night and come morning, figure out the next step.

He lay beside her and turned on his side in order to fit on the ridiculously narrow bed. She seemed unaware her towel had fallen open, revealing her body in all its glory. Memory hadn't done her justice. Too thin but otherwise lovely.

Naturally, his cock jumped to attention, hardening with an urgent need. Only a few inches separated them and that gap effectively closed when his erection brushed her soft, bare hip. She stayed rigid for a minute, mirroring what his cock did. It would have been amusing in another time and place. He flipped the towel to cover her up, then patted her stomach, wordlessly signaling that she shouldn't worry about it

As soon as he touched her, she sighed deeply. She closed her eyes and a soft little humming noise came from the back of her throat. That wasn't the sound of contentment or peace. Rather, that was the sound of her letting go of this nightmarish day. He knew from experience: a long time would pass before she felt true peace or serenity again. There were no shortcuts.

Sadness squeezed his chest. He wouldn't be there to help. She'd have to get through this alone—one night at a time—slowly letting go of the death and destruction she'd witnessed. Soon enough, he would go back to living out of a suitcase, sleeping with a series of women he liked well enough but whom he rarely thought about otherwise.

She'd be safe though, and some day she'd be happy again. He didn't kid himself that he would be happy. Then again, he never expected to be.

~

Rose woke with a start. It must still be the middle of the night. Outside the wind wailed and tossed grit against the window sporadically. She squinted across the dark room, relieved when she spotted Jackson asleep in the other bed. She got up to find one of his t-shirts, pulled it over her head and then burrowed back under the covers.

A rumbling noise wove in and out of her dreams until a mournful howl penetrated her sleeping brain. The crashing boom that followed made her bolt upright and blink into the surrounding darkness.

Jackson wasn't asleep. He lay on his back with his arms behind his head, watching her.

"What was that?" she whispered.

"Mortar rounds."

"Are they close?"

"You don't have to whisper," he said. "We're the only ones here. No, not as close as they sound. We're safe enough, I expect."

She lay back down. "You expect? I hope you're right. With that sand storm blowing, how do they even know where they're aiming?"

"Oh, they know where they're *aiming*. Whether the shells hit the intended target is another question altogether."

"Well, exactly. This is insane."

"Go back to sleep, Rose." His voice was deep and calm. Soon the shelling subsided and she eventually did just that.

Some time later, she woke to a howl that sounded like an evil wolf calling to its pack. When that shell dropped, the whole house shook and the bedroom window rattled.

Another one launched with a long whine. She could see it in her mind's eye, arcing over the city. Sooner or later, one of these missiles would punch through this roof. Images of torn-up body parts flashed through her head. She threw the bedcovers aside and dove under the bed, crawling on her elbows till she reached the center.

The shell landed close enough to shake the window violently. She stayed facedown. There would be no more sleep for her tonight.

In the silence that followed, Jackson spoke right above her, "I'd keep you company down there, but I don't think I'd fit."

She contemplated his bare feet a few inches away and managed to keep her voice more or less steady. "Yeah, the bed would just ride on your back."

"You do realize, if one of those shells actually lands on us, hiding under the bed isn't going to improve your odds."

"At least I won't see the mortar shell coming." His feet weren't as big as she'd imagined. Those were ordinary feet belonging to an ordinary guy. But she didn't really believe that. In more ways than one, he was extraordinary.

And complicated. He'd been mean as a snake last night, when she'd practically begged him to tell her about their past. But then he'd bandaged her knee and even stayed with her until she fell asleep. He wasn't the cold bastard he pretended to be. Not entirely.

"They've stopped shelling," he said.

"How do you know?"

"Come on out. I'll show you."

She crawled out, tugged on her shirt hem to make sure it covered her butt and sat on the bed. He switched on a light and joined her, tablet in hand. He wore only a pair of boxer briefs that were molded to his muscular thighs. She couldn't help staring and he followed the direction of her gaze. Almost immediately the gusset of his briefs filled out and a very healthy erection strained against the fabric.

She flushed while he positioned the tablet over his lap.

She said, "Where did that come from?"

He looked down and then back at her with an expression that said: *you don't know?*

She laughed softly. "I meant the tablet. I thought you lost yours at the hospital."

"Markus left this one here." He pointed to the screen. "See, this shows us what's happening. The government soldiers are on the move. I think they're packing it in for the night."

All she saw were colorful ant-sized dots. "If you say so. How do you know?"

"The data," he said simply. "It tells a story."

"I don't see how you're getting this information. Where is it coming from?"

"From their phones."

"I thought you said mobile networks were down."

He studied her for a moment. "You're full of questions. I'm not used to talking about technical details with anyone other than colleagues. Most people don't care. Why do you ask?"

"Why wouldn't I? My life may depend upon your data. Plus, it's interesting."

He cocked his head as if re-evaluating his opinion of her. "The mobile networks are operational at the moment. That may well be temporary."

"So how do we know all these dots are government soldiers and not insurgents?

"You'd be amazed at what I can glean. More and more every day. That's the beauty of what I'm working on," he said, warming to his subject. "More people have mobile access in sub-Saharan Africa than have access to grid electricity. It will change everything. In a few years, five billion people on the planet will have internet access from a phone. Phones everywhere mean we'll have sensors everywhere, which gives us data. We just have to harvest it. The potential to improve quality of life is astonishing."

This was the most animated she'd seen him. Someone who lit up like this when he spoke about ideas and possibilities was no spy. Nor was he a criminal.

"So you *are* one of the good guys," she said. "Who do you work for? What do you do?"

"I'm a data scientist and a field engineer. I work for a private foundation. That's all you need to know."

"Why were you at the embassy the other day?"

"I had a meeting with the science envoy, which never happened."

"Why not?"

"The roundabout bombing, for one thing."

"Yeah but…" She paused. "I'm confused. You told me you came to this country to check on me. But you had no way of knowing I was out in front of the embassy."

"That actually was a coincidence. I set up that meeting before I even arrived, figuring I'd go find you later."

"Hold it. Nurse Okeke said you saved her cousin from that second bomb. How did you get there so fast?" Then it came to her. "You followed me. Why? You could have said hello outside the embassy."

"I was so surprised, I was speechless. Then you took off before I had a chance."

"I see," she said, though she didn't. "One last question."

He raised a disbelieving eyebrow.

"When and where does a data scientist learn how to kill a man with a mop?"

He looked away. "We'll talk about that some other time."

*Some other time?* As if she'd invited him to lunch. She rubbed her upper arms. This house wasn't heated. The relentless daytime heat made it easy to forget it was mid-December.

Without so much as a sideways glance, he hauled her in against him, so close her ear flattened against his bicep. "Stay here for a minute. You'll get warm faster."

Even with her head at this awkward angle, she wasn't the least bit interested in extricating herself. His heat enveloped her, as did a soothing sense of security that felt even nicer than the warm, smooth skin under her cheek.

He seemed easier with her now and less prone to hold the past against her. The past he refused to talk about. In another time and another place, she would have liked nothing better than to learn more about him and their history. Become friends again. Even lovers.

Jackson still held his tablet strategically over his lap. From here, it sure seemed as though he needed extra clearance. She felt herself flush again. Her fingers itched to walk across his lap and sneak under that tablet. Just to explore. What would he feel like? Taste like? The more she wondered, the more turned on she became. Heat and desire gathered and tightened between her legs.

She lifted the hair off her neck and blew out a long breath.

Jackson didn't take his eyes off his screen. "What? Arousal is perfectly natural."

"Are we talking about yours or mine?"

He did a double take. "I thought we were talking about my hard-on. It's an involuntary reflex. Like a sneeze."

"Bless you."

His grin dazzled her. When he looked at her like this, with an open heart and no hint of resentment or baggage, he was incredibly attractive. It wasn't just his body that attracted her. There was something else at work here, something deeper.

She threw caution to the wind and pulled his head down to kiss him. He froze when she hooked her arms around his neck to give him two short, tentative kisses. His mouth was pliant and warm. He didn't quite kiss her back but he didn't pull away either. She waited for him to respond.

He didn't. With a sigh, she released him but couldn't resist brushing her mouth against his chest in one last caress before pulling away. He tasted good. Warm, salty and sweet at the same time.

His breath quickened and his muscles contracted. He wanted her to keep touching him. She knew it. Yet when she glanced up, his eyes blazed with a warning.

brand new. All new and yet so familiar. He savored the delicate texture of her skin. Her soft ass against his legs. Her lush lower lip. She tasted like herself.

She tasted like hope.

~

She recognized his surrender when his lungs expanded and he released a long sigh.

"It's going to be okay," she whispered. "The past can't be changed and the future can wait. All that matters is here. Now."

She felt certain he would eventually tell her their story. Maybe not tonight, but sometime. Meanwhile, she would give him what he didn't know he needed. Comfort. Loving attention. Mind-blowing release. Anything and everything. With her mouth, her hands, her lips, and tongue.

Operating purely on instinct, she kneeled on the bed and pressed kisses along his collarbone, loving the feel of his hot, dry skin. Then she explored his upper body with tiny nips and tastes, brushing her lips over his nipples and letting the crisp chest hair tickle her nose.

When her mouth trailed down his flat torso, she said, "Do you like this?" though she already knew by his sharp intake of breath. Her fingers massaged his chest while her mouth teased. His stomach muscles jumped under her lips.

She watched him. With no idea of what he liked—or what she liked either—she read the clues. His moves. His temperature. The moist slick of sweat on his stomach. How his breath quickened and his hands alternately guided her and then let go. Every time she went near his lower belly, his breath hitched. When she teasingly went even lower, he planted his palms on the bed and gripped the blanket. He was trying not to touch her. But he wanted to. Desperately. She could tell by the way his fingers flexed. Several times he reached out, only to pause and let his hands float a few inches above her head.

Over and over, he held back. A few times, he started to say something, a word of urging or praise, and then stopped himself. She wasn't sure what that was about. But she wasn't going to worry about it. Unless and until he said "no," she planned to love every inch of him for as long as he let her.

She delighted in figuring out the cause and effect, creating action and reaction. He might be stifling his verbal responses but he couldn't hide his body's unmistakable signs of arousal. With every second that passed, she knew him better and gained confidence in her instincts.

When she skimmed below his navel, his cock jumped repeatedly, almost begging to be released from the boxer briefs. Wickedly, she made him wait, devoting all her attention to learning exactly what he liked, all the while getting wetter and hotter herself. She smoothed the muscles above his groin with feathery strokes, gradually deepening the pressure. Then she slid to the inside of his strong thighs.

"Hold it," he said. "Condom." He got up and left the room briefly and when he came back, sat on the edge of the bed and ripped open the package.

She knelt on the floor and helped. His skin smelled pleasantly familiar, of cherry tobacco and soap. The scent evoked a chain of elusive memories of yearning and happiness. More complex feelings crept in too and swirled around the edges. These were tangled with failure, shame, and loss.

She closed her eyes. "I think…I think I know this. I think I know *you*."

He sat with his hands braced on his knees, watching her. "What are you saying?"

"I'm not sure. It's not clear yet." She didn't understand and right now, she didn't *want* to understand. Whatever she and Jackson had shared in the past or present, it was fragile. Maybe too fragile to withstand scrutiny.

She slipped between his legs and held her hands flat against his taut, trembling thighs. If he was feeling anything close to what she felt, second thoughts were mere speed bumps under a roaring engine of need.

His eyes closed as if he were in pain and his palms hovered above her. She paused, grabbed his wrists and placed his hands on her head. His breath came in a low hiss of need and anticipation.

"Keep your hands there," she whispered, with her lips so close to his cock that she could feel it pulsing, beckoning her. "Guide me. Show me what you like."

As soon as the words left her mouth, his fingers threaded in her hair. He groaned outright when she went down on him, slowly taking all of him in. She gave herself a moment to adjust to his long length. He tightened his fingers and his whole body stiffened as she sucked, using her tongue to swirl and her hand to squeeze the base.

They created a dance, finding their rhythm. She alternated pressure while his pelvis rocked against her. He was already close. She rolled back on her heels to watch his face as she stroked him, slow, then fast. His eyes opened and the look he gave her was fierce and possessive.

He captured her hands and moved them to his hips, effectively bringing all her efforts to a halt. She scowled in disappointment and then realized she had him right where she wanted him. Who needed hands?

She lunged and sucked the tip. For a couple of delicious seconds, he let her do what she wanted while he grew swollen with need. Though her wrists were still pinned against him, she felt his control slipping,

That's when he released her and pushed her back.

"What are you doing?" she protested. "I want to keep going."

"If you keep going, I'll explode." He dragged her back onto the bed, rolling until she was trapped on her back with him above her, elbows braced on either side of her head. He looked so serious, so intent as his gaze swept up and down. "You're beautiful."

"So are you. Why don't you let me finish what—"

He cut her off with his mouth. The kiss started out forceful but quickly morphed into gentle. He took his time, as if she were a delicacy to be lingered over.

Something changed during that sweet kiss. She'd thought this would be a straightforward affair, one where they each gave and took the comfort as needed. Now— now she realized it wasn't that simple. Not for him. This wasn't just any old roll in the hay or quick, enjoyable sex— fast food to be consumed and then forgotten. This meant something to him. With every minute that passed, it meant more to her, too.

His feelings weren't straightforward. She'd known that since the janitor's closet. Sometimes he looked at her like he hated her, sometimes like he wanted her. But never with indifference.

This was a new plateau where like, lust, love and hate overlapped and twisted together in a confusing puzzle. What was happening here? She sensed that whatever he felt, it wasn't for her, the actual woman under him. Right now he was making love to someone he'd known a long time ago. The girl that didn't exist anymore.

He abruptly stopped kissing her. Had he read her mind again?

No, he was too far gone. His hands were everywhere, caressing her breasts and gliding down the center of her body. By now her senses were heightened and she was exquisitely sensitive to his touch. Her body quaked with every caress and she gasped when he stroked her inner thighs. She couldn't control herself. He was making her twitch and jump every time he found another erogenous zone.

He spread her legs and his tongue made her catch fire. She shook and moaned as he teased and rolled her clitoris softly and then harder, flicking it faster.

He had all the power. She didn't like this; she wanted to control the pace. She tried to bat him away, pull him up like he'd done with her but he wouldn't let her.

The wanting became unbearable. He drew her up a long incline till she was half-blind with need. Then he backed down, easing up on the pressure and intensity. Each time he pushed her back up again, she thought this time he'd take her to the top. Instead he brought her almost to the peak and then distracted her with other moves. He even lifted her legs to kiss the back of her knees.

She was almost sobbing. "I can't wait, I can't stand this, you have to—"

His smile had an edge. She hated him.

"What?" he asked. "Do this?" He entered her with two fingers and she convulsed. "What about this?" He curled his fingers and she bucked upward. When he proceeded to lick her with unhurried finesse, she trembled with need.

She was going to die from frustration—she knew it. "Don't do this."

"Now," he said. His tongue came down on her hard and she nearly lost it.

She couldn't talk, couldn't scream, couldn't do anything except feel her body tighten while every ounce of awareness centered on his tongue as he tortured, teased, and soothed her, and finally, finally, gave her a release that broke in undulating waves of pleasure.

From far away, she heard herself exhale on a long moan of animal satisfaction, shuddering in an orgasm that he orchestrated. She lay limp and exhausted, quivering like a bow string plucked one time too many.

He crawled up her body and captured her face between his hands. His hair hung around them like a curtain, shutting out the world. Nothing else existed. Just the two of them inside this private space where he made her feel cherished and peaceful. Where anything seemed possible.

"I want you inside me," she said. "And you can wipe that smug look off your face. Unless you want me to dish it out the way you just did."

He hovered over her. "Which way is that? Like a maestro?"

"You're an arrogant bastard."

"You're just now figuring that out?"

He twitched against her thigh, large and pulsing. But Jackson himself was a study in alert relaxation. He pushed her hair away from her face, untangling a few strands and spreading them on the pillow with care.

She wiggled into a better position, reached around and massaged his glutes. He dipped his head to kiss her and entered her only partially, watching her face the whole time.

"Okay?" he said in a clipped voice.

He had every intention of drawing this out. The hell with that. She pulled him hard so that he had no choice but to sink into her. His long groan gave her a satisfying thrill, even more satisfying that his first, deep thrusts.

After a few startled seconds, she adjusted to his length and girth and soon met and matched him. He drove into her, quickening the pace. She wrapped her legs up and around his waist, giving him deeper access. The first thrust at that angle made her cry out in surprised pleasure.

He immediately stopped and gathered her face in his hands. "Too much?"

She shook her head. He had taken over her body. They were merged so completely she didn't know where he ended and she began. He'd been right after all. This was too much. Too raw. Too intense. And she felt powerless.

"I've got an idea," she said, prodding his chest. "Up."

He hesitated, then withdrew with a wary look on his face.

Once he sat up, she clambered over and settled herself on his lap with her knees bent. Now they were face to face and eye to eye.

"*This* is what I've been waiting for," she said. He found her mouth, kissed her long and deep, and slid his big hands down her back to cup her bottom. She didn't need any more encouragement. She held onto his shoulders and lifted herself. And then sank down, greedily taking every inch he could give.

He filled her so completely she couldn't imagine moving. There was no space between them, no room for anything resembling regret, no way to pretend this felt anything less than amazing. He steadied her trembling body.

A sense of rightness, a certainty that this was where she was meant to be, formed in her head and her heart. The certainty overwhelmed her, so much so that she thought he might see it in her face. She tried to rest her forehead against his. He wouldn't let her. He lifted her slightly, keeping her exactly where he wanted her.

"You can't hide anymore," he whispered. "I'm right here and I see everything. Everything you feel, I feel. I'm a part of you and you're a part of me."

Strangely enough, she believed him. They were fused in body and spirit. His pleasure was hers. And maybe, just maybe his pain was hers.

She clutched his biceps and those seemed to swell, too, bunching with tension as she rode him. Soon she forgot he was watching and moved with abandon, controlling the pace and the intensity. Her inner muscles contracted and held him tightly.

He had her ass in his hands and squeezed every time she moaned. They moved faster, creating something almost tangible. Whatever it was, it coalesced between them.

He pulled her hard and captured her mouth in his at the moment of her most intense pleasure, right as the wave gathered her up, helpless against its power over her. They rose in the wave together, free and yet anchored too.

"I have you," he said.

"I have you, too," She held back, waiting for him.

He surrendered, gasping and shuddering in one long hot burst. That sent her flying with one last shudder that ended in long ripples of pleasure. She kept her legs wrapped around him and rode it out.

They stayed upright for a while, locked in a sweaty embrace, holding on tight, with neither inclined to let go. She would have been content to stay that way all night. After a few minutes, he lifted her off him and collapsed onto his back. Feeling curiously shy after the intimacy they'd shared, she turned on her side.

She was almost asleep when he spoke to the ceiling. "You said something. You said, 'I think I know you.' What did you remember?"

She blinked herself awake. "Nothing specific. My body remembers you, remembers we were together. It's kind of like hearing a remix of an old song. I recognized it...I mean, you. And the emotions that came with that recognition. But now...now the song has changed."

He said nothing and she stared into the darkness, glad she wasn't facing him when she asked the question. "Were we in love?"

She counted in her head while the seconds ticked by. One-Mississippi. Two-Mississippi...

At seven-Mississippi, he finally replied. "We can't go back, Rose. Life doesn't work that way."

Her chest tightened. "I know."

"What did you expect?"

She didn't have a snappy comeback.

"Just so we're clear," he muttered.

"I don't think we are. You don't have to say anything, but for what it's worth, I must have loved you, as deeply as a seventeen-year-old can love anyone. If those scraps of emotion I recalled are any indication, I think you broke my heart."

Five Mississippis passed. He let her twist in the wind, even as the storm outside weakened.

"Oh, for crying out loud," she said. "Would it kill you to throw me a bone?"

His laugh came out of his nose, like it snuck up on him. "I thought I didn't have to say anything." His arms came around her, strong and possessive.

She was so sensitized to his touch that her nipples hardened against his forearm and a twinge of arousal stirred between her legs. He reacted too, stiffening against her ass.

Despite everything they'd just done, a ripple of desire passed through her.

"Ignore it," he said. "Sleep."

## 11

JACKSON WATCHED the morning light play over her hair. She faced him, warm and rosy, curled up with her fist under her chin. Since she would never know, he lay back down and allowed himself five more minutes.

He wanted to wake her with slow kisses and memorize every inch of her. Take her hard and take her soft. Make her forget every other man she'd been with. And then he wanted to start all over again.

Except that what he wanted was monumentally stupid. Not to mention selfish—she wasn't his and never could be. Last night she'd tried to tell him she'd loved him once. Or thought she had. As if he'd broken *her* heart. What was he supposed to do with that?

Nothing, that's what. Today he'd find someone else to serve as a watchdog. Then he'd get the hell out of her life. Soon enough she'd be safe at home. In the long run, after she recovered her memory, she'd be relieved he hadn't stuck around. With any luck, he'd go on as he always had, travelling a lot, working too much and sleeping with women he didn't much care about.

She sighed in her sleep. The sound made him hard. If he wanted, he could wake her now and make love to her again. She'd be warm and responsive, any man's dream. He knew she would. But then they'd have to talk. And he didn't want to lie to her anymore. So instead, he relaxed and kept on watching her with his fingers tangled in her hair.

Just five more minutes.

He twined a strand around his finger and smiled at a long-lost memory of his own. They'd been watching Saturday morning cartoons and while Rose was distracted, he'd braided several gobs of chewing gum into her hair. Her mother had been so upset when she saw the mess, Jackson felt terrible.

Mrs. Slater had slathered peanut butter into Rose's hair for an hour. But no matter how she tried, she couldn't remove all the gum. Finally, Mrs. Slater got some scissors and started chopping the gum out. By the end of the morning, Rose had a pixie cut.

Rose, meanwhile, laughed it off and returned the favor the following Saturday afternoon when she deposited a juicy wad of Double Bubble in his hair while they watched Tarzan. Mrs. Slater had taken one look at him and said, "Get the scissors."

More light poured between the curtains. Five minutes became ten. The morning was advancing. He released her lock of hair and watched it unspiral and return to its original shape. If it weren't for the risk of waking her, he would have kissed her. Instead he picked up a stray hair and wrapped it around his finger. Then, calling on the self-discipline he'd developed over the past ten years, he left her without a backward glance. After a quick shower, he dressed and made coffee.

Local cellular networks were blocked once again. He walked outside to use the satellite phone and that didn't work either. Satellite malfunctions typically didn't last long. When service came back up, he'd check in with Markus. In the meantime, he'd stick with the plan. This shouldn't take more than a couple of hours. She might even sleep till then. He hoped so; she needed it.

He left a note in the kitchen instructing her to stay inside until he returned.

Outside the front door, the only sign of life in the neighborhood was the twitch of a window curtain across the street. He circled the block once, just in case. All was quiet. Two blocks down, traffic flowed as usual and people were out and about. Cafes and street vendors were open for business.

A big man in fatigues and a military green sweater was buying coffee from a stand on the corner. He wasn't armed and seemed harmless enough. This fellow was likely a volunteer militia member whose primary purpose was neighborhood patrol.

The militia man smiled broadly at him. "Good morning, sir."

When Jackson returned the greeting in keeping with local custom, the man nodded his approval. Ordinarily in unstable situations like this, Jackson would take the opportunity to hang out and learn the scuttlebutt. Not today.

He found a taxi on the next block and directed the driver to the embassy. The closer they got, the more deserted the streets. The entire district had turned into a ghostly maze of blast walls and concrete barricades. Three blocks from the embassy, he paid off his driver and continued on foot. A policeman at the final barricade flat-out refused to let him pass, telling him that no one had been allowed in or out of the embassy compound since the diplomatic corps had evacuated.

Just then his phone rang. Markus spoke rapidly. "We have a satellite signal at the moment but it keeps going down so listen up. As of five minutes ago, you and I have orders to leave the country by any means possible. ASAP."

"Is the airport open?"

"No, but the trains are running, for now. I just got an email from the embassy advising anyone who hasn't evacuated to stay off the streets. Personally, I think we're better off hiring a driver to take us across a remote border while we still can. The insurgents control the southern border but not the eastern one. North is remote enough, but travelling through that territory is treacherous."

"Alright, we'll figure that out later," Jackson said. "I've got to find another place for Rose to stay until the airport opens again."

"I know an ex-pat who's still here."

"Who?"

"The woman I've been seeing. There's twenty-four-hour guards outside her building. Rose could stay there. Or we could just take her along with us."

"No. Not an option."

"Where will—"

Jackson cut him off. "I need you to keep watch outside the safe house while I find a passport for Rose. Is Mr. Bobo still in business?"

"Sure he is and fatter than ever. You better get over there quick. Mr. Bobo always looks out for number one, so he'll be closing up shop early. Things are about to get even uglier around here."

"Why? What else have you heard?"

"You know about the kids they've been taking? Over the past three days, the insurgents have been raiding camps, schools and shantytowns, taking both boys and girls. They seized a United Nations camp. Rumor has it they're keeping hostages and kidnapped kids there. To make matters worse, there's talk of a possible outbreak at that camp."

"Ebola? Lassa Fever?"

"Yellow fever."

Jackson thought about the kids he'd played soccer with at the hospital. Even if they survived the missile strikes, they might well have ended up at that camp.

"But here's the bad news," Markus said.

"That wasn't the bad news?"

"I just had this from a reliable source. The insurgents murdered those two nurses at that U.N. camp yesterday. Virtually every aid organization and NGO is pulling their people out of the country."

"Do me a favor," Jackson said, "and get over to the safe house. Make sure Rose is okay. I'll be there as soon as I can."

He disconnected as Markus said, "Wait. You're not there now? Where are you?"

When Jackson tried to call him back, there was no signal.

Mr. Bobo remembered Jackson, or more likely, remembered his crisp U.S. dollars. By late morning, Jackson had purchased a fairly decent U.S. passport, complete with a head shot of Rose they'd found online, and a few pages filled with stamps. This passport wouldn't get past the biometrics sensors used elsewhere; it should suffice to get her on a plane out of here, once the airport reopened. She'd likely be stranded at Heathrow for a day or two. In the scheme of things, not that big of a deal.

He examined her passport photo. She looked younger yet harder and more cynical than she did now. An interesting contradiction that made him wonder about the real Rose, the woman she'd revert to once she recovered her memories. Growing up, she'd always been idealistic—how much had she actually changed? Who had she become? Hollow regret chased the question. He might never know.

The trip back to the safe house cost him double what he'd paid earlier. Once again, flashing a roll of bills had done the trick to convince the driver of the only taxi he could find. Although the curfew didn't go into effect till 6 p.m., far fewer people were out than just two hours ago.

The taxi driver dropped him off two blocks from the safe house, refusing to go any further into the neighborhood. The corner where people had been chatting earlier was empty. All the shops and cafes were closed. A sense of queasy anticipation hung in the air.

Jackson walked up the block. Markus's Toyota wasn't in sight. Either he hadn't arrived yet or he'd stashed the car elsewhere. That Aussie bastard had better be on his best behavior with Rose.

As he drew closer, he realized something wasn't right. Splintered wood lay scattered on the front step. The front door hung open, off-kilter.

He ran in and yelled her name, though he already knew she was gone.

~

Rose leaned forward as far as the guy holding her allowed. Though she couldn't see through the hood, she was certain the man in the front passenger seat was the leader. He'd been giving orders to both the driver and the pissed-off nutcase beside her.

Her only warning had been the sound of the door splintering. They'd grabbed her as she emerged from the bathroom in a panic, barefoot and wearing only the flowered caftan. She'd landed one good kick with her heel before the beefy one dealt her a backhanded slap. Then they trussed her up and hustled her out to a waiting car.

The whole thing couldn't have taken more than two minutes. All in broad daylight. Surely someone—perhaps a neighbor—had seen what happened and could tell Jackson. However, even he, with all his geeky tech skills, wouldn't have any way of knowing where they'd taken her.

If he had been there, they wouldn't have gotten her so easily. On second thought, it was a blessing he hadn't been there. Otherwise, he would have been captured too.

She held back a sob. Better not to think of him at all. She was on her own. At least she wouldn't have the anguish of seeing any would-be rescuers die. That would be way worse than dying herself.

She spoke carefully through swollen, bruised lips. "Where are you taking me?"

Something hard and metallic poked into her skull, right above her ear. She closed her eyes. Either he'd do it or he wouldn't. Screaming wouldn't help. She waited for the click.

"Put the gun down." The order came from the front seat in the deep voice of a big man.

The pressure let up, but the guy beside her was still breathing heavily. He smelled like fish and belligerent male pride.

"Do not speak again," he hissed in her ear, "unless you are spoken to." He pushed between her bound hands and punctuated his words by pressing his thumbs hard inside of her wrists. Under his breath he added, "I will punish you for that tonight."

He dug in, pushing against the veins until she gasped.

He laughed. "Listen. She likes that. These women are all whores."

From a haze of pain, Rose dimly heard the man in the driver's seat say something in another language.

The boss spoke, directing his question to the back seat. "You let her kick you? Is that why you hit her mouth?"

"She went crazy while we were tying her up. Someone had to show her who is boss."

"Ah," the boss man said in an oddly pleasant voice. "You thought it was your duty to hit my hostage."

She wanted to ask these asshats if they knew the American government did not pay ransom for kidnapped citizens. And then thought better of it. Because they might just say fuck it and kill her.

She strained to hear any sounds the men made, noting every identifiable action and filing it away. Thank God she could count on her short-term memory. The one who'd hurt her just now had used both his thumbs on her wrist. He would have had to put the gun down first, and she hadn't heard him set anything on the seat. So he must have set it on the floor. Since then he hadn't bent over or shifted his body weight. Had he forgotten to pick up his gun?

They drove for a long time, maybe an hour. One of the windows was open and Rose listened carefully for any distinctive noises. She heard nothing unusual, except the thumping of the car's low-riding undercarriage when it met deep ruts.

The car lurched to a halt.

"Take her inside," the deep voice ordered.

The man beside her hauled her out of the car, dragged her a short distance and into a structure of some sort. He dumped her on the floor.

She felt a draft on her legs.

*Oh, God.* He had lifted her caftan. She was completely exposed and helpless while he groped between her legs roughly, staking a brutal claim.

Outside the door, someone called out in a language she didn't recognize.

Her captor withdrew his hand. "I will be back tonight. That's a promise." Then he walked out, leaving her sprawled on the floor with the dress pushed up around her hips.

Silence fell. With her feet and wrists still bound, it took her several attempts to roll over and get the skirt back down. Using her elbows and knees for leverage, she managed to sit.

A shout—abruptly cut off—made her jump. A loud pop-pop came next. Gunshots. Almost certainly gunshots.

The door opened again and heavy footsteps approached. She shut her eyes tightly and tried to mentally prepare herself for another assault. A deep chuckle came just before the hood whipped off her head.

She blinked against the unaccustomed light. It seemed blinding at first, though the room wasn't bright. She was in a windowless, concrete block hut.

The face above her came into focus and she recognized the round-faced man who'd pursued them in the jeep. What had Raymond called him? The general. The Red Boys' general.

He sat with a gusty sigh on a stool opposite her. Sweat gleamed on his forehead and he smiled the toothy smile she remembered. He wiped his hands on his fatigues, leaving damp streaks.

"What is this place?" she asked. "Why am I here?"

"You are in a refugee camp," the general said with precise, smooth diction. "Set up by so-called peacekeepers. That's what they call themselves, those thieves and crooks. General Mutan has liberated the camp from our oppressors. Now it belongs to the people. We have taken back what is ours."

"There's been some mistake," she said. "I'm not a thief or an oppressor."

"General Mutan does not make mistakes."

Not if one didn't count how he'd eaten her dust yesterday and then tangled with that chain link fence. Or his habit of referring to himself in the third person.

He went on. "You were foolish to trick me with that quarantine hoax. And then you ran away. You should not have done that. I am your only friend here."

"I think you've confused me with someone else. Which side are you on—the government or the insurgents?"

Though his smile never slipped, there was tension in it. "The winning side. I can protect you if you cooperate."

She wasn't sure if he expected a thank you or what. "Cooperate how? And protect me from whom?"

"Yellow fever has arrived in the camp. Some of my people believe you and other aid workers poisoned our children with vaccinations. They would like to see you pay for your crimes. Lock you up, then put you on trial for war crimes."

"I haven't poisoned anyone."

He chuckled again. "Ah, but General Mutan did not say he believes that. Others do, the backward and ignorant. I know the truth. You and your friends are spies who use your aid work as a cover. You've been allowed to travel freely all over *my* country to protect *your* country's capitalist interests. We both know it suits your purposes to keep my people ignorant and impoverished."

"I don't know where you got that idea. And I'm not a spy. What do you want from me?"

"Your cooperation. Mosquito nets and medicine are in short supply. Your organization stockpiled these resources and kept them from us. Don't insult my intelligence or waste my time with denials. If you help me, I will protect you from others who are not as enlightened as I am."

The general did not strike her as someone overly concerned with his fellow man, much less public health. She didn't know what to say. If she told him she had no memory of the aid work she'd been doing, much less knowledge of supplies, what then?

Maybe he'd let her go. Or maybe he'd kill her. As long as he thought he needed her, she could buy herself time.

"I see you are not convinced," the general said. "We will pay a visit to your friend."

"What friend?"

"The man you were fucking. Did you think you kept that a secret?"

Time seemed to slow down as Mutan waited for her to react, his face full of gleeful anticipation. She kept hers impassive. Jackson had left the house very early this morning. His note said he'd gone to get her a passport. He couldn't possibly be a prisoner. He was in the city.

"I don't know who you mean," she said.

"Of course you do."

She watched him warily. The missile strikes had likely concealed how those two soldiers had died in the janitor's closet. Chances were the general and his men had no idea Jackson was a badass. Not unless Jackson wanted them to know. Should she just play along?

"I should warn you," Mutan said. "He's not pretty anymore." His booming laugh bounced around the small hut as he untied the restraints from her ankles.

He yanked her up and forced her out into the mid-day glare.

Hundreds—if not thousands—of tents encircled the hut, forming a temporary village surrounded by a dense forest. Soldiers with AK-47s patrolled the rows of tents.

The general kept his hand on her neck and forced her to turn a corner. As soon as she rounded it, she stumbled over something and looked down, wondering why her bare feet were wet. A full second passed while her mind absorbed what she saw.

A lifeless man stared at the sky, arms flung out, already embracing death. It was the beefy soldier who had assaulted her just minutes earlier. Minus a chunk of his head. A pool of blood and brain matter spread around him.

Rose skittered sideways and held her throat to contain her instinctive scream. She fought to stay in control. She looked around for help. There were plenty of people all over the place. Both soldiers and camp residents walked by with their heads averted as if nothing had happened. The general chuckled, pleased with her reaction. He'd intended for her to trip over the corpse.

"Why did you kill him?" she asked.

"He wasn't worthy of the uniform."

This is why he had been wiping his hands on his pants inside the hut. He'd just killed a man. Rose wasn't sorry that man was dead, not at all. Nevertheless, the violence and now the cheerful way Mutan regarded the dead man turned her stomach.

A soldier scurried over and grabbed the body by the ankles.

"No," Mutan ordered. "Leave him. I want everyone to see what he looks like in the morning. If the animals don't drag him away before then." He turned to Rose. "What you people would call a teaching moment. Isn't that the expression?"

"Teachable," she said. "A teachable moment."

His smile flickered and she cursed herself for not keeping her mouth shut. A long moment passed. He seemed to make a decision.

He pushed her ahead of him and forced her down a long aisle with tents on either side. Every step across the rocky dirt hurt her bare feet. He shoved her when she walked too slow for his taste. Civilians came and went from the tents, avoiding any eye contact with Rose or the general.

Except for one girl. She was about fourteen or fifteen, carrying a plastic water jug. There was something different about her. Perhaps her posture and air of dignity. Rose might not have known her if it hadn't been for the pink sandals. As she passed, the girl raised her chin with a quick furtive gesture and widened her eyes. Aware that the general was watching, Rose resisted the impulse to acknowledge her.

This girl and her two younger sisters had worn matching pink sandals while playing outside at the hospital. All three had shown off those sandals proudly. The littlest one was so smitten she had refused to go upstairs until they'd found the sandal she'd misplaced.

Rose remembered the girls because they were adorable. Also because of their names: Faith, Patience, and Charity. If the oldest girl was in the camp, were the other children here, too? Unless she had somehow been separated from them. This, at the very least, was proof that the children had survived the missile strikes yesterday. If they had survived, Nurse Okeke may well have survived also.

The general continued to push Rose down the long row. At the end, hard against the forest, a metal shipping container sat apart from the tents. Soldiers stood guard outside. She was shoved through the opening and into a hot, cramped space that smelled of urine and blood.

A man lay facedown, his hands pinned behind his back and ankles tightly bound. Flies swarmed around him. The soles of his bare feet were crisscrossed with deep lacerations.

Relief pumped through her. He wasn't Jackson. This man was blond. When he turned his head, shock and recognition flashed in his bright blue eyes. This was the man she'd seen at the hospital yesterday. The one who had called her name.

"I'm sorry," he said in a choked voice, before his glance slid to the general.

"For what?" she said reflexively.

The general used his boot to flip him and the man immediately curled into the fetal position.

"Your Doctor Oliver is sorry he talked," Mutan said, waving the flies away with a moue of disgust. "He told

General Mutan everything. He signed a confession admitting how you pretended to help my people, posing as humanitarians." He spat the last word.

So this man was a doctor she worked with.

"I'm sorry I wasn't stronger," Oliver said to her, though he stared at the wall. He spoke in a faint accent she couldn't identify. "He tortured me. I'm sorry."

"What are you sorry for?"

"Everything." His voice cracked and shook. "I need you to do something for me."

"Of course."

"If you make it out, tell my wife I love her. Tell her she was the best thing that ever happened to me. I know it's asking a lot. But you're tough, aren't you? You don't feel things so deeply. It's easier for you."

The general cackled at that while Rose stared in bewilderment.

Oliver went on. "Promise you won't tell her the rest. Please. I don't want my kids to know what a prick I was." His chest convulsed and tears seeped from the corners of his eyes.

"Ha," the general said. "He admits it."

Rose raised her voice to be heard over Oliver's sobs. "Listen, you'll see your wife and tell her yourself, okay? Just hold on."

"That's enough," General Mutan said. "This weak cunt bores me." He opened the door and called to the guards. "You, get my jeep. And you, get my machete."

She tried to think what Jackson would do in this situation. He sure as hell wouldn't give up. Nor would he assume everyone in this country was evil.

The girl stopped screaming. Unsure whether that was a good sign or a bad one, Rose cracked the door a few inches and saw only the guard's back. There was no sign of the general. She turned back to Oliver.

"Alright," she said, "What does he want with me?"

"He wants the stuff from the storage unit in town. At least that's what he says."

"This isn't adding up."

"He knows the security touchpad requires two people to provide both a fingerprint and a passcode."

"So what he needs is…our fingerprints? That's what he wants?"

His chin sank to his chest. "His men killed Maud and Lorenzo yesterday. Mutan was pissed about that. Or was that the day before? I can't remember now. They only kept me alive to show them which drugs to steal from the hospital. Now you and I are the only ones left. He needs our fingerprints. That's why he asked for the machete."

She felt cold, despite the stifling heat in the container. "No. He wouldn't—"

"He gets off on inflicting pain. He's looking for a reason to use it."

"You don't know that. He might want the machete for something else. You're not giving up." She raised her voice. "Do you hear me? I won't let you."

"That temper of yours. It's ironic they caught you."

"Why is that ironic?"

"Forget it. It doesn't matter anymore."

She shook her head as if to clear it. "If he wants those supplies so badly, why not just blow the security panel off the door? Things are so chaotic here, no one would stop him."

"Until last night…until he got it out of me, he didn't know where that storage unit was. Now he does. So now we're really fucked. Once he gets what he wants, he'll kill us both."

"Hold it," she said. "You said the general needs our fingerprints *and* our passcodes."

"Two people have to perform the entire protocol, one right after another, within thirty seconds," Oliver said dully. "But he knows my password now. He'll get yours too. It won't take him long."

"Except *I don't remember* mine. I woke up with amnesia two days ago."

His laugh grated on her nerves. "You really can't remember? Maybe not knowing will keep you alive a while longer. Just long enough to wish you were dead." He lifted his chin and for the first time, displayed curiosity about something other than himself. "He's been asking a lot of questions about you. About the villages you all travelled to when I went home last month. Why would he do that?"

"You'd know more than me. You were my boss, correct?"

"Among other things."

She looked at him askance, disliking his tone. "What was my job?"

"Planning and logistics. You assisted in the field too. We provided basic medical aid in remote villages. Vaccinations and primary care."

"Can you tell me…did something bad happen to me, trauma that might have caused the amnesia?"

"Nothing as bad as what's about to happen to you."

She crouched beside him. "How long have we known each other?"

"Since we both arrived, about six months ago. We've been in some intense situations, working long hours, far from home. I didn't plan to get involved. But you know, shit happens."

A sinking feeling formed in her stomach. "Are you saying you and I had a thing?"

"No one forced you. Quite the contrary. I told you I was single. You never questioned that."

Her eyes went to his ring finger and a thin strip of white skin above the knuckle. Plain as day. A wave of mortification engulfed her.

He saw where her eyes went. "I took it off on my first day here. You never once asked me about the missing ring. You didn't *want* to know."

"You're married." It hadn't occurred to her that she might be this sort of person. Either ignorant or selfish. Quite possibly both. A homewrecker, for God's sake.

"Of course I'm fucking well married. Why wouldn't I be?" He choked up. "I've got a beautiful wife and three kids. Don't look at me like that. You're no angel. You have a fiancé somewhere."

She rubbed her temple and a despairing half-laugh bubbled to the surface. "A fiancé. Oh, this is getting better and better."

"A Frenchman, I think you said. Anyway, you stopped sleeping with me when you couldn't ignore the evidence any longer. If it wasn't for that scare you had—"

"What scare?"

"Never mind. It's moot now. Not important."

What had she seen in this Oliver character? Other than his looks. She didn't know whether to believe half the stuff he said. How could she be engaged? She wasn't wearing a ring, had seen nothing in her room, not even a picture stuck in the hotel mirror.

Longing for Jackson overwhelmed her. She missed him. His competence, his humor, and his strength. The way he observed everything and took it all in. He didn't blame or whine. He problem-solved. If he were here, he'd—no, she wasn't going to think like that. Self-pity was an indulgence that made her weak and as useless as Oliver.

By now Jackson must have deduced what happened and reported her kidnapping to the State Department. He would have done that for her before he left the country. He might even be safely across the border by now. She hoped so. She truly did.

"I'll never see my family again," Oliver said. "What happened between you and me…none of that matters anymore."

"It matters to me, asshole. Keep talking."

"You don't know what torture does to a person," he said, sniffing. "You have no idea what happens when they break you."

He was right. She didn't know how she'd break, or what she'd say or do under duress. For all she knew, in his position she'd be whimpering, too.

More gently, she asked, "What else can you tell me? Did anything unusual happen in the last few days, before all this I mean."

"You were acting strange all last week," Oliver said. "Kind of foggy and off your feed. Ever since the shit hit the fan and you found out—" He stopped abruptly.

"What? What did I find out?"

He hesitated, then said, "What my actual mission was."

His words sunk in and the rustling of the forest behind them seemed to grow louder. "What are you saying? What was your mission?"

"Keep your voice down."

"Answer the question," she said through gritted teeth. "What were you doing here?"

"Gathering intelligence."

"What sort of intelligence?"

"You name it," he said. "Since we travelled all over, we had eyes and ears on troop movements, insurgent activity, population shifts, even natural resources that might be useful."

"Who were you feeding this information to?"

"An alliance with interests here."

"That sounds like corporate involvement, not humanitarian. Not even political." It was all she could do to control her voice. "But you're a doctor."

"Yes."

"What kind?"

"General practitioner."

"You were using our aid work as a *cover*? Whatever happened to 'First, do no harm?' Tell me we weren't giving fake vaccinations. Because if we were, I might just steal a machete and kill you myself."

"The vaccinations were real. We didn't hurt anyone."

"How could you do this?"

"I did it because I could make more money in six months here than I would have made in five years as a doctor back in my country." He snorted. "You know what's funny? This is the second time we've had this conversation and it's almost identical to the first time around. Whatever's wrong with your head, it's bound to be temporary. Because your character isn't any different. You're a sanctimonious hypocrite."

"And you're a sonofabitch who played fast and loose with the truth. Innocent people will suffer because of what you did."

"You did your job. I did mine. You're just pissed off because your Mother Teresa fantasies didn't pan out. What you didn't know didn't hurt you."

Fury propelled her to her feet. "Until now. Didn't anyone think about the consequences for real aid workers?

Or the people who will refuse medical care because we've broken their trust?"

She saw no remorse on Oliver's handsome face. He was only sorry for himself, sorry he'd been caught before he could fly home to his beautiful wife, three kids, and plump bank account.

"Tell me something," she said. "When did I find out?" She waited for him to say *a few days ago*. That discovery— the shock of it—might be connected to her memory loss.

"A few weeks ago."

She gaped at him, unable to reconcile this. "A few weeks ago? I didn't quit? Why did I continue to work with you?"

"You insisted you weren't leaving without finishing what you'd started. There were two villages we hadn't gotten to yet."

Rose felt more disoriented and lost than she had since the truck bomb blew up the roundabout. "So the general was right all along. If I went along with this insanity, I'm a spy too. I'm a goddamn spy."

~

The afternoon wore on and Mutan didn't return. Oliver curled into himself, weeping and growing increasingly despondent. She had long since stopped trying to talk to him so it was a relief when a young soldier came in and pulled her to her feet. She recognized the skinny teenager instantly; he was indeed Raymond's brother, Solomon.

He hustled her past the other guard and into a tent in an adjacent row, then pointed to a small bowl of stew and a bottle of water set on a folded blanket.

"Where is your brother?" she asked.

Solomon quickly looked outside and scanned the vicinity before responding. "I sent him to our cousin."

"So he's safe?"

"If he is a good boy and does as he is told. He does not always obey."

This young man spoke with none of yesterday's bluster or antagonism. He had changed, seemingly overnight. Which seemed too good to be true. "Yesterday you nearly choked me to death. Why are you helping me now?"

"My brother would have been killed or captured if you had not taken him away from the hospital yesterday. Sorry I hurt you. I had to prove myself."

"Prove yourself to whom?"

"Never mind. I have to go."

If this were a ruse, she couldn't imagine what the teenager would gain by tricking her. "Wait, where is the general?"

"He was called into town to meet with the new defense minister. He will be back."

"Do you know what he's planning to do with us?"

"He will take you with him tonight to collect supplies."

"Oliver too?"

Solomon's gaze was steady and bleak.

"He won't kill him, surely."

"Do not interfere. You can't save him now."

~

Jackson was working as fast as he could, willing himself to concentrate and focus on the evening ahead. She needed him. Every argument began and ended with that simple fact. If he had to risk everything to find her, so be it.

Hearing a noise outside, he pulled out his Glock and moved into position. Footsteps approached. He released the safety and trained the gun. When the door creaked open, Jackson lowered his pistol.

"Where the fuck have you been?"

"They got her?" Markus said, inspecting the splintered door.

Jackson holstered the gun and resumed his work attaching LED lights. "What do you think? Where were you?"

"Detained by the Red Boys. Lucky for me I had enough cash on me to bribe my way out. Why did you leave her alone?"

"I told you. I had to get her a new passport."

Markus studied him. "You couldn't wait for me to get here first?"

"No." Jackson wasn't going to admit the truth. He had left because he was afraid she'd wake up with dreamy-eyed expectations, or worse, breezily dismiss last night as a fun fling. He'd been so tied up in knots, he hadn't known—and still didn't know—which scenario disturbed him more. His cowardice might have cost Rose her life.

"Have you notified your embassy contacts?" Markus asked.

"No, not yet. Anyway, they're evacuating. I know how these things work. By the time the special ops teams get their shit together and mobilize, she could be dead."

"I see you found the hidden closet."

"That wasn't difficult. Your dry wall seams were way too obvious."

Markus counted the units spread around the room. "Are you planning to use every single prototype?"

Jackson didn't look up. "Whatever it takes."

"You like to live dangerously. Even the Hummingbird?"

Jackson's laugh was dry as dust. "Doubtful. That thing is a piece of shit. A parlor trick with a short battery life. It's got no finesse."

"You know you could lose everything."

"Don't try to talk me out of this."

"I wouldn't dream of it, mate. I've got your back. What's the plan? If you want surveillance, we've only got three hours of daylight left."

"I don't need daylight. I need darkness. Listen, there's no need for you to get involved. Just stay out and maybe Holloway will go easy on you."

"I'm already involved," Markus said, scooping extra battery packs into a gear bag. "You ought to tell him what you're planning. You owe him that much."

Jackson contemplated his phone screen, noting that it was only 6 a.m. on the West Coast. Not the smartest way to wake up your boss. *Good morning. I'm about to create an international incident and there's nothing you can do to stop me.*

He was risking a great deal. If seized, their hardware would be confiscated by their host country and possibly sold off to the highest bidder. Once word got out, anyone savvy enough to reverse engineer the proprietary software would pounce. Years of work might go down the toilet. Most significantly, the entire project could be blown wide open, compromising their plans and dashing hopes. Politicians and naysayers worldwide would rail about "Big Brother" and block future progress. Real people would lose access to life-saving technology. Those weren't theoretical consequences.

Choosing to ignore potential outcomes was selfish. He understood that. Best case scenario, Will Holloway fired him and let it go at that. Given that software development alone on this project had cost Holloway a small fortune, it wasn't likely.

Worst case scenario, the insurgents won this civil war decisively and took over in short order. These rebels were religious extremists with a deep distrust of technology and Westerners. Unauthorized surveillance—by an American no less—would create a shitstorm of Biblical proportions. If they caught him, he'd be lucky to rot in a jail cell for the next twenty years. If he escaped, he'd face the music at home. The State Department would call for his head and the Justice Department would assemble the guillotine.

It would be worth it.

Will Holloway picked up after only two rings. A baby babbled in the background.

"Sorry for the early call," Jackson said.

"I'm a farmer, remember?" Holloway said. "I've been up for an hour."

*Farmer, my ass.* Holloway drove an ancient truck and lived in the middle of a vineyard, but he was hardly your typical farmer.

"What is going on over there?" Holloway asked. "You and Markus ought to be well over the border by now. Yet you're still at the safe house."

Naturally, Holloway would know their exact location.

Jackson began, "We have a situation."

"And why would—" Jackson's phone pinged. He checked the screen. "Shit. We've got a problem. There's a truck full of troops on an intercept path with Markus. He won't be able to get through to pick us up."

Rose made a beeline, glad for an excuse to go to him. His solid presence bolstered her courage. With Jackson here, she could cope with her sore feet, the dropping temperature, and her ever-present fear. This sweet rush—the glad reassurance from just looking at him—was the only thing keeping her going.

Maybe *this* is what happiness felt like: a certainty that you could count on someone, that he'd look out for you, no matter what. It surprised her. She hadn't expected this intense connection and near-magnetic pull to be liberating. In a weird way, she realized, Jackson represented...freedom.

"Where is this jeep?" he asked Solomon.

The teenager pointed in the opposite direction. "I moved it to the other side of camp."

"Give me the keys."

Solomon handed them over. "We can circle back through the forest."

"Go back? Not likely, kid."

"Solomon's right," Rose said. "They won't expect us to return. It's a good idea."

"He could be tricking us."

"He's not," Rose and Faith said in unison.

He angled his head in Rose's direction, not meeting her eyes, speaking at her rather than with her. "You really think we can trust this kid?"

"Yes."

"Let's do it then," he said grimly. "The sooner we're out of here, the better."

She limped behind the other three as they beat their way through the trees. Jackson kept his distance though she had the impression—she wasn't sure how, perhaps from his body language or the subtle tilt of his head—that he knew exactly when she winced. An impression that didn't jibe with his cool attitude. She'd just assumed that Mutan's accusations—the stuff about her being a spy, about fucking Oliver—wouldn't carry much weight. Apparently she'd been wrong. Had Jackson heard the reference to Oliver's wife, too? Shit, of course he had.

Ten minutes later, they emerged on the other side of the refugee camp. The jeep with the cracked windshield sat in the middle of a clearing. No one guarded this isolated spot; all the guards must be out searching for them and likely for those drones, too.

Jackson held his arm out to bar their way and produced his gun again. A shout from the camp galvanized him and he continued, signaling for them to follow. Something became apparent as they slowly edged towards the vehicle. A large bundle of clothes sat in the back seat. Those had not been there when the general pulled in earlier.

The bundle moved. A girl huddled beneath a scarf and watched them through terrified eyes. She couldn't be much older than thirteen. When Faith pushed past Jackson and into the back seat, the younger girl threw herself into Faith's arms and buried her face against her chest.

"Who is she?" Jackson said, herding them.

"My cousin," Solomon said.

When Rose tried to get behind the wheel, Jackson dug his hands into her shoulders and guided her to the back.

"Come on," she protested, "you can't do everything. If I drive, you can follow what's happening with Markus. And plot our course."

"Do as you're told," he said, getting in.

"But—"

"You're putting all of us at risk." His words were like ice water in her face. Then he jabbed a finger at Solomon. "I want you where I can see you."

She settled beside the girls and the jeep lurched forward, headlights off for the first few minutes as they quietly crunched over the gravel road. They crept past the empty guard post, before accelerating to barrel roughly away from the camp.

So much for her dreamy thoughts. Either Jackson had been repelled by the general's nasty remarks or he wasn't able to deal with a woman in the driver's seat. The latter didn't ring true, so she had to conclude it was the former. Yet he hadn't asked a single question about Oliver or given her a chance to explain. Even if he *had* asked, she didn't have any answers.

She turned to the young girl beside her and put a gentle hand on her shoulder. "I'm Rose. What's your name?"

The girl shrank away and hid her face.

"Her name is Sunday," Faith said.

"What happened to her?"

"One of the guards," Faith said, in a resigned, unemotional tone that broke Rose's heart.

Solomon turned around and his eyes glittered with rage. "She needs medical assistance. Can you help?"

"I'll do what I can, but I'm not a doctor. Or even a nurse."

"But the general said you were on a medical team."

Unlike her earlier spurt of happiness, this awareness of her own futility was familiar, a pall that spread from her chest, suffusing her with hopelessness. Much like the ineffectual anger she'd felt over and over in the last three days, and equally draining.

Good God, what if this was her normal state? What if she recovered her memory to find she was perpetually angry, or worse, a habitual victim? That had not occurred to her. Surely a good sign in itself.

Jackson would know, she thought suddenly. Of course he would. As her childhood friend, he'd know her true personality. Even if disgusted with her, Jackson had a core integrity. She could trust him to tell her the truth. Painful though it might be to hear, he'd be honest. She might not like it but at least she'd know.

Regardless, she did have free will, did she not? Once she got out of this mess and recovered, she could be whatever sort of person she wanted to be.

They hit a bump at high speed and the girls gasped and held onto each other. Rose, with nothing and no one to hold onto, flew up a few feet and bounced on the landing.

Jackson's gaze found hers in the rear-view mirror. "Okay?" he asked.

"I'll survive."

"Yes, you will. You're tough."

It's what Oliver had called her, too. Tough. Not a *survivor*, not even *resilient*. No, she was "tough." Durable and hard-wearing. The implication being: like that black polyester travel dress she'd discovered in her suitcase, unwanted stains just slid right off after a quick swish in the sink. She'd managed to give both men the impression that dirt, blood, sweat, and tears wouldn't leave a mark.

The idea made her grimace. The mental image that followed—popping unbidden into her head—made her suck in her breath. She had remembered something. Not everything, just one life-changing incident too vivid and gut-wrenching not to be real. Now, of all times, stuffed into a back seat with two traumatized girls, her frazzled brain made a leap, connecting dots to summon up one significant fragment.

It arrived not as a fully-formed coherent memory, but as scenes running like a film loop in her head. She saw herself hunched over a bathroom sink, scrubbing blood-stained panties, watching the stain dissolve into a faint brownish ring. She remembered weeping, then catching a mirrored glimpse of her ravaged face as she grappled with what had just happened.

The details were hazy. Not the grief. The grief was crystal clear. That was the moment of reckoning, when she'd understood what a mess she'd made of her life.

A terrible thing to face all alone in a sterile hotel bathroom.

~

Jackson concentrated on the road, glad he didn't have to look at Rose. Putting the kid up front with him had been a defensive move, but a good one, as it turned out. After seeing the teenager's concern for his cousin, Jackson shoved his doubts aside and tasked the kid with navigating. So far, Solomon had done a fine job, finding enough strategic detours to put plenty of distance between themselves and the camp. They hadn't encountered any government troops or insurgents on these back roads. For now, they were on a quiet stretch, passing small villages that were evidently not important enough for the insurgents to bother taking over.

Rose had been very quiet these last fifteen minutes. Damned if he couldn't ignore her, despite his best intentions. Was it his imagination that he could feel her grieving? Presumably for the owner of those dismembered hands. Her lover, if the general could be believed. When he'd mentioned a third man, a fiancé, Rose had not looked surprised. She'd kept that secret well.

And then there were the contradictions in her behavior. She'd shot Mutan square in the ass with efficient, practiced ease. Then expertly disarmed the weapon. Come to think of it, where did she find that gun?

Markus had not trusted her. Maybe Markus was right.

Behind him, Rose broke her silence. "Where are we going?"

"To Beatrice Okeke. These kids will be safe with her, or as safe as we can hope."

He heard her—or felt her, more like—perk up. "Beatrice. You mean Nurse Okeke? You know where she is?"

"Yep. I spoke to her earlier today, and I've been tracking her movements. She's in a village a few hours from here. Unless my data's wrong but—"

"Data doesn't lie," she said, saying it right along with him and sounding wry, but subdued.

She tapped Solomon on the shoulder. "How can I know for sure that Oliver is dead? We left him behind without verifying. Mutan could have been lying. We didn't even *try* to find him."

Solomon said flatly, "The Danish doctor? I saw them throw his body into the pit before I came to find you. He was dead."

"You're certain?"

"Very certain."

"I see," Rose said and sat back. "Thank you," she added unsteadily.

Jackson couldn't help a quick glance in the mirror but the shadows shifted and obscured her face. Had today's events jogged her memory? She must have loved the guy.

He wasn't surprised. These things happened all the time with expats: young, attractive people thrown together in intense situations. She'd fallen for someone on her team, a doctor no less. Likely a paragon of humanitarian virtue. A true hero. Women went gaga over that type. No doubt handsome as hell.

*Wait a second.* The general said *his wife* would want the hands. So, he was a married martyr.

His sympathy for her ebbed. This new drama only reinforced his original plan to go his own way and leave her behind at the first opportunity. He'd kept his word to her mother, saving Rose's ass enough times in the last few days that he'd lost count. She should be fine now, if she could keep herself out of trouble. All she had to do was lay low until the airport opened.

Her head was bowed and she had withdrawn into silence, much like Solomon and those young girls. They were a sad quartet, and he couldn't wait to deliver every single one of them—Rose included—to Beatrice Okeke, someone far better qualified to heal them than he.

Rescues weren't his gig and never had been. Though he'd witnessed civil wars, natural disasters, outbreaks—just about every misery that human beings and mother nature were capable of—he'd never had any illusions about who and what he was. He wasn't a hero or a humanitarian. He was a data geek, that's all.

It was well past midnight by the time they drove into a remote village far from the capital city. The landscape was different in this region, more bush than forest. The wind swept over them with a clean, sweet fragrance he couldn't identify.

The girls in the back seat were asleep. The younger one had her head on Rose's shoulder. Rose herself hadn't slept. She alternated between stroking the head of the sleeping girl and staring out the window. Perhaps all her thoughts were for Saint Oliver.

They pulled up in front of a modest home with one lit window. Jackson got out, motioning at Solomon and Rose to stay put. She lifted her head, then nodded. Her compliance worried him, as did that brittle, fake smile. What was wrong with her? He wanted to shake her and bring back the vivacious girl he used to know. Earlier tonight, when she'd thrown herself into his arms, she'd been her old self, radiating pure relief and joy. Not so much now.

Whatever. Her mental state wasn't his problem. *She* wasn't his problem.

Beatrice Okeke answered the door, though for a moment he didn't recognize her. Instead of her nurse's uniform, she wore a bright green wax-print caftan and a matching head scarf. Her warm smile was the same and the comprehensive glance she gave him conveyed the same intelligence and insight. He realized she was much younger than he'd supposed, perhaps in her mid-thirties, only a few years older than him.

"Jackson," she greeted him. "I've been expecting you. How many of the children did you find?"

"Two. Well, three if you include Solomon."

"Solomon is with you?" she said, surprised. "Samuel will not like that."

"Who is Samuel?"

She peered around him. "Ah, I see him now. Surely you know Samuel Mutan is the boy's father."

Jackson nearly slapped his own forehead. "You're telling me that kid is the general's son? Wait, is he the other one's father too? Raymond? Are you fucking kidding me? Er, sorry."

Beatrice was unfazed. "You had better hide that jeep. The village is asleep now, but there are some who rise early."

"If I'd known I wouldn't have let his kid come with us. Why didn't he say anything?"

"You answered your own question."

"Beatrice, before I bring them all in…"

She watched him as if she knew what he was about to say.

"…I need to leave Rose here with you."

She cut him off. "You must both leave in the morning. Samuel will not rest until he finds her. If you don't take her with you, you will put the children at risk."

"How do you know that?"

"We grew up together, Samuel and I. We are from the same village."

"Here? This village?" Jackson said, alarmed.

"No, no. Not this village. This is my auntie's home. He does not know this place. However, I do not make the mistake of underestimating him. Nor should you." She stepped around Jackson to scan the dark road in both directions.

"Mutan was shot tonight so that ought to slow him down."

Beatrice snapped her attention back to Jackson. "He was? Not seriously, I do not believe. I would have known if he had passed." She half-smiled again, but her eyes were sad. "He will have his men looking for her."

"More likely he'll be looking for his son."

She shook her head. "No. He will not forgive the betrayal. That is Samuel's tragedy. He is not capable of forgiveness. At one time I thought he wasn't capable of love, but I was wrong. He can love but it is a stunted love, an extension of his love for himself. If someone displeases him, he casts them off. Today he sent young Raymond to an outer province to train with the Red Boys Junior Brigade."

"Jesus. The kid's what, nine or ten? Let's not share that with Rose just yet. She doesn't need any more bad news. But back to the general. Why is he so obsessed with Rose?"

"She knows something of value. Information he wants for the insurgents, I believe. That's all I know. We should get those children inside."

"We weren't followed," Jackson said. "You can trust me on that."

"Samuel has spies in many places. He used to be with the secret police."

"So why did he join the insurgents?"

"Samuel cares very deeply about our country. He always believed corrupt politicians were the greatest evil. Now he turns a blind eye to the rebels' evil deeds, pretending the end justifies the means. Once Samuel makes up his mind, there's no going back. You must be vigilant. Your lady will need you when he finds her."

"Okay first, she's not my lady." He decided to ignore Beatrice's snort. "Second, by the time he's on his feet again, she'll be long gone. I'll make sure of that."

"He is like a dog with a bone. He does not know about her memory loss, does he?"

"Honestly," Jackson said. "I have no idea." He didn't want to think about the goddamn general any more. He had complete confidence he'd get Rose safely across the border. "I'll make sure she's beyond his reach."

"You had better be certain. If he captures her again, you may not get her back."

## 15

ROSE HELD the door for Jackson, who carried Sunday inside. Faith followed with Solomon. The nurse directed them to a bedroom where a dozen children slept on pallets lining the floor.

When Faith saw her younger sisters, she rushed over to wake them. The girls sat up and threw their arms around each other, then rocked back and forth as one unit, eyes closed, humming a wordless song of relief.

Tears filled Rose's eyes. There had been so much fear and misery today. Here was confirmation, badly needed, that love mattered. That sometimes it prevailed.

Jackson set Sunday down and straightened. She caught his eye and whispered, "You remember the sisters' names? Faith. Charity. Patience."

"Right. No Hope." He turned away, leaving her to wipe her cheeks with the backs of her hands.

One of the older boys stirred and came up on one elbow. "Jackson. You came back for a rematch? You are ready to prove your football worthiness?"

"Not this time kid," Jackson said. "I won't be here in the morning."

The boy hissed, then said, "How will you reclaim your manly pride?"

"Someday I'll come back for that rematch."

"By then I will be much bigger," the boy said. "You will be the one with no hope. You will have to bow before my excellence."

Rose followed Jackson out of the room. When she touched his arm, the muscles in his bicep jumped under her fingertips. Though he tried to pull away, she wouldn't let him and deliberately prolonged the contact. She needed to touch, even if he did not. Anyway, he needed to hear this.

"You did good tonight," she said. "You rescued those two girls and reunited a family. You saved Solomon, too. I want you to know how much I admire your courage and resourcefulness. Thank you."

"You rescued them, too. In fact, if it had been up to me, I wouldn't have taken them with us."

"Yes, you would have."

He looked around the small house impatiently. "Look, we're only staying long enough to catch a few hours rest. I thought I might leave you here…"

She kept her face blank. "Oh?"

"…but Beatrice thinks the general will be looking for you."

"Why would he? I don't have anything he wants. He told us some bullshit story about needing medical supplies from the aid organization's office. Oliver said—" She broke off and swallowed hard. "He said they wanted our fingerprints—his and mine—for the security system. That didn't make sense either. I still don't understand why they kidnapped me. Unless they were hoping for a ransom? Even that doesn't add up because the general's not stupid, I don't think."

"Go talk to Beatrice if you think you should stay here and risk everyone."

Heat rose in her cheeks. He knew quite well she wouldn't dream of endangering the children. "That's not what I meant. We can leave now. Just give me five minutes."

"That would be stupid," he said flatly. "The roads are too dangerous at night. Especially where we're headed. We were extremely lucky to make it here without a problem. No, we'll leave before dawn. I suggest you go find a place to sleep."

She pivoted. A stabbing pain made her regret the sudden move.

He grabbed her arm and looked down at the blood-streaked tile. "What did you do?"

"Ran through a forest barefoot, that's what." She lifted her feet, one and then the other, to inspect the soles of her feet. Thorns had punctured in a few places. "I'm sorry," she said to Beatrice Okeke, busy in the adjacent kitchen. "I dripped blood on your clean floor."

Beatrice motioned Rose to a chair and filled a pan with soapy water.

"I'll do it," Jackson said curtly, taking the pan and elbowing the nurse aside.

Beatrice made a comical face behind his back for Rose's benefit. "Doctor Jackson, here are some first aid supplies. I will go check on the children." She ushered Solomon out, leaving them alone in the kitchen.

Jackson knelt in front of Rose. His tense, closed expression contrasted with his gentle touch as he meticulously cleaned the blood and dirt from her feet. The cold water felt good. His hands felt even better.

The water in the pan turned brown. She thanked him and sat up, assuming he'd leave her to finish alone. Instead, he continued soaping her ankles, then her calves. His fingers were strong and sensitive and the way he caressed her reminded her of last night, how he'd known exactly when and where to touch her. All over. He had found all her sensitive, most responsive pressure points, intuitively knowing what she liked.

The tingling spread from her feet to her legs, up her inner thighs and between her legs. The most secret intimate spots. All the places he'd explored last night with his fingers, lips, and tongue.

He sat back on his heels and his face darkened when their eyes met. He knew what she was thinking and was as turned on as she was. He acted all grumpy and tough, but she was on to him.

This shared link enhanced their mutual understanding in so many ways. Pleasure in each other's bodies wasn't the only dimension, but it was a pretty damn good start. Her memory loss didn't affect her certainty of that, one way or another.

For the first time all day, Rose felt optimistic. Events of the last few days had taught her that life consisted of more hardship and uncertainties than not. So many things were out of their control. It could all be over in a blink—lives ended randomly and without warning. A bomb, a virus, a madman—or woman—could change one's destiny at a moment's notice.

Jackson could not deny what they had. How foolish it would be—how pointless—to deny something so wondrous as a deep, elemental connection to another human being. This bond they shared could not possibly be an ordinary one. When they got out of here, when they had real privacy, they would talk. She didn't care if she was the one to broach the subject. He was worth embarrassing herself. *They* were worth it. Anyway, how could any bond this lovely and profound be embarrassing?

He dried her feet and meticulously bandaged her up. She gave him a blinding smile, fine with letting him see her true feelings. Was this love? Well, why not? A foundation had already been laid, years before. They had started something, even if she couldn't remember the whys and the wherefores. With time, they could keep building.

He got up, dumped the dirty water in the sink and spoke over his shoulder. "I know you prefer honesty, so I'll just say this straight up. These romantic fantasies? Drop them. There's no point in fantasizing about what we can't have."

Her mouth dropped open and the room seemed to tilt. "What are you talking about? So you've decided to push me away? I don't think so, buddy."

He dried his hands. "I'm not interested in arguing with you. The situation isn't what you think. I'm not who you think. We'll be going our separate ways the moment I get you across a border, any border."

She forced herself to breathe through the hurt. "Why would you—"

"Look Rose, whether you're aware of it or not, you're behaving true to form."

That confused her anew. "How so?"

"This is your old pattern. You want what you want and you think you're entitled. Well, not this time. Consider this: in the space of a day, you transfer your affections from that doctor to me? Your feelings must not run deep. And what was all that about a fiancé?"

She started. "I forgot about that. You know, I'm not even sure—"

"You *forgot*. Add him to the list. Even the general knew about him before I did. Rose, even if I were inclined to trust you, which I'm not, I'd think you were a very confused person."

Their link was a double-edged sword. He knew exactly how to hurt her. But only if she allowed him to. After all, there were two sides to every story. At least two sides.

She stared at him stubbornly. "Maybe I am and maybe I've done things I'm not proud of, but I'm not heartless. Or shallow."

Meanwhile, Solomon wandered into the kitchen to look for food.

"Go get some sleep," Jackson said to her.

"Not quite yet," Nurse Okeke said from the doorway. "I need a few minutes with Rose."

"In that case," Jackson said, "We'll be outside." He pulled Solomon along and went out the front door.

Beatrice placed a glass of hot tea and a sliced baguette with butter in front of her. "Tell me, do you remember our conversation at the hospital?"

Rose ate the bread and sipped the sweet, minty tea. "Of course."

"Do you recall what I said to you about forgiveness?"

Rose frowned between bites. "Something about how I must learn to forgive myself?"

"Ah. That is a good sign. Your short-term memory is not affected. You are starting to remember other things as well, yes? Your affliction will soon pass."

Rose regarded her curiously. Beatrice hadn't phrased her observation as a question. What's more, in the hospital, the two of them had spoken only of Lassa Fever and not once about the amnesia. She'd been careful not to disclose that to the nurse. "How did you know I'd lost my memory? Did Jackson tell you?"

Beatrice waved the question aside. "No, he doesn't like to talk about you."

Surprise. "How then?"

"That is for another time," Beatrice said. "It is a long story, the history of gifts passed down through the generations of women in my family."

"Never the men?"

"Never," Beatrice said and she giggled, looking younger. "We just let them *think* they are wise."

"So you think my memory will return soon?"

"My auntie kept medical journals before she passed on last year. One in particular was left clipped open, as if she wanted me to see. She made sure I couldn't miss that one. Certain anti-malarial medications can cause severe side-effects, including psychosis and amnesia. Amnesia is usually a short-term effect, though some people never recover all their memories."

Rose leaned forward. Whatever she'd expected, this wasn't it. "How is this possible? I brought that prescription with me from home. I thought an anti-malarial is standard procedure for expats here."

"I expect if you had undergone tests, if you had proper care, we would have diagnosed this within a day or so."

"So, this was just...bad luck all around. What is the cure?"

"The passage of time."

"It's that simple?"

"Or that complicated," Beatrice said. "You have received a gift, you know."

"A gift," Rose repeated dubiously.

"It's a paradox, but a very good one. The amnesia has taken away your memory, but it has also given you a second chance. A chance to let go of past mistakes. Your memories no longer define you. Now you will rediscover your true self, your best self. As will Jackson."

Rose would never insult this wonderful lady with a wisecrack; however, she felt perfectly free to think it. A gift. Seriously?

Beatrice went on. "You'll regain the memories gradually. Childhood memories are more likely to come first. Habits, too. Skills you have. That is called procedural memory. So if you played an instrument, for instance, you will remember how. The most recent memories will come last. I should warn you, however..."

"What?"

"You may not recover everything. Experiences in the days or weeks just prior to the onset, well, some of those memories may be lost forever. You should expect that some events may never come back to you in full."

"As it happens," Rose said, "tonight I did remember something that must have occurred in the last three or four months."

"You must be sure to tell Jackson so that he can—"

"Oh, he won't want to hear about that," Rose interjected.

"Hear what?" He had quietly slipped back into the room and leaned against the wall, watching her with an enigmatic expression.

"Nothing important."

"It could be."

"I'll tell you later," she said, with no intention of doing any such thing. For better or worse, his good opinion meant something to her. No way would she share that she'd lost another man's baby. If he thought her shallow and feckless now, what would he think of her then?

~

A few hours later, after a sleepless three hours on the floor, Rose got up. Jackson and Solomon had bedded down in the other room. From the look of him, Jackson hadn't slept much either.

While Beatrice packed food for them, Rose used the bathroom, gladly shucked the now-filthy caftan and washed herself with a washcloth. She borrowed a brush and tamed her hair. With low expectations, she examined the outfit Beatrice had pulled from her deceased auntie's closet. The skirt was brightly patterned and long. To her surprise, the skirt fit perfectly, snug and low on her hips. She added a scoop neck shirt, a jacket and flip-flops. The clothes were prettier and more flattering than anything she'd seen in her own suitcase.

When she returned to the kitchen, Beatrice and Solomon nodded their approval. Jackson quickly looked away.

She hugged the nurse goodbye. "When will I see you again?"

"Hopefully never," Jackson said. "If you do, it means we failed." He said his goodbye to Beatrice, speaking quietly and holding her hand. For one foolish moment, Rose wanted to knock his hand away. So he could be nice to Beatrice, but not to her?

To hide her petty jealousy, she looked in on the sleeping kids one last time. No matter what happened now to her or to Jackson, these kids were safe. That's what mattered. Solomon joined her and she saw his eyes linger on Faith, sleeping the sleep of the innocent. Then he walked Rose to the front door.

When she tried to hug the teenager, he looked surprised. "I'm going with you."

Beatrice deposited a bag of food into Rose's arms, along with a couple of blankets.

"What's this for?"

"You'll see," Beatrice said and stood at the door to wave them off.

The sky was still dark. Dawn must be an hour away. An ancient Peugeot station wagon, much like the overloaded taxis Rose had seen in the city, was parked outside.

"What happened to the jeep?"

Jackson appeared beside her, popping up with his usual stealth. He steered her into the back seat, saying, "It's hidden where it won't be found. Turns out Solomon has an interesting skill set."

The vehicle wasn't much more than a metal shell retrofitted with three rows of benches to accommodate the maximum number of passengers. Amenities such as upholstery, seat belts and door handles were long gone.

Solomon got behind the wheel while Jackson swung into the front passenger seat.

"You're letting him drive?" she asked.

"If he weren't, it'd be waving a red flag to anyone who sees us coming. I'm a tourist who bought up all the seats in his taxi."

"Why?"

"I'm an uptight American in a hurry."

"What am I?"

"You're cargo. You'll be on the floor."

Rose looked at the rusty metal beneath her flip flops. Exposed bolts and screws stuck out here and there. No carpet, no rubber pads, nothing. A gaping five-inch hole near the door exposed the gravel road below.

"You don't mean *this* floor."

"Afraid so. We were very lucky no one pulled us over last night; I don't expect that luck to hold. I'm not taking any chances with you—lay down now." He paused and regarded her with a wary expectant look that said he was waiting for her to complain. He obviously thought of her as an entitled princess.

When she folded her lips and kept her face blank, he went on. "We'll be passing through numerous checkpoints. When we do, I'll throw the other blanket and random stuff over you. If you're out of sight, that should buy us enough time at checkpoints."

She folded a blanket lengthwise, spread it, and lowered her butt. He wasn't going to hear her bitch and moan. Even if it killed her.

"Enough time for what?" she asked, scootching to find a more comfortable spot. There was none.

"If I hand over the cash quick enough," he said, "we'll be gone before they start poking around and asking questions."

Solomon reversed with a screech and put the car in motion. Rose rolled backward, then forward, and grabbed a bench leg.

Too bad her short-term memory was fully operational. She would have liked to forget the hours she spent rolling back and forth under the Peugeot's back seats, breathing in exhaust and road dust that kicked up through the hole. As hellish and bone-bruising as the ride was, she kept her mouth shut. She endured, hanging on for dear life when the car turned, braked, or accelerated and almost got used to her teeth rattling around in her head.

The ride was too brutal for much sleep and the intermittent checkpoint stops too nerve-wracking for her to relax, though their progress was uneventful. She caught only fragments of conversation from the front seat. At one point, Jackson asked about Solomon's plans for the future, since he obviously wasn't returning to the Red Boys.

"Why do you Americans want to talk about terrorists and politics all the time?" Solomon complained. "I'm going to be a businessman. When my brother is older, he will join me. Maybe Sunday will join us in the business when she is out of school."

"What kind of business?" Jackson asked.

"Making blast walls. I already know how to pour the concrete into the forms. Blast walls are a very good business. Lots of growth potential."

"I hope not, kid. Look, when you're ready to start a business, get in touch. I'll help you get started in something that's more forward-looking and innovative than goddamn blast walls. I mean it. I'll give you my email address."

After that, they were mostly silent as they bumped and rattled along on the road north. As the hours passed, the weather turned and the day grew dark and cold. The blanket insulated her, but only up to a point. She wasn't going to freeze to death; it just felt that way. Jackson reached back from time to time to re-tuck the blanket. His hands were warm but his voice wasn't. Not that he said more than a few words.

The imposed solitude gave her plenty of time to think. Her mind inevitably returned to the sad memory she'd recalled earlier—her only retrieved one so far, if you didn't count the vague feelings stirred up when she and Jackson made love. She discounted those now as wishful thinking.

She found both comfort and bitter amusement in the unexpected privacy the noisy old car provided. For hours now, she'd carried the knowledge of her loss and hadn't let herself think about it, much less allow herself to feel. Now that she had nothing but time and no one to see or hear her, she broke down. Once the floodgates opened, she cried in gulping, hiccupping sobs that she muffled with her hand.

She didn't cry for Oliver, as horrific a waste as his death had been. She cried for a baby she never got to meet. For a pregnancy, over before she'd understood what it meant. For her own stupidity in making a series of bad choices. And finally, for not being sadder about losing the man who'd been the father of that baby, which must say something about her fickle nature. It would really suck if Jackson turned out to be right about that.

She had to come to terms with what she'd learned. The personal stuff and her involvement with a married man was the least of it. The bigger things, the bigger lapses in judgement worried her more. What kind of person would agree to vaccinate children as a cover for dubious intelligence gathering? Even if she hadn't been spying herself.

Without memories of her career or training, she couldn't put these questions to rest. What or who had she started out as? And what had she become? Surely she hadn't always lacked a moral compass.

Finally, the station wagon rattled to a halt. Her ears rang from the constant whine of the engine so, unsure if they were at a checkpoint, Rose stayed put. No voices or other sounds could be heard outside the car, except the wind.

The door opened and the blanket covering her came off. Frigid air iced her wet face. Jackson leaned in and lifted her up and out as easily as if she were a toddler. He set her down with a thump on the side of a remote highway. There were virtually no signs of civilization or passing traffic. The sun had already set. She could see nothing of their surroundings.

When she took a wobbly step, Jackson held her arms to steady her. That didn't help her dignity either, so she made a production of straightening her skirt.

Solomon tapped her on the shoulder. "This is where I leave you," he said.

She glanced at Jackson for confirmation. He was shaking Solomon's hand. Before she fully understood what was happening, Solomon had hopped back in the car. As he took off, she yelled, "Say goodbye to Raymond for me. Be careful."

The station wagon's taillights disappeared around a bend and they were left in the middle of nowhere on a moonless night.

"Now what?" she said.

Jackson fiddled with his device. A flashlight beam clicked on, pointed right in her eyes.

She held up one hand to deflect the light. There was no hiding the effects of an ugly cry. Not from someone as observant as Jackson. "What is that, a flashlight app?"

He scanned her face. "You should have slept while you had the chance." Then he pushed her hair away from her eyes. "You've been crying. That's not like you."

She liked how he touched her, though she would never admit it. "You don't actually know me that well though, do you?" She kept her tone neutral.

"You're still the same person. You don't give up and you don't give in."

"Yeah? I sound obnoxious."

Abruptly, he pulled her into his body so that her face pressed into his shirt. At first she thought it was a hug and then realized he was simply blotting her soggy face.

"Thanks." She tried to disengage.

He wouldn't let her go. He kept her in the circle of his arms and put one big hand behind her neck. The base of his palm felt warm and reassuring. She had the odd notion that if she couldn't hold her head up, he'd do it for her.

"I'm right here," he said.

She pulled back. He was doing it again, reading her mind. The intrusion wasn't welcome, not now.

"I promise," he said, "you'll feel better when you're in a warm bed."

She surveyed the surrounding wilderness, pitch dark and impenetrable. "I'm sure I would. Do you know something that I don't?"

# <u>16</u>

HE'D HEARD her under the engine noise. A faint sound. Then she'd started to cry her heart out. Rose didn't do anything partway; however, he knew she wasn't looking for attention or sympathy. As much as he hated hearing her despair, the meltdown reassured him. He couldn't have said how he knew she was close to remembering. He just knew. Same way he knew she was running on fumes right now.

He had to hand it to her. She hadn't complained about being dropped off on a cold, dark highway in the middle of nowhere.

"Where are we?" she asked.

"We're in a game reserve. Like a national park. We'll camp here tonight."

"That's…unexpected." Her voice was a thread, barely hanging on. "Game reserve. The kind with wild animals?" She moved closer.

"Let's hope so. If not, it wouldn't be much of a game reserve."

"Why not keep going and power through to the border?"

"My intel says the town up ahead is in the hands of insurgents. Unofficially. Which only makes it more dangerous; we can't risk Solomon getting caught up in the net, too. It's like the Wild West out here. Anything can happen, especially at night. Outlaws and gunslingers could start shooting up the saloon, so to speak. So we'll get some rest and tomorrow we'll catch a northbound train to take us over the border."

He picked up his backpack, put his arm around her waist and set off to find the path. She leaned on him heavily, taking painful, hesitant steps.

"Where is Solomon going?" she asked.

"First he'll pay off the ranger. He'll tell him we're crazy American eco-tourists, eager to experience Africa in its natural state. He'll also mention you've been exposed to a virus recently. That will ensure the ranger doesn't bother us."

"I'm more worried about the wild animals bothering us. No, I meant, where is Solomon headed next?"

"He's got…family business to take care of. As far as animals go, we'll be in a platform tent for the night. It's perfectly safe. You can't see it, of course but it's down a path off to our right."

"How do you know where the tent is, or for that matter, whether it's unoccupied?"

"I have my ways."

"You sound like a comic book villain." Her steps had slowed noticeably. He expected her to ask how far they had to walk. Instead, she soldiered on. He would have picked her up, but she wouldn't like that. He wasn't going to add to her unhappiness.

Using the thin beam of light, he found the path fairly easily and they cut through a long meadow. Night birds called and insects buzzed in the underbrush. A sage-like fragrance wafted in from the savannah. There was no cloud cover, which meant the night was cold and getting colder. The stars glowed at maximum brightness due to the new moon.

"It is beautiful out here," she said. "So there's already a tent set up?"

"Something like that. More than a tent, less than a cabin."

"I've been meaning to ask, did Markus get away from the camp safely?"

"Yes, but it was close."

"Did he have time to retrieve the drones?"

"You knew that's what they were?"

"Of course. Your fingerprints were all over that light show. It was spectacular, by the way."

"Thanks. We lost most of the equipment. But we knew what the odds were going in."

"Are you in a lot of trouble?"

"Almost certainly."

"I'll pay you back. I must have savings. I mean, I should, right? And if not, I can get a loan or something. After all, you did that on my behalf, it's my responsibility to—"

"No," he said. "Just no. Whatever I work out with Will Holloway—my boss—it's on me." He would have said more if they hadn't rounded a corner and reached the path's end.

The platform tent came into view as an elevated bulky shadow. Rose halted at the base of a steep flight of stairs. She looked up and slumped at the prospect of mounting them.

He swung her into his arms. "Oh come on," she protested. "This isn't necessary."

"Yes it is," he said brusquely. "You've had a hard day. Don't worry, I won't make a habit of it." He ran up the steps and ducked inside the big tent before setting her down. There were no lights on so all she could see was the side of the tent open to the night sky.

"I spent most of yesterday in a tent," she said. "Here I am again."

"This is no ordinary tent."

"If you say so," she said under her breath.

He located the propane lantern and turned the key. It cast a moderate pool of yellow light, enough for her to take stock.

He waited for her small gasp of pleasure. There it was.

She turned in a circle and gawked at the elaborate gathered fabric walls and ceiling, the wide bed draped with luxury linens and a fluffy duvet. The bed sat at the center of the suite, topped by an elaborate canopy and draped netting. Part of the tent was a deck open to the sky, save for screens that kept insects and birds out. Two willow rocking chairs faced the interior valley of the nature reserve.

"No way," she exclaimed. She launched herself at him and threw her arms around his waist to hug him. He held on and closed his eyes. Her head fit perfectly under his chin.

While she explored, he found matches and lit the dozen or so candles strategically placed around the room and in the small bathroom.

He came out to find her at the huge screened window. Billowing curtains framed the view, though there wasn't much to see in the dark. The night sounds and the wide, starry sky contributed to the illusion that they were all alone in the world. Adam and Eve.

"It's perfect," she said. "Like a private paradise."

"Exactly," he said.

"How did you know about this place? This is an incredible find."

"I've been here before—after a mission."

"A mission?"

"In another life."

She gave him a long look. "I'd like to hear more about that life. When you're ready to tell me." She rubbed her arms. "Only thing is…"

"What?"

"I'm freezing my ass off." She laughed, making an observation, not a complaint. Other women he'd known would have been irate, demanding central heat. Not Rose.

"The down quilt will keep us plenty warm, once we're under."

She ran over to see it like a little kid and stopped at the last second. "Shoot. I don't want to get it dirty." She stepped out of her flip flops and skirt and pulled her shirt over her head.

He watched, fascinated. The candlelight illuminated her pale, peachy skin. Her breasts were small and perfect, her waist slim, her hips small but curvy. She didn't have enough weight on her frame but time would take care of that problem. To his mind, she was perfect and always would be.

She slipped under the heavy quilt and let out a huge sigh. "Oh. My. God. Jackson, wait till you feel this. It's…there are no words."

"I'll be there in a minute. I need a shower first."

"There's a shower?" she said, enthralled. She hopped out of bed and limped into the bathroom, laughing wickedly as she beat him to it.

He zipped the tent door closed, more of a symbolic gesture than an actual security measure. If anyone wanted in, they'd get in. The only thing that door would keep out were adventurous critters. He checked the perimeter of the platform and thought about various scenarios, none of which were likely. His training was part of him now; even if he wanted to ignore the evening ritual, he couldn't.

She emerged in less than five minutes, damp and rosy from her fast shower, and dove for the bed with her hair still wrapped up in a towel. He paused to watch her burrow under the covers then took his turn in the bathroom.

He took the world's fastest shower. Since the water was ice-cold, it wasn't difficult to rush. When he came out with a towel wrapped around his waist, he walked over to the bed and looked down. She was curled into a blissful ball, sleeping like a contented kitten. Practically purring.

His mouth twitched in a smile. He flung his towel on a chair and slid in beside her. He moved slowly so as not to wake her and settled in. For the first time since getting up today, he let himself relax.

Still fast asleep, she gravitated to his warmth and slipped her leg over his. He got hard immediately. He wanted her. Then again, he always wanted her. In a minute, he'd get up, turn the lamp down low and blow out the candles. For now, he would watch her sleep, and listen to the night.

~

She opened her eyes with a snap. The bed faced a huge curtained window with a panoramic view of the stars. It only took a moment to remember where she was and why the air was so sharp with cold.

She slid farther under the quilt where delicious warmth and a sense of well-being had given her the best sleep of her life. But it wasn't morning yet. She could stay right here. With him.

She felt aroused, as if she'd been having erotic dreams. And then looked sideways at the reason why. One of his arms was flung behind his head and the other rested on her leg. When she moved experimentally, his fingers went with her. Which wasn't as creepy as it sounded. His fingers were long and stealthy, much like him, as he soothed and stroked the tender skin of her inner thigh. If he'd been touching her like this all night, no wonder she felt so turned on.

She peered at him suspiciously. He wasn't faking it. He was asleep.

She didn't want to disturb him. Well, maybe she did. She ducked under the covers. There was no light under here but she didn't need any light to know that he had a long body, hot skin, lean hips and a flat stomach. She traced his wide chest and shoulders with one finger, skimming his skin lightly. He was so...big. Naked like this, he was pretty impressive.

Strange thing was, she didn't remember any other man's body. There must have been a few but Jackson was the only one she *wanted* to remember.

She snuggled against him, at peace.

~

He woke her in the best of ways. Stroking her hair back from her forehead. Kissing the nape of her neck. His lips tickled her ear lobe, saying something she didn't understand. Another language. Instinctively she knew those were words of love and desire. What he wanted to do to her, with her, for her.

This time they took it slow and sweet. She followed his lead, arching in pleasure, reveling in the exquisite torture of his lips on her neck. She turned into him, needing that mouth anywhere. Everywhere. Her breasts felt swollen and hot. She pulled him to her. He sucked her the way she needed, hot and sweet, then lowered his head to her stomach and kissed his way down to her legs, lingering there, finding all the secret sensitive places.

Just watching him go after her with that wide soft mouth of his brought her close to coming. She wasn't going there without him.

He turned so his body half covered hers. His cock brushed her thigh. He must have gotten up and found a condom somewhere. Now he teased her with laughter in his eyes. He knew exactly how she felt right now. Because he felt it too.

She was going to make him pay. She climbed up and positioned herself over him. His cock was heavy and insistent, poised at her entrance. Maybe not quite yet. With a triumphant smile, she lay full length covering his body for a long sweet kiss.

She drew back. This close, she couldn't miss the fleeting expression that crossed his face. Hunger and pain were mingled. Need and ambivalence battled there.

He wanted her too much. What else could such a desperate expression mean?

"If you don't take me now, I'm taking you," he whispered.

His breath tickled her ear, hot as his skin, as hot as his cock as she slowly guided him inside her. He thrust with one hard, claiming plunge. She met and matched him. Though she couldn't hope to equal his strength, she could squeeze and milk him with her inner muscles, contracting when he finished a thrust, holding him for an extra heartbeat, taking him prisoner. He groaned when she did it the first time and bucked. The second time she squeezed harder and though he must have been expecting it, he groaned more deeply.

His hands were shaking when he stopped to cup her face and kiss her with an unexpected tenderness. His tongue probed her mouth, seeking something from her. She kissed him back, just as desperate to show him how she felt. He was everything. He was the center of her desire. The cause, the effect, the question and the answer.

Meanwhile, his cock kept expanding inside her. He held back, exerting his considerable will and strength to stay within her without thrusting. He kissed her hard one more time and then surged into her again. This time, she went with him. Higher and higher till she shook with it. He convulsed with a long shudder. There was no separation between them. No past or future. All that mattered was the pleasure they gave each other. Sweet release.

Those hushed moments when they floated down from the high, reminded her of his drone butterfly, trapped and free at the same time. That's how she felt, too. She was trapped in this state of not remembering. Paradoxically, this gave her a sort of freedom. After all, how could she be held responsible for things she couldn't remember? It had its advantages, this amnesia. Beatrice had been right. The amnesia *was* a gift in its way.

She relaxed and watched Jackson drift off to sleep. And she slept, too.

~

The next time she woke, the sky was a wash of dawning pastels. She felt amazing, deeply relaxed. A memory surfaced right away, without any effort. It was, as Beatrice had predicted, a childhood memory.

She recalled standing in front of a mailbox with her mom and going up on tiptoe, trying and trying for the handle and not reaching it. That had *really* ticked her off.

She shook Jackson's arm. "I remembered something!"

He sat up, instantly alert. "What?"

"A really vivid memory. I was a little girl and I was trying to mail a letter. I wonder why I'd remember that, of all things?"

He looked at her blankly, so blankly she wondered if he'd understood. There were shadows under his eyes. He pushed hair off his forehead and got out of bed.

She watched him walk over to his backpack, distracted by his nude body in the dawn light. He really was something. Tall and powerfully built, with all that smooth olive and gold skin. His dark hair, rumpled from sleep, stuck out in the back.

He removed a yellowing paper from his wallet, took his time unfolding it and tossed it so that it landed in front of her.

A note in child's handwriting read:

*Dear Jacksun,*

*I luv you. Do you luv me? I doant want to liv a way from you. Sum day we well look bak on this and laf.*

*Or I will. You never do.*

*Your frend,*

Rose

She smoothed the paper gently. The folds were so worn they were about to rip. "You've been carrying this around? For how long?"

"No idea." He came back to bed, affecting that same detached expression.

"I have a vague memory of a hissy fit about moving."

"I can hear your mom's voice in that note. You were parroting her. She was probably trying to calm you down. You were a high-strung kid."

"But you weren't," she said, as a rush of memories flooded her mind. "You hardly ever laughed, just like I said."

"Have you remembered everything? All of it?"

"Only the years when we were little. I think it's only a matter of time now before it all comes back. So, did you answer this letter?"

"I always wrote back. Until you stopped writing. It was years before we saw each other again, during the summer before you started college. That's when we had our short-lived romance."

"Why *didn't* you laugh more?"

"Might have had something to do with my dad backhanding me whenever I made too much noise."

She reached for his hand. "I wish I'd never left you. I wish you could have come with us."

"Don't feel sorry for me. I learned self-control and discipline. It made me tougher."

She tucked her head under his chin. When he didn't react and just sat there like a lump, she picked up his arms and put them around her. "I'm so glad you came to Africa."

He was very quiet then. She stifled an impatient sigh, found one of his hands and kissed the back of it. "It's okay, Jackson. I know."

His arms tightened around her. "What is it you think you know?"

"Talking about the past is hard for you. Maybe I'm the lucky one after all. What I can't remember can't hurt me. Except there is one thing. Do you recall what you said in Beatrice's kitchen about me following a pattern? What *is* my pattern?"

He stiffened and not in a good way. "Do you really want to go there? What's the point in dredging up the past?"

"I need to know why you don't trust me. It's got to be more than teen heartbreak. I mean, come on. A break-up? That's not so unusual or tragic."

He lifted her from his lap with annoying efficiency. Then he lay back with his hands above his head and kept his eyes on the draped netting. "We split up at the end the summer. Three weeks later, I surprised you in your dorm room. You had gone off the rails completely."

"What? How so?"

"All you could talk about was your new freedom, how you were partying with a different guy every night. You showed me a list of conquests you'd posted on your wall. Within five minutes, a frat boy knocked on the door to make a date for later."

"We'd broken up, right? So I was acting out, sexually. Guys do it all the time."

"You had a supersize box of condoms displayed like a trophy on the shelf above your bed. You said your minimum criteria was a nice smile and a thick shaft."

She winced. "No. I said that?"

"That and more. We'd been through hell that summer and…and I needed to talk to you. I see now, looking back, that's why I went after you, why I couldn't let you go. We had unfinished business."

"What do you mean, 'we'd been through hell'?"

He didn't answer. Her heart broke for him. She'd let down her oldest, truest friend, who was much more sensitive than she'd guessed. He'd been right. She really did not want to hear this.

"You're the one that pushed me into telling you," he reminded her. "You asked."

"Go on," she said firmly. "Finish."

"I walked out of your room that day and we never saw each other again. You might have written once or twice, but I didn't respond. We were through."

"Until the other day," she said and then paused to breathe, to concentrate on keeping her voice steady. "For what it's worth, I'm sorry. It's not enough but it's all I can offer. I'm so sorry. After the way I treated you, I'm surprised you came all the way to Africa."

"I was on my way to Senegal anyway. I did this for your mom."

The last traces of euphoria fled the room. So that's why he'd come after her yesterday as well. A sense of obligation. To her *mom*. She wanted to pull the covers over her head and stay there. "Hold on. Why would she ask *you* to check on me? Why woudn't she ask my fiancé—assuming there really is one."

"I have no idea. You've got a complicated life. Whoever this fiancé is, maybe he's a douche bag who didn't step up when your mom asked."

"I hate that word."

"Douche bag?"

"Well, that too. I meant the word fiancé. It seems foreign to me, something I would never even say."

"Maybe because it *is* a foreign word," he said dryly. "Now it's my turn to ask a question. Yesterday in the car—

when you were on the floor—what or who were you crying about?"

"Myself. Which fits with everything you've said."

"Not the martyred doctor?"

"I suppose I cried for him, but more for myself. I'm self-involved, so there you go. Stands to reason."

"Rose—"

"I'll tell you the unvarnished truth, as I understand it. The general accused me of spying. Then Oliver confirmed we used our aid work as a cover for gathering intelligence. He said I knew all about it."

"That's it? No, there's something else that's hurting you."

She swallowed hard and looked away.

"Rose. Just tell me."

"Sometime in the last few months, I lost a baby."

Jackson regarded her. "And the father?"

# 17

"OLIVER. Presumably." Though Rose understood his disgust and even shared it, his repulsed expression hurt. "So now you know the worst. I was pregnant by a married man. And I wasn't just an innocent aid worker here. Something a lot darker was going on. I still can't make sense of it."

"Because it makes no sense," Jackson said. His eyes were hard and his voice was cold. All the warmth and passion they'd just shared seemed like a dream. "For all you know, Mutan was just blowing smoke up your ass."

"Thank you for that mental image. No, Oliver confirmed I was aware, which means I was complicit."

"I'll admit you were surprisingly handy with that pistol when you shot the general square in the ass. You've had training, that much is obvious. You must have practiced at a range or something. But a spy?" He dismissed the idea with a wave. "Give it some time. You'll sort out what really happened."

"Assuming there's anyone alive who knows. Before he died, Oliver told me that the other two people on our team were killed. What if there's no one left who knows the truth?"

"Trust me, someone knows. As for the...other thing, your mom didn't know about your pregnancy. I think you would have told her."

"I can't imagine being eager to share the news, given my circumstances."

"It's good you didn't. She's got enough to deal with. Your dad is ill."

Rose gave a start. "With what?"

"Prostate cancer."

"Why didn't you say this earlier?"

"She asked me not to. She wanted to tell you in person. You're supposed to go home for Christmas—but she said you kept putting her off and you didn't book a flight. When she couldn't reach you, she began to worry."

Rose jumped out of bed and winced. Her foot hurt more than it had yesterday. "I'll send an email so she doesn't worry."

"I already did. She knows you're with me. She's not worried."

"We better find an internet café or something in the next town."

"There may not be any access. Whoever is in charge of the government has a chokehold on all communications and media. You can use my satellite phone to call her later, assuming we get a signal."

She was already headed for the shower, moving gingerly to keep her weight off her right foot. "I'll have to pretend to recognize her voice and act as if everything is fine and dandy. That's going to be a short call."

They took turns in the bathroom. By the time Jackson finished, Rose had stepped into the skirt and t-shirt she'd worn the night before. She found a coffee maker and, miraculously, an electrical outlet. While the coffee brewed, she unwrapped bread and cheese Beatrice had packed for them.

They ate breakfast on the deck overlooking the game reserve and settled into an uneasy truce. Mist rose from the valley floor and hovered over the treetops. The faint hum of insects and birds rose and fell in a pattern, creating a distinctive song. Jackson pointed out a distant herd of elephants.

Rose set her coffee down. "Listen, I got to thinking while I was in the shower. That dorm-room melodrama you told me about? Does that even sound like me?"

He quirked an eyebrow in response.

"After all, you do *know* me," she said. "I mean, you should. We've been in more than a few intense situations. That ought to count for something in the getting-to-know-you department."

"It does and it doesn't," he said slowly. "You admitted to making bad decisions. Maybe I don't know the real you; maybe you're a different person without your memories. What's your point?"

"What if I staged that little drama ten years ago?"

At first he didn't hide his irritation. "For my benefit?" Then he paused a few seconds and looked out at the savannah. She watched his face while he thought. A flicker of amusement came and went. "The ginormous box of condoms. A list of conquests. You only too happy to show me all of it. It does sound like a badly written farce. A telenovela."

"Right?" She bounced in her seat. "Exactly."

"A set-up implies you were expecting me. Except I'm positive I showed up unannounced that night."

She held up her hands in a gesture of surrender. "Just sayin'. I can't help but wonder."

He had the grace to angle an amused glance at her. "When you recover, I'll look forward to hearing what that was all about. Meanwhile, we need to check out of here and find our way to the train station in Obwele."

"How are we going to do that? We're in the middle of nowhere."

"We'll travel like the locals."

"What does that mean?"

"Bush taxi." He grew still and cocked his head. "Do you hear that sound?"

"Yeah, it's lovely, isn't it?"

"Not the birds. Listen." A whirring noise, separate and distinct from nature's soundtrack, buzzed high above them. She knew that sound.

Abruptly, he yanked her out of her chair and hauled her inside. The whirring sound grew louder. He snapped the canvas drapes together and then did the same at every window.

The drone flew over the platform tent several times. It circled the structure.

"Holy crap," she said.

He shushed her and retrieved his tablet from his backpack. Rose stood as close to him as she could without touching him or getting in the way. She wanted to ask if the evil flying robot could detect audio. He shook his head, as if he'd heard her silent question.

The drone came around and hovered for an excruciatingly long minute right outside the curtain, a few feet away. She clutched the waistband of his jeans and held her breath. It continued to float on the other side of the canvas. She knew the thing wasn't sentient, knew it had no way of detecting how close they were. Yet it certainly felt like that thing watched and waited for them to make a move.

Jackson put his palm on the back of her neck and kept it there for a few seconds, warm and steady. He'd done that once or twice in the last few days. As before, she immediately relaxed. She breathed easier and her heart rate slowed.

He resumed working, calmly tapping and sliding his fingers over the glass as if nothing were amiss. Finally, the drone buzzed off and faded away.

"Two possibilities," he said and then held up his hand to forestall her questions. "I'll explain in a minute. Get ready to go."

Rose organized her things, which didn't take long since her belongings consisted of a jacket and flip flops. Too bad she didn't have better shoes for walking. She inspected her sore feet. The bandages had come off in the shower. The left foot wasn't too bad. The other foot was swollen with red spidery lines fanning out from the deepest thorn puncture. That could not be good.

Still skittish, she gasped when his hands landed heavily on her shoulders. He forced her to sit, folded her skirt out of the way and then picked up each foot in turn. He probed, pressed and watched her reactions.

"Your right foot is infected. Don't move."

He disappeared into the bathroom and came back with a first aid kit—another miracle. While he tended to her feet, she watched him. Here was a man who was good with his hands. Whatever he did, he did with intense concentration, whether that was analyzing data, applying bandages or making love. He knew exactly where to touch her and when. Even now, under less than ideal circumstances, as soon as he put his hands on her, she nearly shot off the bed. Electrical impulses sent from his fingers raced to her lower belly and tingled between her legs.

He taped the last bandage and straightened. "I'll take this first aid kit with us." When she tried to stand, he pushed her back down. "Not yet."

"Bossy."

"Sorry," he said, not sounding sorry at all. "That's the way it's got to be."

He rummaged in his backpack and came back with a pair of tube socks. "My last clean pair."

"I'm honored." When he slid the huge socks on her and pulled them all the way past her knees, she started to giggle.

"You're wearing a skirt," he said. "No one will see."

"Small favors."

"Are you ready?" He stuffed his things in his backpack, added a bottle of water he'd found somewhere and swung her into his arms. Over her protests, he carried her down the stairs.

Rose hung on and glanced over his shoulder for one last look at the platform tent. This place had a magic of its own. She'd found her old friend at last and he'd found her. He didn't trust her yet, but he would. Whether it took weeks, months, or years, she would earn his trust again.

Jackson strode down the path that led out to the highway.

"You can put me down now."

"No." He didn't elaborate.

She repeated herself a minute later and he ignored that too, unperturbed. He didn't even break a sweat. She resigned herself to the indignity of it all.

"As you should," he said. "It's just till we get to the road."

Interesting that this mind-reading thing no longer surprised her. "We're out in the open now. You're not concerned about that drone finding us?"

"I set a geofence around this location and redirected it. Plus I switched off its video camera so even if it comes back, it won't see us. We're good."

"What were the two possibilities you mentioned earlier?"

"One, Markus had another prototype I wasn't aware of and sent it to look for us."

"Or…"

"Or two, the insurgents have people that are more tech savvy than I guessed. Since I haven't been able to get in

THE AMNESIA PARADOX 223

touch with Markus, I have to conclude that someone out at the camp picked up our drones. Whoever's flying it mastered the interface pretty damn quickly."

"How did they know where to send the drone?"

"Not sure." He juggled her in his arms and then lifted her so that they were eye to eye. "What the hell do you have that they want?"

"Not a damn thing."

"Or is it something you know? Keep thinking sweetheart. The answer is hiding somewhere in that stubborn head of yours."

~

Jackson heard the minibus engine coughing and wheezing well before it puttered into sight with an untidy heap of luggage strapped to the roof. The bush taxi was later than he'd expected, although that concept didn't really apply. There was no such thing as *late* or *on time* when it came to public transport here. Your ride showed up when it showed up.

Rose lifted the scarf he'd improvised for her and watched the bush taxi's approach. "Is this really necessary? I'm not going to fool anyone and this thing still looks like a freakin' pillowcase."

"Since your hair is so bright, it reflects like crazy. You may as well have a mirror on your head. You want people squinting and noticing you?"

"I suppose not," she said.

He didn't tell her about the kind of attention she'd attract in remote villages and smaller cities. Her hair would make her very popular.

He paid the driver and helped Rose into the minibus. She hesitated. The vehicle seated seven. Every seat was occupied by men, women and children of all ages. Bags and suitcases jammed every available surface.

A young mother picked up her toddler to make room on the middle seat. She smiled and pointed at the vacancy. Jackson slipped in to claim the seat and pulled Rose onto his lap where she perched straight-backed and wobbly on his knees.

"This can't be legal," she muttered. When the minibus accelerated, she swayed awkwardly and tried to hang onto his kneecaps.

He pulled her hips so that her soft bottom rested more securely on his quadriceps. Travelling this way wasn't comfortable, but it had its compensations.

She twisted around to eye him suspiciously. "That sounded like a laugh."

"Just happy to be on the road again."

"That's all it takes to make you laugh? Please tell me this won't be a long ride. What do you estimate?"

"Ha. That's a fool's errand. Don't even think in terms of ETA. You'll only get mad and turn into the Ugly American. If this contraption doesn't break down more than half a dozen times, we'll make it to the station in time for the three p.m. train. If not, we'll catch the next train. Or the next one."

"You're relaxed."

"No, I've just learned not to get wound up. Getting upset is a waste of time and energy. Some of this—most of this—is out of our hands. I plan to sleep. I suggest you do the same. You didn't get much of that last night."

He watched her neck and ears turn pink and smothered another chuckle. She was right about one thing. He was happier today than he had been since that rush of euphoria when he'd discovered her alive and well, smiling down from that hospital window. Even with his knees jammed against the seat in front of him and elbows tucked into his ribs, he didn't mind the discomfort. It occurred to him that this was their first road trip. And then he wondered why he'd have such a random thought. In all likelihood, this would be their *only* road trip.

Rose was smiling at the toddler beside them, who stared at her with an open, drooling mouth and wide eyes. The baby grabbed a handful of her skirt and shoved it in his mouth. Rose let him chew on it and laughed with his mother. Before long she'd made friends with the people behind her, in front of her, and on the other side of him. She talked to everyone. No one was immune to her charm and virtually everyone, including the toothless old man on his right, fell under her spell.

When it came to Rose, resistance was futile. Better not to fight it because things would change soon enough. She might imagine they could skip hand in hand into the sunset. He knew better than to plan any further than tomorrow. That way lay—if not madness—despair.

Astonishing that she seemed to have forgotten the douche bag she was engaged to. What kind of asshat couldn't be bothered to get on an airplane to check on the woman he loved? For that matter, what kind of woman so casually dismissed her commitment?

He felt himself getting self-righteous and he hated that, too. Four days ago, he'd truly believed he had no angst about her. He had made a decent life for himself that revolved around work, a few good friends, and girlfriends wise enough not to expect much from him. The woman he'd been seeing on and off knew better than to plan on seeing him more than one weekend a month. Neither of them bothered to call or text unless it was to make specific plans. He'd never heard any complaints, nor had she pushed for more. He was almost certain Trina dated other men; he would have been surprised if she didn't.

Rose wiggled to get comfortable and her soft ass felt warm and sweet. He could tell she wasn't wearing underwear under that skirt. His penis woke up and leaped in his pants, seeking her heat. He'd been half-erect ever since he'd pulled her onto his lap. Now he had a raging hard-on to contend with. He sighed inwardly. So much for philosophy. This was going to be a long day.

Every twitch brought back memories of last night. She'd been everything he could have hoped for and more. If this is how good sex could be when they were exhausted and stressed, what would it be like if they were safe, healthy and unencumbered. He couldn't imagine it. He literally could not wrap his head around what that would be like, and he wasn't sure he wanted to try. What would be the point, after all? Hopes? Dreams? Plans?

No. He was back to where he started. Better to just get some sleep and try not to think. The packed minibus grew warmer as the day advanced. Rose was occupied, playing peek-a-boo with the toddler. Jackson put his head back and drifted off.

He woke when the bush taxi braked at a checkpoint. The driver got out to speak to the soldier on duty. Jackson slid lower in his seat, trying not to look his size. Inconspicuous was too much to hope for. He'd settle for non-threatening. It was the chief reason he dressed like a student and avoided tight clothing that emphasized his size or his muscles. In baggy jeans and long-sleeved shirts, people wrote him off as a tourist. A nobody. That's the way he liked it.

Their driver began to argue with the guard. Something to do with the "fee." It seemed the market rate had gone up.

Rose poked him in the ribs. "Should we chip in?"

"No. We're low-profile. Especially you."

The dispute escalated. The other passengers grew restive. One of the men got out and joined the driver, adding his voice to the argument.

Finally, one of the women behind Rose passed forward a packet of garish yellow hard candy. It made his teeth ache just looking at it. The baby grabbed for the candy as it passed over and knocked the packet to the floor. Rose bent down to retrieve it and passed it up to another passenger who handed the candy out the window.

The solider looked relieved to be given a face-saving out, accepted it as his due and went back into his booth. The driver got back in and they were back in business.

As the taxi passed the booth, the guard's head turned and tracked Rose through the window. Too late, Jackson realized the improvised scarf had slipped, exposing her bright hair.

If General Mutan truly did have a network of spies, as Beatrice had claimed, he would soon know exactly where they were and where they were headed. There wasn't a damn thing Jackson could do about it now, except to be prepared.

Half an hour later, the minibus chugged up a long incline that became a winding mountain road. A ravine flanked one side of the highway, a steep slope on the other. The minibus went around and around hairpin turns. Everyone in the bush taxi grew quiet, either from carsickness or fear. Even the babies kept quiet.

The toddler next to her threw up on Rose's left foot. A few of the men berated the child's mother. Windows were rolled down. Jackson gagged. Happened to him every time someone got sick in his presence.

Rose kept her smile. "It's not his fault. I get carsick, too." She bent down and removed her flip flop and sock. The mother used the sock to clean up the kid.

"Thank goodness I was wearing that sock," Rose said. "Told you."

She stretched forward to catch the hot breeze coming in the window and then sat back quickly. "Oh shit. There's only a few feet between us and that cliff."

He glanced out at the narrow shoulder and sheer drop-off. Not much margin for error. He'd been keeping an eye on the driver, however, and the guy seemed alert and competent.

Rose shifted in his lap and her breathing rate changed. He leaned around her to see her closed eyes and a thin film of sweat covering her face. Her pulse sped up. Even if he hadn't noticed her pulse hammering in her throat, he would have known she wasn't well. Her skin had taken on a green tinge.

"What is it?" he said. "Are you gonna' be sick too?"

"It must be the view. I'm trying to go to my happy place."

"You want to go to Fiji again?" He knew she smiled, though he couldn't see her face.

"Been there. Done that."

"What about...Yosemite. In a meadow looking up at Half-Dome."

Her throat worked as she swallowed repeatedly. *Uh-oh.*

"No mountains," she hissed.

"You want sea level? The Seychelles then, where the sea is an electric blue. The water is so warm it feels like a bathtub. Blinding white sand. Can you smell suntan oil on your arms?"

"I better *not* be smelling suntan oil. I'll turn into a broiled lobster."

"Okay, you smell sunblock. It's zinc oxide. You're covered in gooey white paste. Happy now?"

Her cheek curved in another smile that became a yawn.

She didn't protest when pulled her against his chest and tucked her into his shoulder. He swept her fine, slippery hair away from her damp forehead.

He knew the second she fell asleep. All tension left her body except for the hand she kept curled in the waistband of his jeans. He liked this. Loved it, in fact, though he ought to know better. She stayed in his arms all the way up the mountain.

# 18

ROSE DREAMED about the birthday party. She had a secret. She kept her hand slapped tightly over her mouth to keep from telling and watched Jackson get ready to blow out his candles. She thought she might bust with excitement. He didn't know about the trick candles. This was going to be good. If Katie didn't tell first. Katie always told.

She woke with a start when the minibus swerved. A hard thump came from under the car. Something flopped and thumped on the pavement. Passengers were yelling, kids were screaming, and luggage tumbled around. She didn't. Jackson kept her securely anchored on his lap.

The bush taxi skidded to a halt in a spray of gravel. They had stopped on the downhill run of the mountain highway, still at a high elevation. Though the driver shut the engine off, the vehicle rocked and its metal chassis groaned.

Rose's stomach dropped when she looked out the right window and saw nothing but the horizon. Just air and a brown valley in the far distance.

"All okay?" the driver shouted. "Do not get out on the right side."

He assisted the passengers able to scramble out his door, the only door that opened to solid ground. Jackson helped lower other passengers and their kids from the left rear window. Rose went next. He hoisted himself out last.

Heat rose from the asphalt in shimmering waves. The wall of rocks on the interior side of the highway gave off more heat. Since there was even less space on the inner side of the road, Rose moved higher on the outside shoulder to a spot with more breathing room.

She had a clear view from here. The taxi's right front tires hung in mid-air. If it had skidded any farther, the minibus would have sailed off that cliff. While passengers milled around, the driver inspected the blown-out rear tire. Jackson and several other men helped push the vehicle well away from the edge.

He glanced up from time to time. Checking on her, she thought, which felt nice. She wondered anxiously about the train schedule and tried to adopt Jackson's philosophical attitude. It wasn't easy to roll with the punches, especially when it became apparent that this would not be a quick stop. The wheel's rim had been bent by the blowout.

By now, most of the men were out of sight on the other side of the minibus. A couple of kids, immune to the heat and grown-up worries, were playing tag. They chased each other up and down the road, weaving in and out, annoying the adults who were busy changing the tire. The boy leading the game zig-zagged cleverly, first towards the gravel shoulder then back onto the asphalt. The boy giving chase pivoted on the gravel to follow his friend.

Quicker than she would have thought possible, the kid slipped. His feet flew out from under him and he went over the edge with a short, surprised yelp.

She ran, dove flat, and looked down.

The boy was still there, about ten feet below, wedged against a tree stump. Something of a miracle since it was the *only* tree stump. He clutched at tufts of grass, which weren't going to hold his weight when he moved off that stump. He stared up at her with big petrified eyes.

Rose screamed for help and then swung her feet over the edge. She stayed on her butt and slid, digging her toes in, cursing the flip flops that were worse than useless and using grass and woody shrublets for handholds.

By the time she reached the boy, other voices were calling out above them. She pulled him into a rocky outcrop near the stump, a ledge of sorts. The boy huddled with her, safe for now.

Jackson yelled her name.

"Yes?" She refused to look up. If she did, she might do something stupid. Like cry. Or look down.

"Have him grab my hand," Jackson called.

She dragged and pushed the boy till he was above her and then shoved at his butt to get him within Jackson's reach. She shoved hard, aware she was most vulnerable now with her arms outstretched and occupied. She had no way of hanging on to anything. The boy's flailing foot caught her on the temple. She took the blow and clung like a limpet to the slope.

Then her hands were empty. Jackson hauled the kid up and onto solid ground. The boy's mother and other passengers exclaimed excitedly.

Rose stayed flat against the hillside and rested her face on dry grass. This dizziness would be from adrenaline, most likely. The kid hadn't kicked her that hard.

"I'm gonna' rest," she announced, without looking up.

"The hell you will." His deep voice sounded close.

"No, I'm fine. Stay. I'll be right up." She clawed at the dirt and inched her way slowly upward.

His hands latched onto her wrists and dragged her up and over the top. She landed on her stomach and briefly considered kissing the dirt. Instead, she crawled a few feet and turned onto her back.

Jackson stood above her, a shadow blocking the sun. She closed her eyes and laughed with pure relief, taking a minute to recover her equilibrium. That dizziness had hit her like a ton of bricks.

He moved away and then landed with a thud beside her. She knew it was him by the grunt and by his scent, spicy sweat mixed with soap.

She turned her head and shaded her eyes. He had a funny look on his face and his color was off. "Hey. You okay?"

"No I'm not fucking okay."

She folded her lips and let him be. While they lay there quietly, a memory niggled at her. Someone else had fallen. Another time.

She broke out in a cold sweat. She didn't want to remember this. Someone had fallen from a great height. It hadn't been a movie or a story. It had been real. Except that time, she hadn't gotten there in time. She hadn't saved...her.

The memory pounced like a deadly predator.

She sat up abruptly. "Katie."

It all came back: the shock, grief, and shame. She knew then why her mind kept this time capsule buried. Because remembering hurt like hell.

Jackson sat up too. His gaze was steady and calm. But the emotional distance was unmistakable. He still didn't trust her. With good reason.

"Coward," she blurted. "You could have told me." She would have gotten up and stalked away from him if her feet weren't so messed up, if she didn't feel so—raw. Now she had the memory back, she had to re-live it, re-live the sound of her sister's body hitting the tile floor three stories below.

They were at the mall when it happened. Katie had been behaving like her usual fourteen-year-old self, scowling over some perceived slight. Rose and Jackson were nearby, ignoring her drama. They didn't see her swing her legs over the third floor railing. She'd hung by her fingers, waiting for them to notice. As soon as they did, as soon as they both ran to her, she looked Rose in the eye and simply let go.

Rose didn't want to talk about this. The question burst out anyway. "Why didn't you tell me?"

"Beatrice thought it best if you recover the memory on your own. I wasn't sure you'd believe me anyway."

"That's a bullshit excuse if I've ever heard one." Rose glanced away, shocked by how fresh her perceptions of that long-ago day seemed. "Katie knew exactly what she was doing, didn't she? She looked right at me. God, that smile. That tiny smile of triumph before she let go. How could she do that to us?"

"Do you remember everything now? Are all your memories back?"

She massaged her temples as if that would bring them back, once and for all. "I remember that summer. You and me as teenagers. My family. What happened between us. Everything after that is fuzzy. But that's two decades I've just recalled in one day. Decade three can't be far behind." She glanced at him sharply. "Why? What else haven't you told me?"

"Nothing else. You remember how you were—afterward?"

She nodded. The memory of how she'd treated him after her sister's suicide flooded back, like a toxic river of guilt and shame.

"Why did you throw me under the bus?" he asked quietly. "Why didn't you defend me when the cops questioned us? They accused me of encouraging her. You blamed me."

"I never blamed you," she said, astonished. "I blamed myself."

"You were pretty angry."

"With myself."

"You couldn't even look at me."

"Because of the pain. I couldn't separate my feelings for you from the pain. Later, when I realized what they'd put you through, I was ashamed." She sighed and stared at the valley below. "I failed her and then I failed you. I recognize that now."

"You were young," he said.

"So was she. And that's how she'll stay. Forever young. Forever fourteen."

"And now? Do you really believe you failed her? If anything, you might have been too tolerant. Too loyal. You let her tag along with us all the time."

She looked down at her laced fingers. "I guess I knew something wasn't right with her. I thought I could fix her. We didn't realize—none of us—how obsessed she was. Did you know she truly believed I stole you from her?"

"What?" he said, startled. "She was a kid. I knew she had a crush on me, but I thought it was harmless."

She wondered if he'd forgotten how they used to laugh at Katie behind her back. An awful memory. The guilt had eaten her alive for years. As did the anger. She'd been furious with Katie for doing what she did. An ugly emotional backlash no one wanted to hear about or acknowledge.

"I didn't understand anything until I finally went to a therapist," she said. "Those were delusions she was having. If I had known, I wouldn't have laughed at her. But my family didn't know enough to distinguish mental illness from teenage angst. As you say, her infatuation should have been harmless. If it wasn't you, it would have been something else. If I had a new dress, she wanted it. If I had a friend, she wanted that friend, too. She wanted something *because* it was mine, not because of the object itself."

"So I fit the pattern. I was yours. She recognized that, even if you did not."

Rose wrinkled her nose. "That's a bit extreme. I didn't own you."

"You may as well have."

The driver called out. The bush taxi's repairs were complete. Time to get back on the road. Jackson helped her get up and brush the dirt off.

She refused his arm and hobbled back to the minibus on her own. Her life was too damn complicated. She'd liked herself much better when she didn't know about her fucked-up past. When there was no shame and no guilt. Ignorance really had been bliss.

~

By the time they rolled into Obwele's market square, they'd missed the 3 p.m. train. The time was now 4:45 and nearing sunset. Another northbound was scheduled for 5 p.m.; however, the trains rarely ran on time. Unfortunately, Rose moved slower than molasses once they left the bush taxi. She refused to let him carry her so he ran interference, using his shoulders to clear a path.

The colonial-era square teemed with civilians. They too were headed to the northern border to avoid the escalating civil war. The train was the preferred mode of transport since this rail line cut across a vast expanse of desert with notoriously bad roads cursed by deep potholes and modern bandits.

Jackson didn't like their odds of getting tickets on short notice, but there weren't many other options. He scooped up Rose only once, to save her from being trampled by a small herd of longhorn cattle. When he set her down, he noticed her skin felt hot; she'd gotten too much sun today. Other than thanking him, she said nothing. She plodded on, resisting any more help.

The dense crowd was both a blessing and a curse. They were definitely safer in a crowd; however, progress wasn't easy or fast on the brick and cobblestone paved streets. If he put his head down and plowed through, as he easily could, he'd only draw unwanted attention.

He scanned for signs of trouble. Soldiers were everywhere, some armed, some not. Problem was a uniform meant nothing. Insurgents often wore a government uniform as a disguise. Also, soldiers switched sides on a whim, depending on which side was winning that day. Since his data wasn't reliable at the moment, a situation he found deeply aggravating, he didn't know which side prevailed. He didn't trust the government forces any more than he trusted the rebels but when he got it, that info would factor into his decisions.

The screens in cafes and storefronts—usually tuned to a soccer match—were dark. Whoever was in charge at the moment had shut down access to all mass media. He thought there might be radio, however, from reading the body language of a group of people huddled in listening stance on the sidewalk. Something about the intensity with which they listened caught his eye. He saw now that there were numerous clusters—civilians, not soldiers—listening in multiple places along the square's perimeter.

The back of his neck prickled. He didn't like this. Was it his imagination that a few of the men had their eyes trained on them? They'd made it almost to the station door when a familiar voice boomed at them. Rose jumped and looked around.

General Mutan's voice emitted from a speaker mounted on the wall, saying something about a national security threat. Another voice—an interviewer—asked about UFO sightings reported at the United Nations refugee camp. The reporter used the camp name without irony, as if the U.N. forces hadn't been forced out days ago.

He exchanged glances with Rose. Virtually all mass media here operated under state control. Mutan being chosen for this interview said volumes. If the insurgents hadn't gained official control of the government, they soon would. Rose paused to listen but he pushed her on.

Inside the station, travelers jammed the large room, sitting, standing, or sleeping on their bags and bundles. Most had the glum expressions of those who'd been waiting a long time, with no expectation of moving anytime soon.

He parked her in an inconspicuous spot. "Stay here. I'm going to talk to the station agent." When she didn't respond, he frowned and did a double take.

She leaned against the pillar with closed eyes. Though she'd been on his lap for hours, she'd been facing away from him. He saw now how pale she'd become and even though the early evening air had cooled considerably, her face and hair were damp with sweat.

He kept an eye on her—and on anyone too interested in her—while he spoke to the agent. When he returned five minutes later, she didn't show much reaction to his update. "The five o'clock was cancelled. So is the seven o'clock."

"So we wait," she said in a voice so low he had to bend close to hear. She didn't open her eyes.

"No more trains tonight. I'm taking you somewhere you can rest." What he didn't say was, she looked like shit and near collapse.

Her eyelids flickered and she half-smiled. "That bad, eh?"

He took her arm and steered her to a side door, thinking the fresh air might wake her up. Instead, she wilted further.

He made a decision. "We're finding a room for the night. You need a bed."

She didn't say much after that and walked as if the ground were a bed of nails. Every step cost her. He kept his arm under hers to prop her up.

Two hotels were nearby. A decent one and a lousy one. He thought about the possibilities. Anyone looking for them would go to the decent one first. Then they'd go to the lousy one. Either way, they'd check all the hotels.

He flagged down a tricycle taxi, got himself and Rose inside, then gave the driver instructions. Rose swayed beside him with her eyes closed, looking like death warmed over, yet stubbornly attempting to stay upright on her own. After she almost fell off the bench seat, he wrapped his arm around her and pinned her head against his shoulder with the heel of his palm.

The driver had the radio tuned to the same broadcast they'd heard earlier. Jackson didn't doubt it was the only station available. The driver turned up the volume, so distracted by Mutan's rant that he paid no attention to the odd tourists he'd picked up.

"Last night the terrorists unleashed a swarm of drones on our people. Innocents—not soldiers—were the target of parachute-drops of biological weapons. Our citizens were exposed to a highly contagious virus—used as weapons of mass destruction by Western interests who want our country's resources. We are lucky that the fever outbreak is confined to the U.N. camp. A countrywide curfew will be in effect tonight while a joint task force investigates the health risks to our citizens. We will maintain the utmost vigilance and defeat these avaricious foreigners who want only to exploit us and our country."

As they turned into the hotel grounds, the driver clucked his tongue, apparently buying all this. Jackson directed him to the dusty service road. A few years back, his team stayed in one of the relatively luxurious private bungalows flanking the hotel. They'd holed up there for nearly a week between missions.

Mutan was still going on:

"The current administration is a sock puppet for Western interests. This is unacceptable to anyone who is a true patriot."

So the administration hadn't been ousted. Yet.

To be on the safe side, he had the driver stop at one of those fancier bungalows. Once he'd paid the guy, he picked up Rose and, keeping to the shadows, carried her to the small bungalow he recalled. The caretaker's cottage wasn't luxurious but it had the advantage of obscurity, completely hidden in a grove of neem trees.

He left her under a tree before knocking on the door to give the old gentleman enough cash to retire in exchange for vacating his home for twenty-four hours. He hoped they wouldn't need a safe house that long, but, this being Africa, better to plan ahead.

He returned to find her sitting against the tree, arms wrapped around her knees and her head bowed. When he lifted her, she blinked at him in vague recognition.

This couldn't be good. He carried her inside, placed her on the bed, then turned out the lights. She immediately curled on her side and went to sleep.

He rested his hand on her forehead. She wasn't hot from sunburn. She was running a high fever.

# 19

SHE WOKE up in a dark room with her heart pounding. When she sat up, a wet washcloth fell onto bare legs. She was naked, with no memory of how she'd gotten into this bed. Hadn't they been at a train station? Her breath hitched. Oh, no. Had her mind betrayed her again? The darkness swirled around her like an evil entity, heavy and oppressive.

Then she saw him beside her and immediately breathed easier. Peace and gratitude returned. He was her constant, her North Star. He always had been. Ironic that amnesia helped her to remember that.

He turned on a small lamp and sat up, so close she felt his breath on her cheek.

"Sorry to wake you," she whispered.

"You didn't." His cool hand slid to the back of her neck. "You're still too hot."

"How long was I out?"

His gaze grew heated as it flickered over her. "Four hours, give or take."

"I'm so lucky to have you." Quickly realizing she may have presumed too much, she amended that. "I mean, I'm lucky. If it weren't for you, I'd be sleeping on the floor of that train station."

His dimple appeared. "You had it right the first time."

The ambivalence she saw in that crooked smile did not put her fears to rest. Not ready to push her luck, she lay facing him and listened as he explained how they had gotten there. She let his deep voice wash over her.

She must have fallen asleep again because next thing she knew, he was nudging her to drink water and take some pills. "These aspirin will help. You might need antibiotics but that's one thing I don't have." She swallowed the pills and he took the cup from her. "We lucked out—our host had just cooked his dinner when we got here. He wanted us to help ourselves. Are you hungry?"

She shook her head.

He left the room and she lay down again. The darkness no longer frightened her. Now she understood its power to heal. She dozed until he came back and made her sit up.

He handed her a bowl of rice and beans. "Don't argue."

She ate half of it and then put it aside. "Thanks. Can you point me to the bathroom?"

He draped his shirt over her shoulders and insisted on going along, arm protectively around her as if she were a fragile little thing. Which, though unnecessary, she kind of enjoyed. She kissed his cheek when they got to the bathroom door. "Thank you. You're the best."

His glance was cautious, perhaps disbelieving.

She paused. "Have I been so difficult that a 'thank you' shocks you?"

"Lately? No."

She laughed, as he'd meant her to, and said ruefully, "I get it." She limped into the bathroom, propped one hand on the sink and waited for him to leave. "You can go. I'm okay in here."

"I'll stay."

"To watch me pee? No thank you."

He looked ready to argue the point but then left.

While she used the bathroom, she reflected on the most recent memories she'd regained. Bad memories *were* better than no memories. Even the horrific experiences mattered.

These things were integral to who she had become. She wasn't the teenage girl who'd shut down after her sister's death, nor was she the do-gooder that Oliver had mocked.

Until she got all her lost time back, she couldn't know for sure. Nonetheless, with every passing day, she had a better sense of the woman she had become. She wasn't a saint *or* a sinner. She was herself.

When she stood up, she became so dizzy she had to brace her palm against the tiled wall and clutch the sink. She leaned heavily on the sink in order to wash her hands. Opening the bathroom door, she nearly bumped into Jackson.

"Have you been waiting there the whole time?" she asked.

"Always," he said.

"I changed my mind. I need you."

He came in with a fiercely glad expression. "It's about time. What do you need?"

"Other than you?" When his dark eyes flashed with a warning she didn't understand, she added, "A shower, desperately, and I probably shouldn't do this alone."

"We'll do it together."

"I must really smell bad for you to agree so quickly."

"No worse than me," he said. "You realize it's ice-cold water?"

"I'm burning up right now, so cold is perfect."

She stood back to give him room to undress. As big as he was, he moved with such grace, even doing something as mundane as undressing. They'd made love multiple times in the last few days, gone through so much, and yet she'd never taken a shower with him, brushed her teeth with him, or any of those ordinary, day-to-day intimacies. So many things they hadn't shared.

He undid his belt, then his shirt came off, exposing that wide chest. She loved his body, loved how he looked in those low-slung jeans. He unzipped his jeans and her mouth went dry while she watched him pull them off, stripping down to his boxer briefs.

"Enjoying the view?" he asked and his lips relaxed into a bona fide smile. If she didn't know better, she'd say it was a *shy* smile.

"Yes, as a matter of fact."

"I'm going to find towels," he said. "Don't go anywhere."

He made her sit and she watched him go. He wasn't muscle bound and yet she had no doubt of his power and strength. He must be the most beautiful man she'd ever seen. And she was prepared to stick by that statement, even without remembering any other men she'd seen naked.

Because, honestly, who could compare? Certainly not Oliver, who, though very handsome, hadn't been handsome on the inside. She wondered what she'd seen in him, other than his movie-star looks. Probably not a whole hell of a lot.

And the mystery fiancé? For days she had struggled to remember the man, what he looked like, sounded like, how he made love even. Yet nothing pinged, no matter how hard she tried to summon up an image or a shred of emotion.

Jackson returned and guided her into the shower, taking the utmost care with her. He dwarfed her and she shifted awkwardly, not sure where to stand. He wasn't hairy on his chest or back, which she liked. His skin was smooth and olive-gold all over.

He adjusted the nozzle and turned on the handheld shower. He hadn't lied. The water was freezing.

"You first," she said, shivering.

"Not a chance. We'll do this in order of importance. Your feet first." He braced his back against the tiled wall and beckoned to her.

"Come on," he coaxed and turned her so that she stood between his legs with her back to him. He nestled her bottom against his thighs, bending his knees slightly so she could sort of sit against him. With one arm wrapped beneath her breasts, he balanced her there easily and held her up at the same time.

"Lift your feet," he said and then removed the bandages he'd applied that morning, a million years ago. The bandages were disgusting and she made a sound of distress when she saw them. He tossed them in the trash and cleaned the inflamed cuts without flinching.

Jackson kept her in that half-sitting position while he washed her hair. Though the water was cold, the heat of his body against her entire backside, ankles to shoulders, kept her warm and kept her body temperature bearable. As he massaged shampoo into her scalp, she folded her lips to keep herself from groaning aloud. He rinsed her hair and then washed the rest of her, soaping her torso and in one blink-or-you'll-miss-it-moment, slipped his fingers to her inner thighs.

She jerked in response, already so sensitized she was halfway to coming.

He pretended not to notice and kept his arm around her waist while he quickly washed himself and dumped shampoo on his hair.

"May I?" she asked.

He lowered his head to give her access. His hair felt good under her fingertips. Strong, thick and full. When she finished, he angled his head to look at her, for once at eye level. Brown eyes asked a question.

She framed his face with her hands and nodded before she kissed him. Their lips met, his colder than hers. She didn't hold back and kissed him deeply, exploring his beautiful mouth. He let her take control at first, then returned the favor aggressively, nipping, sucking, and teasing with his tongue.

When she tasted bitter shampoo, she drew back sputtering, then cupped water to splash inside her mouth, giggling the whole time. He kept a hand locked on her arm while he tilted his head back. She slid from his legs and stood on one foot like a stork so that he could finish rinsing.

Suds streamed through his dark hair, down his body, sluicing his powerful back and sliding between his buttocks. She leaned around to watch where the suds went and ran a curious finger along the crack there. His butt muscles clenched and he went rigid.

His cock, already erect, stiffened more, growing engorged and thick. She reached out, unable to resist. He made a noise low in his throat when she closed her fingers around its base and squeezed.

As it grew larger still, she indulged herself with a brief, private fantasy. What if she could claim Jackson just as easily as she claimed his body, with the same open, uncomplicated desire? What if she could mark him as hers and give him pleasure whenever, wherever she pleased?

He twitched eagerly. The head of his penis darkened. She touched it with the tip of her thumb. His cock leaped in her fist.

"We have no condoms," he said. "Wait and I'll see if—"

"Ask me if I care."

"You'll care when you've come to your senses."

"Still don't care." She bent down and pressed her lips to his stomach, then lost her balance. He caught her before she fell. He wasn't going to let that happen. Not on his watch. He moved his hands to her hips and she felt the tension and need in his grip. "I want to go down on you," she said wistfully.

"Sweetheart, you're literally on your last leg and you still have a fever."

She let go of him reluctantly and angled herself between his legs again, this time facing him and resting her bent knee along his thigh. His cock poked her stomach insistently. "Shall we find out how hot I am?"

He snorted, then laughed at her.

She looked up, not minding at all, delighted by his laugh. She didn't hear it nearly enough. Her hands slid up his chest and she circled his nipples with the center of her palms. "I do love touching you."

He sucked in his breath and his head went back. She kissed his exposed throat and the hollow beneath it. With a growl, he lifted her high in his arms. Her legs wrapped around his hips without missing a beat. She rocked against him, open and completely vulnerable. His big hands held her bottom, tilting it, positioning her front and center, almost but not quite touching his cock. He rocked her, already showing her the rhythm he needed.

Desire pooled between her legs. He touched her with delicate precision, curling his finger and making her moan. He stroked the outer folds, the inner ones, then the tender aching bud of her clitoris. The icy shower was the only thing that kept her from catching fire.

When he withdrew slightly she grabbed the back of his head, kissed his lower lip, then the upper one, very softly. He was all she needed, all she'd been waiting for. The soft folds between her legs were wet, slick, and aching.

"Now," she begged.

He pushed inside her, filling her deeply. He was breathing hard, arms and legs trembling, as he waited for her to adjust to his length and girth. "Okay?" he breathed.

"More than." She wanted to give him everything: her body, her mind, and her heart. This was real, she told herself. Everything they'd been through, all the pain and loneliness and long years apart—all led up to this moment. He would either open himself to her—or he would not. It was out of her control. All she could do was show him, tell him, love him in any and all ways.

He'd accept her body—she knew that much. As to the rest, who could say? So much had happened, so much time had passed. It might be too late for anything other than this deeply satisfying physical connection.

He surged back and this time, there was no hesitation, no doubt. No more waiting, no more dancing around and delaying the inevitable. They found their rhythm. Together. He gave and she received him with joy and deep satisfaction. He stretched her to the limit, going deeper than she thought possible.

She balanced with him there on the edge between pleasure and pain, fulfilment and need so deep it hurt. She hadn't even tried to touch herself, too caught up in his pleasure to care.

He pulled out abruptly.

"Did—?" But she knew he hadn't. He pulsed against her thigh, still heavy with need.

His voice was barely audible above the shower. "Not without you."

He kissed her deeply while he reached between their bodies and touched her. Then the need built quicker than she would have thought possible.

"Stay with me." The words burst from her. She didn't know why.

She kept her mouth on his shoulder for the long upward climb. He held her at the top for agonizing seconds. She froze, trembling, with her whole being focused on the intense pleasure he gave her. The pressure built and built until he pressed her hard and pushed deep inside her at the same time. She contracted around him, squeezing his cock while she came. Then he took her there again, with those sensitive fingers that were touching her in erogenous zones she didn't even know existed. Climbing the third peak, she rode him in undulating long waves, milking him until he too cried out and shuddered inside her.

They stayed that way for a minute with the icy water pounding them, foreheads touching. He turned off the shower valve and lowered her to the floor.

Her knees felt like rubber and her head swam. Maybe it was the wild sex, maybe it was the fever. She felt bereft.

He wrapped her in a towel and carried her back to the bedroom. She watched him while he sat her down and found one of his t-shirts to tug over her head. He turned on a fan and put a towel under her wet hair. He never made a big deal about the things he did. He just did them, quietly giving her what she needed even when she didn't know what she needed.

He kissed her and pulled the sheet over her. "I have to work for a little while."

"It's the middle of the night."

"It isn't back home. You sleep. I'll join you soon. Meanwhile, I'm right here." He sat up in bed cross-legged, fingers dancing across the screen. He stayed immersed in what he was doing, as always. Yet his left hand found her forehead and stroked her hair.

The inconsolable girl she'd once been had written him: *"I luv you. Do you luv me?"* That girl knew theirs was not an ordinary friendship. Now, twenty-odd years later, the grown woman knew it as well: this thing between them was extraordinary.

She loved him. She'd always loved him.

As to his answer to that question? He hadn't ever said. Her memory of any reply was lost, gone forever like so many childhood memories.

However, she'd seen how he'd unfolded the brittle paper from his wallet. Carefully. Painstakingly. Over the many years apart—busy years filled with school, work, other friendships, and other lovers—he'd kept that note. He hadn't forgotten. They were connected now and always had been. Tangled up in each other so deeply that logic couldn't really explain it. No logic she understood.

~

Jackson checked intermittently throughout the night for news. The signs were ominous. Virtually all media networks were blacked out. Even satellite signals weren't reliable. Finally, just before dawn, he walked outside and finally managed to reach Will Holloway.

"You better get your ass in gear," Holloway said. "BBC News just reported the coup attempt is escalating. My sources tell me a new government is mobilizing. Official word could come as soon as a few hours from now. Which means you need to get out of that country. I don't care what you have to do. Just *get out*."

A silence fell. Jackson wanted this conversation over with but he knew Holloway's methodical style and he knew better than to interrupt. He waited for the other shoe to drop.

"I don't know why it's taken you this long," Holloway said. "Scratch that. I know and I still don't care. No more delays."

"What about Markus?"

"I don't know his status yet. He's been radio silent for over twenty-four hours. Look, Markus can take care of himself—just get yourself and your friend out of there. When you get back, we need to have a talk. Those drones were earmarked for a medicine delivery network, as you well know."

A "talk." Jackson knew what that meant. Years of work and buckets of Holloway's money had been wiped out by Jackson's unilateral decision to use the drones. His decision had compromised their primary mission: improving health and quality of life for mothers and children.

After disconnecting, he returned to the bedroom. He sat next to her and watched Rose sleep. All these years he'd compared other women to her, a bad habit he'd never broken. No one ever came close. About five years ago, he'd concluded his perceptions were heavily biased by youth and sexual longing. Turns out he hadn't imagined his perceptions. If anything, he'd underestimated how desirable she was. Then and now.

He rested his hand on her forehead, as he'd done numerous times during the night. Her fever had come down, marginally. This might be the last morning he'd have her to himself, the last time he'd wake her like this.

With a longing so deep it manifested as an ache in his chest, he watched her wake up. He wanted to start every day with her. He wouldn't even mind if she took him for granted. For some, that would be a bad outcome, something to dread. Not to him.

She stretched and smiled at him, lovely and rumpled in one of his t-shirts. "Did you get any sleep?"

"Enough." He handed her a glass of mint tea.

Her smile faded. "I heard you on the phone during the night."

"And?"

"I'm afraid history is repeating itself. I've messed up your life. Just like before."

"That fever has you confused."

She watched him with a furrowed brow. "Mr. Lee had it right after all. You know, being a shithead doesn't make him wrong."

"Are you talking about my father?"

She clapped her hand over her mouth. "I'm sorry. I'm missing the filter between my brain and my mouth."

He snorted. "What was he right about, exactly?"

She spoke to his chest. "A few weeks after my sister's funeral, when I finally came to my senses, I drove for twelve hours straight and knocked on your dad's door."

"This is news to me."

"I missed you by one day. You had already left home."

"That's because he kicked me out of the house."

"He didn't tell me that," she said. "Anyway, I didn't make it past the front door. He said I was the reason you were dropping out of engineering school. That I'd messed with your head so thoroughly you had thrown away your scholarship."

"He told you all that, did he?" Jackson said coolly. "My failure reflected badly on *him*. I'd embarrassed *him*. He never bothered to sit down and talk to me. He just yelled."

"He said I'd ruined you. A nice Korean girl would never have messed with your head and turned on you the way I did."

"Funny, considering *he* didn't choose a nice Korean girl. Hypocrite."

"When he told me to leave you the hell alone, I took his words to heart."

"You shouldn't have."

"I was only seventeen, remember? I wasn't prepared for his hostility. Until then I thought grown-ups only wanted the best for young people."

"Clearly not," Jackson said. "Especially not him."

"Why was he such a jerk?"

"Probably started with the name he was saddled with. After his parents emigrated from Korea, they gave him an American name. Oswald. The choice was not fortuitous. A few years later, Lee Harvey Oswald assassinated John F. Kennedy. You can guess how that played out for a freakishly tall immigrant kid named Oswald Lee. Yet no one ever thought to change his name. That's as good an explanation as any to explain why he grew up to be such a bully."

"Do you ever see him?"

"Once or twice a year. He's retired now. Spends his days at the roulette table with a cigarette in his mouth and a drink at his elbow. Alone."

"That's sad."

"No one else thinks so. Certainly not me."

"For better or for worse, his accusations forced me to take responsibility for my behavior. I *had* failed you after a terrible trauma. Then, by refusing to see you or talk about what happened, I twisted the knife. He was right. I did bring you only sorrow."

"Not true."

"So now you know why I staged that scene in my dorm room. I truly thought I was doing right by you. I thought you'd go back to school and forget about me."

His eyes darkened.

"Why *did* you drop out?"

"I'd been thinking about it for months. I knew I'd never be a bench engineer, but I kind of threw the baby out with the bath water. Which I figured out eventually. My decision was hasty but it had nothing to do with you."

"We never spoke about any of this. Or am I forgetting?"

"No, if you'll recall, we didn't do a whole lot of talking that summer. We were intimate strangers."

"I didn't really know you at all then, did I?"

"No."

"I wish I'd tried harder," she said. "I hope you can forgive me someday."

"Done." He leaned over and kissed her hard. Her mouth opened under his and she gave a tiny moan of surrender, a sound he loved. If he heard her moan like that every day of his life he'd be a happy man.

She hauled him down onto the bed. She was surprisingly strong for such a little thing. He braced his arms on either side to avoid crushing her with his weight. He would have liked nothing more than to make love to her again, to sink into her delicious body to demonstrate what he could never say aloud. Instead, he reluctantly removed her arms from around his neck and frowned. Her eyes were bright. Too bright.

"That could be from your skillful lovemaking," she said, taking up the thread as easily as if he'd made the observation aloud.

"I'm not that good."

"Yes you are." She rubbed her knuckles under his chin. "In so many ways."

He kept his face expressionless. She meant the words, but he couldn't help thinking that the circumstances fueled this infatuation. He'd come to her rescue when she was in desperate straits. He didn't miss the irony. Rose had no clue how he'd leaned on *her* from the time they were small. Yet he'd always known she wasn't his to keep. He'd first learned that lesson when her family moved away. He'd had to face the hard truth that he'd been left behind and would have to go on without her.

Her mother had unwittingly reinforced that belief in her Christmas cards. She'd reported all of Rose's milestones: her summer jobs, her college graduation, her moves across the country. He'd understood the messages. Rose had gone ahead and made a life without him, thank you very much.

He pulled away. "Up and at 'em. Time to go."

## <u>20</u>

THIRTY MINUTES LATER, they rattled towards the train station in yet another tricycle taxi. Jackson remained as subdued as he had since she'd woken to find him staring at her with that love/hate expression she loathed.

She wanted to see the same deep longing she'd seen last night, right before they kissed. Or even the way he looked at her before she went to sleep, with thoughtful reassurance. As if he saw her as she was now, not the girl she used to be. As if she were his best friend again. What they needed was time together and dull, everyday experiences. Then he'd know he could rely on her.

When he redirected the taxi driver, she said, "You've been to this city before. What were you doing here?"

He jerked his chin to remind her of the driver's presence. "Later."

"You'll have to tell me some time," she said evenly. From the way he acted, you'd think he had been in the CIA or something. "You'll be happy to hear that more memories surfaced this morning."

"How does that work?" he asked. "Do they come back all at once?"

"No, it's like the memories are grains of sand, piled up there at the top of an hourglass waiting their turn. Every day, more grains filter through."

"What filtered today?"

She saw his gaze go to where her hand rested on his thigh. If he didn't like it, too bad. Time he accepted that she wasn't going anywhere, figuratively speaking. "Memories of what you were like as a young man."

"You say that as if I'm an old geezer."

Good, she'd gotten a rise out of him. "What did you do you after you dropped out of school?"

"I bummed around for a year then joined the Naval Reserve Officer Training Corps. That's how I managed to finish my degree."

She didn't have time to ask any more questions. The driver had pulled up in front of the train station.

Thanks to Jackson's skill at greasing palms, they boarded with far less difficulty than she'd expected. He'd negotiated for two seats in the first-class car, which was newer than the rest, with theoretically operational air conditioning and a theoretically operational toilet compartment.

There weren't many niceties, not even boarding steps. Jackson donned his backpack, picked her up and deposited her on board. He jumped up to join her. They found seats and watched their fellow travellers queue up. More and more people crowded the platform.

"What's happening here?" she wondered aloud.

"People are desperate to get out of the battle zones. All this luggage is a bad sign. No one thinks the civil war will be short."

People lunged and leaped aboard any way they could. One rather large and aggressive lady attempted to board with an entire pot of soup. In her struggle to get herself up and into the train, she spilled the contents on the people behind her. Then she scolded those who'd been soaked, evidently angry they had absorbed her soup.

A fight broke out and the line fell apart. People abandoned the door altogether and climbed through open windows with help from those already aboard. After they piled into the train, passengers sat on every available surface, including seat tops, aisles, and even luggage racks. A few people stared as they passed them; none did so in a threatening way. Most were preoccupied finding a seat, minding their luggage, keeping their kids in line.

Through it all, Rose kept quiet, mindful of not drawing attention. She wore the new scarf Jackson had fashioned for her. He'd embellished this one with a length of ribbon from his backpack so that it looked less like a pillowcase. He had an endearing habit of performing small, thoughtful gestures like this, without expecting thanks or attention.

Two of the families from the bush taxi yesterday paused to greet them like old friends before making their way into the next car. The mother of the boy she'd pulled from the cliff stopped for a long hug and a few tears.

Just as the train began to pull out of the yard, a convoy of trucks appeared nearby. Several were personnel trucks, the same type that rumbled past her and Jackson when they hid in the dumpster. Dozens of soldiers in red berets packed the open cargo beds. One truck cut across the train yard. It drew alongside and parallel to the moving train. The driver called and gestured wildly from his window, presumably at a conductor or engineer, but the train kept going.

"What's up with that driver?" she said to Jackson. "Does he really think the train will stop? There's no room anyway. We must be at twice the maximum capacity as it is."

The soldiers on the cargo beds stood at eye level with the train passengers. They were mostly teenagers, some even younger. Rose hid under her scarf and didn't make eye contact. Then a flash of red caught her eye.

Just outside her window, leaning over the side of the truck, was Raymond. His teeth gleamed white against his skin in a blinding smile. He'd recognized them.

She kneeled on her seat and pressed her hands against the window. "What's he doing with those soldiers? I thought he was sent away to a cousin. Isn't that what Solomon said?"

Jackson didn't respond. His gaze stayed on the truck that kept up with the train as it chugged out of the yard and out of town.

"You're not surprised he's with the Red Boys," she said. "You knew. Why didn't you tell me?"

"What good would that have done?"

"He's too young to be a soldier. We have to do something to help him."

"What Rose? What would you suggest?"

"I don't know. But I can't do *nothing*. He's like a little brother to me. I don't—I don't know if I can stand this."

"You don't have a choice," Jackson said.

She kept her eyes on Raymond. He'd had to roll up the floppy sleeves of his uniform. "They wouldn't make kids that young fight, would they?"

"I would guess they've got them drilling and practicing. None of them look any the worse for the wear."

Soon the train picked up speed and began to outpace the truck. Raymond fought his way to the rear tailgate so he could maintain eye contact. As the truck dropped farther and farther behind, he watched them with a wistful smile. Then he began waving his beret in slow overhead arcs.

Rose craned her neck. Without her glasses, Raymond was a blur. He wouldn't know that though, so she stayed plastered to the window for as long as she thought *he* could see *her*. When the train rounded a bend, she finally lost sight of the truck and sank back into her seat.

"So we got to say goodbye after all," she said. The ache in her chest had nothing to do with the fever.

Jackson took her chin and turned it so she faced him. "Haven't you ever stopped to wonder why you are the way you are?"

She folded her arms and regarded him with misgiving. "Meaning what?"

"You keep trying to save people. Had you not noticed?"

"What...oh, I see what you mean. Because of my sister."

"You couldn't save her and ever since, you've been running around trying to save anyone and everyone you think needs saving. Enough, Rose. It's time you save yourself."

She scoffed. "Save myself? No one's forcing *me* to fight a war. I'm perfectly fine."

He put his hand on her forehead. Then he looked out at the passing scenery and said matter-of-factly, "You're still running a fever. You're not perfectly fine. You're a fucking mess."

She flinched. "I didn't know you thought that. I thought——" She stopped herself.

"Your risky behavior affects other people, too."

"What are you referring to?"

"I'm talking about the choices you've made in the last months."

The first stirrings of righteous indignation prickled. "That's not fair. Given that these last few months are still a blur. Not even a blur, actually."

"How do you think it feels to watch someone willfully disregard her own safety and health? You've been selfish, Rose."

She waited a moment to calm herself. He didn't need to know how much he'd hurt her. "Hey, it's not like I haven't been doing worthwhile work."

"In one of the most dangerous countries on the planet. You've put me at risk also. Is your need to save the world more important than the people who love you?"

Arrested, she looked at him. He wasn't talking about her parents.

"Forget about it," he said. "It's done. We'll get you out of here and you'll recover. Once you're home and feeling better, give some thought to what I said. Try and forgive yourself while you're at it."

Feeling vulnerable and uncertain, she didn't know what to say. It sure sounded like he wasn't planning on being around while she did all that thinking and forgiving. She'd gotten so many things wrong. Very wrong.

She ventured, "Forgive myself for putting you in danger?"

"No, for what happened to Katie."

"I realize it wasn't my fault. I get that now, but I'll always be sad that I let you down."

"Time to let it go," he said, staring out the window. The terrain had changed, becoming dustier and more desolate. Many of the villages they passed had been torched and abandoned.

"I can if you can." Then, gathering her courage, she asked him point-blank. "Is it too late for us?"

He looked startled, then uncomfortable.

Mortified, she spoke quickly to smooth over her blunder. "We've been through the fire, haven't we? It changes a person. That's understandable."

"You're talking about your experiences here? Trauma?"

"Yeah well, that too," she said. "Some seriously fucked-up things are fixed in my head." She shook her head. "Unless amnesia strikes again."

"It won't."

"You can't know that."

"No, of course not. You'll need to see a doctor or two to sort yourself out. You'll do that when you get home, right?"

"Of course," she said, studying him. "Why are you asking me that now? You're not going anywhere, are you?"

"No, just wanted to make sure."

She grew pensive. "I wonder if we can ever be the same again. Do you ever feel that way, that maybe you've seen too much? That you'll never be normal again?"

"All the time. I'm used to it. What's bothering you?"

"Some things shouldn't be shared. You'll think I'm a psychopath."

"No, I won't. I'll think you're you."

After a long hesitation, she said, "Right after the truck bombing, I saw a young man on the ground. He must have died instantly. I keep remembering him."

"Okay."

"His face and upper body still glowed with life. This wasn't long after the bomb, maybe a minute or two. If I hadn't looked lower than his torso, if I hadn't seen the unspeakable mess where he'd been cut in two, I would have thought he had just fallen asleep."

"No question a sight like that is a shock," Jackson said. "It triggers a primeval horror, I think, to see one of your own kind mutilated."

"Yes, but that's just it," she said, willing him to understand. "He was beautiful, even though he'd just been torn in half. I know that's a vile thing to say, I know it's awful."

He said nothing, watching her with those wise, steady brown eyes.

She went on, letting the words tumble out of her, both afraid and relieved to get them out in the open. "What kind of person sees beauty in horror? As twisted as that is, what I saw and felt was true. For me. But no one else will ever understand. My family would be aghast to hear me say something like that aloud. I could never tell anyone."

He reached for her hand. "You can tell me. I've seen things too, remember?"

"I forgot about that poor girl at the checkpoint. Thanks to you, I didn't see much."

"I wish I could have prevented you from seeing any of it."

"Too late for both of us, I guess," she said.

He kissed the back of her hand and wrapped it in both of his. "You can always tell me what's in your head, good and bad."

He probably had no idea how much his steady calm helped. How much he meant to her.

They didn't talk much for the next hour. He held her hand, holding tighter as the passing scenery became more depressing, with signs of recent battle in every village they passed. Charred mud-brick walls and twisted iron roofs were increasingly common.

The train passengers grew quieter, except for the children who continued to chatter and fidget. The little girl in the seat behind her tugged on Rose's scarf and played with her hair. Eventually Rose pulled the scarf off and let the girl braid her hair. The child's mother was so glad to have her kid occupied, she offered to share their lunch.

Jackson wouldn't eat. His body language changed. Even though they were safe inside the train car, he grew tense and hyper alert.

"What is it?"

"I've been here before," he said. "We're approaching a military installation that's strategically important. The base is close to the railroad and a major highway that leads to the border. If the insurgents don't control it yet, they'll be actively trying."

They entered another burned-out town and the scenery became grimmer. Burned up vehicles of all types lined the roads. Corpses littered the streets. No one had bothered to remove them. God only knew how long the bodies had been there.

Suddenly the train jolted and the brakes protested in a high-pitched squeal.

Jackson cursed. His arm shot out to keep her anchored as they shuddered to a long, screeching stop. Their car erupted in shouts, screams, and tumbling luggage. The brakes released with a whoosh.

Jackson said, "Okay?" He checked her up and down then lowered his arm.

Taking a collective deep breath, passengers retrieved their kids and belongings. Then an armored car zoomed past their window, headed for the front of the train.

"Now what?" Rose said.

Jackson pulled her scarf over her hair just before three loaded personnel trucks lumbered past. The men in the trucks wore gray knit caps instead of red berets and their uniforms were dirty and tattered. They were older than the soldiers she'd seen with Raymond and leaner and more battle-hardened. The men glared at the train passengers with open hostility.

"Which side are those guys on?"

"Government. They're regular military," Jackson said, unzipping his backpack.

Another few vehicles raced past the halted train. By now, most passengers were up and checking the windows. Those seated at the far end of the car were pointing at something. With numerous languages and dialects flying around, Rose didn't understand any of it. She asked the young mother sitting behind her to translate.

"They say the train is blocked," the woman said. "Trucks are parked across the track and soldiers have gathered."

Jackson had his head down, preoccupied. A series of clicks emanated from his pack.

"Is that what I think it is?" Rose whispered.

"Probably."

"I didn't think you were carrying."

"You were wrong."

"Will it come to that?"

He shook his head in a clipped motion, an answer she didn't believe. She'd seen that face before. He was in ninja warrior mode, watching and waiting with a set expression.

The door to the next car slid open with a bang.

## 21

TWO SOLDIERS CHARGED through the door, using their rifles as battering rams to clear the crowded aisle.

"Everyone off the train," one announced, indicating the door with his thumb. "Except you and you," he added, pointing his rifle at Jackson and Rose.

The rest of the passengers immediately began to exit the car. Anyone who dallied or tried to collect every bit of their stuff got smacked with a rifle butt.

Jackson recognized the men for what they were. Not by their uniforms. By their dead eyes. He'd seen men like this in every hell hole he'd had the misfortune to visit, men who had seen and inflicted so much violence they'd lost their humanity. At his lowest point, before he'd switched careers, he'd seen those dead eyes every time he looked in the mirror.

He acted the terrified tourist and clutched his backpack to his chest like a teddy bear. Rose stayed calm, even nodding reassurance at various passengers she'd spoken with earlier. People touched her shoulder as they passed, communicating silent support. Rose being Rose, she'd made a dozen road friends in the last twenty-four hours, including four toddlers, various mothers and fathers, and the combative fat lady now squeezing past with her cast iron kettle.

He watched the parade of exiting passengers from the corner of his eye, keeping his attention on the soldiers who now appeared more disgruntled than hostile. He noted where their eyes lingered. Both men wanted the remains of Rose's lunch, some sort of roasted yam wrapped in a rubbery leaf. The fat lady's kettle had gotten their hopes up until she showed them it was empty.

He shouldn't have been surprised that Rose also noticed. She unwrapped the yam and presented it as if serving a plate of cookies at a tea party. The bigger, tougher soldier grabbed the yam and crammed it into his mouth. The short one, with his empty hand still in mid-air, looked ready to stab the greedy one in the back.

Rose pointed to a bag of crisps someone had left behind. The short soldier ripped into it and emptied the bag into his mouth. When she stood to show them where to find more snacks, Jackson tried to pull her back down but she evaded him. He nearly had a heart attack when she limped away.

"I think I saw some water bottles over there," she said, holding on to the seat backs to support herself and scavenging alongside the soldiers. She didn't act frightened, ask any questions, or pay attention to anything other than food and drink. Within a few minutes, both men had lowered their guard and their rifles. They followed her around the train car like puppies.

Jackson looked on in genuine amazement. He, who prided himself on his observational skills, wouldn't have known which rows to search. She went right to various stashes of food, continuously supplying the ravenous soldiers and keeping them well occupied for at least five minutes. Even feverish and unsteady, she was braver and cooler under pressure than anyone he knew.

Watching her, he felt unsettled, like the rules of the game had changed. Or as if he'd landed in a parallel universe. He'd been *this* close to firing. Shooting two soldiers with fifty odd of their buddies gathered outside wouldn't have been smart. He knew that very well. He also knew logic wouldn't have stopped him. If those two had hurt Rose, he would have blown them away without a second thought.

When the men's backs were turned, Rose caught his eye. He couldn't imagine what she saw in his face, seeing as how he couldn't decide whether to be proud or petrified. That's when she winked at him.

Winked!

He set his jaw, far from amused, and went on loading the second pistol. She was more of an adrenaline junkie than he'd guessed. If they made it out of here alive, he might tell her mother to chain her to the refrigerator.

He took advantage of the soldiers' distraction to send a text message to his boss, which may or may not have gone through, and to hide his phone in his sock. As he did so, a distant buzzing sound brought his head up. He couldn't see shit from his window but he knew what it meant. That couldn't be anything but a drone, not with that particular buzz.

The soldiers were peeling oranges as they ambled back, trailing Rose and in no particular hurry. A fresh citrus smell filled the air. The men were relaxed, far less threatening than only a few minutes before. They didn't seem to notice the faint buzzing outside.

"These men haven't been paid in months," Rose said softly. "They were promised back pay plus a cash bonus to stop the train and wait here."

"Wait for what?"

"I don't know."

"Now we go outside," the bigger soldier commanded. He hauled Jackson out of his seat and took his backpack. Jackson didn't protest. He went along, staying in character.

Rose gave him a questioning glance. He shook his head slightly before they emerged into blinding sunlight. Their fellow passengers had been herded from the train and down the line to stand by the steaming locomotive, along with the conductor and engineer. Surrounding them were more than double the number of troops than Jackson had supposed. Five empty trucks were parked on a road parallel to the tracks.

Jackson jumped from the train and held his arms out for Rose. When she hesitated at the edge, one of the men shoved her hard and she pitched forward. Jackson caught her around the waist and set her down on the gravel slope. She braced her hands on his shoulders and closed her eyes briefly, which told him what he needed to know. No way would she be walking anywhere, much less running.

He helped her down the slope and kept his arm around her in case she needed help. But mostly because he didn't want to let her go. Anything could happen now.

One of the soldiers asked, "What is taking the Red Boys so long? If they don't get here in time, who will go in as the first wave tonight?"

"The general knows we need cannon fodder," the older one said, chuckling. "They will be here."

Jackson heard Rose's low gasp. He put his hand on the back of her neck, which seemed to steady her. To his relief, she understood his warning and controlled her temper. He could tell it cost her. He felt her anguish and worry for Raymond, as clearly as if she'd voiced it.

"Cannon?" the short soldier asked. "There are land mines around the military base, not cannon. What is this fodder?"

The older, tougher soldier spat out an orange seed. "It is an English expression, stupid. You should learn not be in such a hurry to fight. Not until he shows us the money. First, we get paid. Then we fight. In that order."

Jackson considered this. These men wore government uniforms. If they were planning to attack their own military base, that meant both they and the Red Boys had joined forces with the insurgents.

The unmistakable whine of the arriving drone caused everyone to stop and look up. It flew in wide circles above them. Once more Jackson wondered about the pilot. Someone had figured out the user interface remarkably quickly. Who had the technical skill required? Piloting one of those wasn't as easy as it looked, especially given the proprietary software. They all watched as the drone settled into a perfect landing on top of the locomotive. It perched there in triumph like a smug kid on top of the monkey bars.

A shiny new Range Rover arrived next. General Mutan emerged, dressed in a fancy uniform dripping with gold braid. He was all smiles and bluster, despite the gunshot wound that had put a hitch in his step. He quickly commenced glad-handing, shaking hands with the soldiers. From the soldiers' wary reactions, Jackson thought they weren't fooled by his phony good humor either.

Then Mutan turned his attention to Rose. "I told you we'd meet again. If I had known about your diminished capacity"—he tapped his head—"I would have killed you right away. You and your dead friends must be the most incompetent spies I ever knew. What a joke. I no longer need you. But you," he said to Jackson, "you I can use."

Mutan waved at his driver with a "go ahead" motion.

The driver opened the back door and dragged out a teenager clutching an orange briefcase. Jackson didn't recognize him right away. Solomon had been knocked around and his face was bruised and puffy.

With a quick indrawn breath, Rose reached for Jackson's hand. He squeezed it in another warning. Mutan watched the interplay; he hadn't missed her reaction.

"How did he get you?" she asked Solomon.

Solomon looked at his feet. "His men caught me that night I left you at the game reserve. I never made it to that training camp. Never found my brother."

Mutan inspected Jackson up and down. "The rest of the drones are in the back of the Range Rover. My son says you were responsible for these."

"Your son?" Rose echoed.

"Only when he wants something," Solomon said.

Without missing a beat, Mutan cuffed the back of the teenager's head. "Shut up." He smiled broadly at Jackson. "You know your way around my country. Possibly we encountered one another in the past."

"Could be," Jackson said laconically. "You were secret police?"

"And you were a mercenary," Mutan replied.

"We prefer the term 'private security consultant'."

Rose released his hand. He knew without looking she was aghast. He'd expected nothing less.

"Our meeting must be fate. You've given me the technology I needed most." Though his words were triumphant, Mutan's laugh sounded forced.

"What are you planning?" Jackson asked. "My boss fired me for losing the drones. I'm open to a new gig."

Mutan paused, appearing to consider the idea. "I checked you out. You're not like her, playacting the humanitarian while stealing my country's natural resources."

"As long as I'm well paid, your money is as good as anyone's."

"That's what I like about mercenaries," Mutan said. "Honesty."

Shouts went up from the crowd near the locomotive. A fistfight had broken out. Mutan made an impatient noise, directed the guards to surround Jackson, Rose, and Solomon and walked up to investigate.

The fat lady was scuffling with someone. They watched while he directed the guards there to restore order. His men waded into the crowd and whaled on anyone in their path.

Rose whispered to Jackson, "You said you had missions here. What exactly were you doing?"

"Guarding assets, countering insurgent attacks, and providing tech support for the team."

"Why did you tell Mutan you'll work for him? You don't expect him to believe that, do you?"

He pitched his voice so the soldiers heard every offhand, careless word. "Why not? I've worked in more fucked-up situations than this. On every continent except Antarctica. For oil companies, mining companies, governments both large and small. As long as they paid me, I followed orders. To the letter."

It felt surprisingly good to say that aloud. He'd stated the truth. His truth. The various elite teams he'd worked on had never really solved problems. They'd *handled* them, applying tiny bandages over gaping wounds. In some cases, their attempts to quell an uprising, rescue a hostage, or protect an asset had, in effect, poured gasoline on an open flame. And what had he and his fellow "consultants" done when each mission ended? Checked into a five-star hotel and waited for their incoming bank deposits.

Rarely had he or his team truly fixed anything for the locals, invariably folks who didn't have the means to escape whatever hellhole they were stuck in. It had gotten to him after a while—not just the missions—but the way his team viewed civilians. One day he realized he had begun referring to human beings as "it" and "them." That's when he'd called it quits. By then, of course, he'd made a shit-ton of money. None of which he planned on returning, that was for damn sure.

Rose still gaped at him, tilting her head as if reevaluating him. He expected the fever and stress had made her more gullible. The confusion wouldn't last; she was too smart for that. For now, her bewilderment suited his purposes.

For good measure, he added loudly, "Money is money."

"I hear you, brother," the tough soldier said. "He's paying us in gold."

The young soldier chimed in eagerly. "A new deposit, top secret. No one else knows, just the villagers and they are so backward, they don't even know what they are sitting on."

Solomon raised his voice, too. "He's not going to pay you. Any of you. He is full of shit. There is no mine, just a village with a pile of rocks. He doesn't even know which village. He's still looking."

"What are you saying?" the tough soldier said. "Is there gold or isn't there?"

"If he finds it, yes, there will be gold flakes. But that's after they grind the stones and separate the gold from the ore."

"Mutan promised us gold *coins*," the tough soldier said. "Today." He wheeled around and stalked away to confer with another group of soldiers.

"More lies," Solomon said to Jackson. "Two village chiefs in the east have boasted of a new deposit. The government covered the news, but he has ears everywhere. He learned of new lead poisoning cases in the outer villages."

Rose recoiled and went very still. Jackson felt something change in her.

"Lead poisoning," she said and put her palm against his chest—for comfort? For reassurance?—without seeming to notice what she did. "That must be what he wanted."

"What have you remembered?"

"It's fuzzy but I remember a clinic." She then gripped her elbows and stood rigid. "Kids were coming in with convulsions. Going blind. Paralyzed. Some died." Her voice broke.

Jackson worried for her. She was tough but so were these memories. If this is what remembering did to her, far better if she didn't. He hated her hopeless expression. He wanted to take her in his arms and tell her everything would be okay. Even if it weren't true.

"In other words," she said, regarding him as if he were a stranger, "you want to lie to me."

Of all the times for her to tune in to their private frequency…on the other hand, she might be better off this way, distrusting him. Whatever. Anything that kept her away from this brewing shitstorm.

The general's voice boomed out as he addressed the now subdued train passengers. "You will be transported somewhere safe from the coming battle. Then you will have the honor of helping our noble cause. You will be hailed as heroes." He paused as if he expected them to cheer. The silent passengers stared back. He tried again. "With your help, we will take back our country from the corrupt politicians. Our national treasures do not belong to the Chinese or to Western investors. This gold belongs to us. You will find the gold and liberate it from the rocks that imprison it."

"…And breathe in clouds of contaminated lead dust," Solomon said, disgusted.

Up by the locomotive, Mutan ordered, "Load them up."

Soldiers began to herd the passengers to the empty personnel trucks parked nearby. A few of the passengers balked. One of them argued. A shot rang out. The passenger who'd refused to obey dropped to the ground. He lay in the dirt, unmoving. People were forced to step over him as he twitched and bled out.

Mutan walked back, smiling as if nothing unusual had happened.

"Open it," he said to Solomon, nodding at the orange briefcase. When Solomon didn't do it fast enough, Mutan pushed him aside to unclick the briefcase and set it on the Range Rover's tailgate. He lifted the lid to reveal an industrial laptop and a satellite internet terminal. "Thanks to my new drones and global wi-fi, I have all the tools I need to locate that gold today. I even have high resolution mineral maps."

This close, Jackson saw beads of sweat on Mutan's forehead, the way his hands shook and how his eyes darted at the restless soldiers. Though the general successfully pulled up a satellite image of geological features, he stared at it for a long minute, and hit the space bar repeatedly for no good reason. He obviously had no idea how to interpret the color-coded data. Nor did he know what to do next.

Suddenly Mutan unholstered his pistol and pointed it at Jackson. "Go ahead. Your turn."

"Is this a paying gig or what?"

Mutan cocked the gun then turned it on Rose, though he still spoke to Jackson. "If you don't get to work finding my gold, I'll put a bullet in her, same as she did to me. It won't kill her, not right away. She'll bleed for a long time. On second thought," he reflected philosophically, "the flies will come. I hate flies. My men will put her in the truck. *Then* I'll shoot her." He beckoned over his head.

"Relax," Jackson said. "I'll find your gold for you."

Rose stared at him, white-faced. She didn't see the soldiers coming up behind her.

## 22

THEY SNATCHED her arms and began to drag her away. Rose let her body go limp, making them work to carry her. They struggled to get a grip, giving her a moment's reprieve. In the meantime, other soldiers seized Solomon.

"There's no need for that," Jackson said calmly. "Put those two on the train. In fact, why not put everyone back on the train? Then they'll be out of our way."

"The train is here to transport soldiers," Mutan said. "Soldiers are my priority. *Those* people," he added with a distasteful wave at the loaded trucks, "those people are worthless, except as labor. The universe has delivered what I need, once again. It is a sign. The more hands grinding that stone, the better. I'll have my gold that much sooner, right boys?"

"Hold it," the tough soldier said, walking over.

The soldiers manhandling her hesitated. Their grip loosened and their heads swiveled back and forth between the general and the soldier who spoke with authority.

"Did you say 'my gold'?" the soldier said, scowling at Mutan.

"A slip of the tongue. Our gold. It belongs to all of us." His laughter rang hollow, possibly even to his own ears because he glanced around at the circle of hostile faces that surrounded him.

None shared his mirth.

"Take the boy and the woman," Mutan commanded. "Load them on the trucks with the other sheep. In fact, put them on that last truck with the big auntie. She'll keep them in line."

The soldiers holding Rose and Solomon still hesitated.

Infuriated, Mutan said, "Don't you know this woman is a spy? She helped spread viruses and spied on our country. This boy helped her to escape custody."

The tough soldier looked at Mutan with barely veiled contempt. "Isn't that boy your son?"

"Not anymore."

The soldier shrugged and turned to the men who held Rose and Solomon. "Don't shoot them just yet. Mutan's right. We'll get work out of them first."

They resumed dragging her and Solomon toward the trucks. As they pulled her farther and farther away, Rose watched Jackson, overcome by the sudden conviction that she'd never see him again. Even now, with those beautiful emotionless eyes pretending to ignore her, she also knew that whoever he was or would become, he was a part of her. No one could ever take him from her, not really.

An arriving group of recruits distracted the soldiers. The moment they looked away, Jackson's gaze found her. His hands were clenched by his sides and she sensed the agitation he kept well hidden. Though the two of them were separated by at least fifty feet, she heard his voice in her head, as easily as if his lips brushed her ear.

*We're going to make it. I'll find you.*

She was a part of him too. He was her oldest friend and the love of her life. Nothing could alter that. As the distance between them widened, she relayed her own message.

*I love you. Always.*

Hot tears filled her eyes, but not from sadness or loss. What moved her most was gratitude for the insight. They would always be together. No one could separate them completely and nothing could break their bond. Not distance. Not time. Not even death.

Jackson called out to her but his words were lost on the wind. Her pulse quickened and she strained to hear. She shook her head slightly to convey she hadn't heard him. He had something else to tell her. Something profound and meaningful.

He yelled, "Keep your scarf on."

She glanced down at the scarf around her neck and then back at him blankly.

"For protection. From the sun," he added, even pointing at the sky for emphasis.

So much for loving last words. Crestfallen, she nodded and watched his tall figure until the soldiers threw her in the back of the truck. Too weak to get up, she lay on the cargo bed until Solomon crawled over to help her. The truck roared to life, then followed the other trucks onto the highway. She assumed they were headed to the camp the general had mentioned or, she supposed, one of the places Jackson would soon identify. While she knew he had no intention of aiding the general and that he *must* have a plan, she couldn't imagine how he'd pull it off.

Only one soldier guarded them. The driver. There were no other passengers other than her, Solomon and the aggressive woman who had been put on this truck alone for a reason.

Rose edged closer to get a good look at the cast iron kettle. It was hefty and strong, like its owner. The woman eyed her with deep suspicion and braced her hands on either side of the pot as if debating whether to fling it in Rose's face.

Rose tipped her head in sympathy. "Too bad about your soup. Did you make it yourself?"

As if she'd been waiting for someone, anyone, to ask this very question, the woman uttered a long, heartfelt sigh and then told Rose all about the soup that got away. She recited a long list of ingredients and then described each step of the recipe in exhaustive detail.

Rose listened and commiserated. Then she scooted closer and began to tell her own story.

~

Jackson had nothing to work with now except his wits. He asked the question as casually as he could. "If you don't know the gold deposit location, where are you sending those trucks?"

"For now, they will drive east," Mutan said. "The lead driver has a sat phone. I will direct him to the village. As soon as you find it. Enough talk. Find that gold." His phone rang and he turned to take the call.

Jackson's fingers flew over the keyboard, ignoring the men around him, ignoring everything but the task at hand. He downloaded all his software, including the "return to the hive" pattern he'd designed for the drones. Then he quickly installed the app he'd developed to monitor the embedded sensors in Rose's scarf. A minute later, he had his finger on her pulse, or as good as.

Her heart and respiratory rate were normal. He exhaled in relief and kept the app running in the background, hidden from view. Even if the general saw the screen, he wouldn't know how to interpret the columns of numbers. That data could mean anything.

The general was winding up his call. As he did so, he watched Jackson through narrowed eyes. In those few seconds, Jackson located the nearest airstrip thirty minutes north and memorized its GPS coordinates. There was no time to log in to email or a messaging app to communicate that information to Holloway.

With help from one of the general's flunkies, Jackson launched one drone to follow the trucks and three more to search for the gold deposits. He then switched on the gold-hunting drones' cameras and showed the general their location in relation to the satellite images. He kept up a stream of techno-babble about the infrared colors and what they meant, speaking in jargon that sounded convincing even to himself. He was certain the infrared satellites images Mutan was so proud of weren't suited to this purpose. The presence of gold would not be as easily identified as copper or other minerals. Of course he wouldn't point that out. The general's over-confidence bought him time.

Mutan stayed at his elbow and took a series of phone calls. Jackson listened with half an ear while he kissed someone's ass and predicted a decisive victory in tonight's takeover of the military installation. It was obvious that the strategic win Mutan had just promised would pave the way for a high status job with the new regime. He had just boasted complete control over the combined forces, no problem. Which wasn't what Jackson saw.

Truckloads of soldiers of all stripes were coming in. The only thing they all had in common was the promised gold. An army was gathering, including "volunteers" from regional militias and the Red Boys who patrolled the cities. If Raymond had arrived, Jackson hadn't seen him. As the afternoon shadows lengthened, the soldiers became more restless. When they started grumbling, Mutan went from group to group, making more promises, even upping the ante, promising the men a bigger payout.

The number of troops mobilizing surprised Jackson. The military base couldn't be that well guarded. Many of those ostensibly guarding it were out here waiting to be paid. How hard could it be to take over that place?

A short time later, another drone he'd sent out as a scout revealed a huge convoy coming up from the south. The vehicle markings indicated they were government. So unless that entire convoy had switched allegiance, this battle wasn't just about the military installation. This was an orchestrated showdown between the government and the rebels. If Mutan knew this, he wasn't saying.

When Mutan was briefly called away to deal with another group of irate soldiers, Jackson switched camera views to scan other major roads. Several scattered trucks packed with men were headed in this direction, on a direct intercept path with that convoy. At the rate they were moving, Jackson estimated all the trucks would converge at a nearby highway crossing in an hour, give or take.

Zooming in on one of the trucks, he saw caps on their heads. Berets. These would be Red Boys coming in to assist in the base takeover. Possibly even young Raymond's group. If so, those kids would soon be face to face with a small army. An actual army that would regard every one of them as traitors. Jackson knew only too well what would happen next. The vastly more experienced and hardened military would murder every one of those kids without hesitation. They would be viewed as rebel sympathizers, even though most, like Raymond, had been pressed into service.

Jackson switched over to the camera feed for the drone following the convoy. Rose's truck had dropped far behind the others. It now appeared to be pulling over to the side of the highway. What was going on?

Though the drone offered a decent bird's eye view, he could not see Rose, just indistinct figures on the cargo bed. The combative woman would be one of those figures. Was she turning belligerent again? Rose did have Solomon with her; however, that other woman outweighed the two of them put together.

He switched screens to check on Rose's vital signs. Damn. Her heart rate had rocketed. It sure looked like she was moving around more than someone who could hardly stand should be moving. Her temperature spiked while he watched the screen, climbing to 104 degrees. The fever wouldn't kill her. Still, she must be feeling pretty lousy.

A lump of dread formed in the back of his throat. He had data out the ass, but all of it was either too micro or too macro, with not much in between. He needed to fly lower to see her. As he prepared to do just that, Mutan returned and demanded to see the satellite map. Jackson had no choice but to close the tab and go back to the gold-hunting drone.

Worry for her hit him hard. She needed him. If only he had his gun…but they'd already found that and taken it away, along with the one in his backpack and the phone he'd stuffed in his sock earlier. He needed to send those airstrip coordinates to Holloway and then find a way to go after Rose. The private jet his boss kept on standby for dire emergencies was, more than likely, already in the air. That plan would have been activated as soon as Holloway received the text he'd sent from the train.

Mutan had returned to stand over his shoulder, demanding arbitrary course corrections as if to prove his superior knowledge to the men listening. His agitation grew with every passing minute, directly correlated with the increasing number of soldiers. Even he seemed surprised by the waves of men and boys showing up.

Jackson scanned the hundreds of massed troops who now filled and overflowed from the train. Quite a few lounged on the roof, some even slept up there. They wore many different uniforms and their weapons ran the whole gamut, from long knives to grenade launchers. This was a motley crew by anyone's definition. Some, like the Red Boys' "recruits", were from regional militias, some were from the regular military, and others were from God knows where. Most of these men wouldn't know one other. As time passed, the men only grew edgier.

Jackson was counting on that. His plan would only work on a group of men who didn't trust each other. In casting their lot with the insurgents, they were about to commit treason. If they'd bet on the wrong horse, they were fucked and they knew it. The tough soldier who'd boarded the train earlier had quietly disappeared, along with his original squad of turncoats. They must have sensed that the tide had turned.

Creating more chaos would not be particularly difficult. Unfortunately, he stood in the eye of the storm. The crazier things got, the better the odds he'd be shot himself. If he were wounded or killed, Rose would be in even deeper shit than she already was.

When the general got on the phone again, Jackson checked the video feed but couldn't see Rose's truck. He pulled back and located the first three, still trundling east, but the fourth one wasn't where it was supposed to be. He'd seen that truck pull to the shoulder only minutes ago, in real time. It had disappeared.

He quieted his mind, blocked out the babble around him, and pretended to stare at his screen. What was happening out there? A wisp of reassurance popped into his head. Or was that his heart? She was up to something. Of course she was. *That's my girl.*

Not that she was Superwoman. Except she did have superpowers. Witness all the times she won people over. He still didn't know how she pulled that off, time after time.

He checked her numbers. She might be up to something but she wasn't okay. Her temperature had spiked to 105 degrees. Her blood pressure was elevated. She was breathing way too fast. That did it. He couldn't wait any more. To have any prayer of catching up with her, he would have to hurry things along. He rigged the camera feed so that it looked normal, then set the video to loop the previous half hour. As long as Mutan didn't check the time stamps, he'd never know the difference.

Mutan wrapped up his call. Eyes on his phone, he was disconnecting and walking back to the tailgate. With the soldiers becoming more and more restive, the pressure on Mutan was ratcheting up. Since shit flowed downhill, the general would expect Jackson to produce fabricated proof or outright lies any minute now. Given these men had already shown themselves to be willing to betray on a dime, when they turned, things would get even uglier.

With only seconds to spare, Jackson initiated his standard "return to the hive" sequence and then queued up the World War I dogfight pattern he and Markus had programmed last year. They'd done it purely for fun, for no better reason than that they were boys with new toys.

He entered the final command. The pattern was set.

~

Rose nodded at Solomon and moved out of harm's way. His delighted grin made him look exactly like what he was, a boy with a new toy. She was tempted to play, too. However, there was no point in pretending she had sufficient strength or agility. Her body shook with chills and her eyelids begged to close. Still, she didn't want to miss this. Unable to get warm despite the hot sun, she curled shivering into a corner of the cargo bed to watch their game play out.

Her new friend, Doris, took her cue and launched into a tirade about someone touching her kettle. Doris got louder and louder. After a strategic pause, she tossed the cast iron pot so that it slid down the truck bed like a bowling ball. It pinballed and banged off the metal surfaces louder than any of them had expected. She was a natural.

Solomon caught the pot and shoved it like an air hockey puck back at Doris. He responded with an improvised rant of his own at even higher volume. They passed the pot back and forth, playing the game faster and faster, repeatedly aiming for the back of the truck cab to create maximum annoyance and impact.

The driver shouted at them through his open window, bemoaning his thankless duty and all the crazy civilians he had to put up with.

Rose actually felt sorry for him. He didn't know the half of it.

Solomon called to Doris, "You're so fat, when you go to the beach, Greenpeace will come and tow you back out to sea."

Taken aback, Doris blinked, then heaved the pot so hard that it dented the panel right behind the driver. The pot skipped and bounced across the truck bed, missing Rose by a hair.

At the end of his rope, the driver braked and pulled to the shoulder, spewing curses. Solomon, meanwhile, handed the pot to Doris with an apologetic smile. She took her position closest to the driver and waited.

The engine cut out. If the driver wondered at their abrupt silence, he didn't show it. Rose, Doris and Solomon all froze and watched the driver emerge from the cab. He had one foot on the running board.

Doris swung the pot. The cast iron hit his temple with a sickening thud and the driver flopped to the ground, out cold.

"Soup's on," she said.

## 23

COMBAT WOULD HAVE BEEN EASIER than playing this
waiting game. Jackson went through the motions while the
bogus video continued to fool Mutan into thinking the
drones were still finding his gold. Jackson watched the
clock, counting the minutes until the mock dogfight
commenced. This promised to be a thing of beauty. He
wished Rose and Markus were here to see it.

The first drone came in low and fast, skimming right
above the soldiers on the roof of the train. Men yelped and
slid off the train, certain they were under attack. Some fell,
hitting the gravel with bone-crunching impact.

Mutan looked around wildly. "What was that?" He
hadn't seen the dogfight start. He'd certainly heard it
though. Even so, his disoriented expression revealed his
belief that the drones were miles away. He still believed in
the mythology he'd created.

The general spun around when a second drone
swooped down to buzz dozens of men near the
locomotive. Some of them ran. Others lifted automatic
rifles or handguns and shot at the departing aircraft. Mutan
rushed after it, emptying his pistol into the sky as he ran.
He didn't come close.

Jackson took cover behind the car. If only he'd taken
Markus's suggestion of weaponizing the drones. That
would have made things really interesting. But of course he
hadn't. Their mission was humanitarian and the drones'

sole purpose was medicine and food delivery. If Will Holloway had even suspected they'd flirted with the idea of air-to-air combat, just because it sounded awesome, he would have blown a gasket.

The other two drones arrived in quick succession. One circled high and the other climbed to meet it, looking for an angle of opportunity to take down the enemy aircraft with its make-believe machine guns. Both drones flew in an upward spiral and jockeyed for an advantage. Then one dove straight down, as if on a suicide mission. It whined at high speed right at the nucleus of massed soldiers. The other drone gave chase and both zeroed in on the men.

The soldiers reacted predictably. Their weapons came out and they fired in all directions, including straight up, heedless of the men around them and of gravity itself. One guy loaded his shoulder-held assault weapon and veered in a manic circle, attempting in vain to get a bead on the drones that whizzed past him. A rocket-propelled-grenade hit a jeep. The explosion created a black cloud that would be visible for miles.

The cries of the wounded added to the pandemonium. Some of the younger, wiser soldiers dove under the train. Others scrambled into the train cars and ducked under the seats. Bullets continued to fly.

Jackson leapt for the Range Rover's door, half-expecting to be shot in the back. If that happened, the show would go on. Thanks to him, those aircraft were powered by the best batteries on the planet. He'd be out of here by the time they died. Either that or he'd be dead himself.

He jumped in, hit the locks, and started to search. He found his backpack but no guns and no phone. This was a problem. If the pilots did not soon receive the coordinates for the nearest air strip, they would divert and land across the border to await instructions. Such a delay could be fatal.

Outside, confusion reigned as the soldiers ran back and forth, trying to decide who was attacking whom. All four drones now flew very low and chased each other in a manic zig zag pattern that sent them darting back and forth between troops and vehicles. Soldiers continued to fire at each other. As more vehicles arrived for the impending battle, the confusion and weapons only multiplied.

Mutan stowed the satellite terminal and laptop back into the orange briefcase then picked it up and stalked over to the train. At first Jackson thought he must be looking for safe harbor because he stooped to look under the cars. Seeing only terrified kids, he stood back up and turned in a slow circle. By now most of the men had scattered, leaving him isolated.

Jackson saw the precise moment when the general realized there was only one place he hadn't checked. Mutan moved deliberately toward the Range Rover, disregarding the bullets that flew around him. He knew exactly who to blame for this debacle and he wanted blood.

On that thought, Jackson remembered his Hummingbird. He reached in his backpack to find the micro-drone, one of his first designs. He'd kept it for sentimental reasons and because Markus had asked about its single-minded ferocity.

With Mutan less than twenty feet away, Jackson switched on the micro-drone and tossed it out the door. It hovered in place briefly. In those first few seconds, the Hummingbird seemed harmless, even cute. It flitted in a wide aimless circle, moving so fast its propellers were invisible. In a vacuum, it chased its own tail. Once it honed in on a heat source, however, the game would be on.

Mutan ignored it. He kept coming for Jackson with murder in his eye.

Safe in the front seat of the Range Rover, Jackson offered a jaunty wave. When Mutan leveled his pistol, Jackson ducked.

No shot came. The windshield remained intact.

He cautiously raised his head. The Hummingbird had found its target.

Mutan batted at the micro-drone and hesitated, surprised when the tiny aircraft became a blur. He tried to run, only to be sliced by the propellers as the tornado spun tighter and trapped him within its vortex. Mutan raised his pistol to shoot at the drone and the pistol was knocked out of his hands. When he bent to retrieve the gun, the Hummingbird hit his butt. He screamed and dropped the briefcase. Its propellers must have sliced at his gunshot wound.

Mutan twisted and contorted inside the whirlwind. He tried to kick his way out. If he'd been wearing combat boots, that might have worked. Too bad he chose dress shoes today to go with his fancy new uniform. That Italian leather would never be the same.

Within a minute, his hands and arms were sliced open in a dozen places. The cuts weren't deep, but they would be painful. Jackson had learned that the hard way. Given enough time, the general would die the proverbial death by a thousand papercuts.

Unfortunately, there *wasn't* enough time, because the Hummingbird wouldn't last long enough to kill him. Within three minutes, the aircraft would simply drop dead. Until then, the drone would go full throttle, which gave him some breathing room.

Jackson got out of the car, careful to keep his distance lest his body heat confuse the drone. He looked around for something to poke the briefcase out of the whirlwind and soon found an old railroad tie that did the job.

For the moment, he was safe. The confused troops were still shooting at each other and the drones; most had moved to take up positions near the end of the train. Seeing the general's plight, they simply backed away. At some point, these guys would stop shooting at one another and go home. Unless the government convoy got here first.

He quickly set up the laptop and satellite terminal and logged on to a messaging app. Maybe two minutes remaining in the Hummingbird's battery life. He typed the airstrip coordinates, hit "send" and looked up to see a new truck rumbling in. Every other truck that had pulled in this afternoon had been full. But not this one. Solomon was at the wheel and the fat lady stood in the back.

His stomach dropped when he spotted a bit of bright hair through some cargo netting. But the angle wasn't right. She would never lay down on a filthy truck bed. Not Rose.

He ran to intercept them. When the truck came to a stop, Jackson jumped into the back. She lay unmoving on her side with her head on her arm.

He rushed over and shook her awake.

She opened her eyes with an achingly sweet smile of recognition. He wondered how he'd lived without seeing her smile all these years. When they were kids, she used to greet him with this same exact smile that said, "*There* you are. I've been waiting for you."

In all those years spent apart, no one else had ever made him feel as alive and as essential as she did. No one.

"I'm okay," she announced and held her hands out.

Understanding the gesture, Jackson dragged her to a sitting position. "Ah, no. No you're not."

"Yes, I know I'm a fucking mess. You said that."

He knelt and framed her face with his hands. He wanted, badly, to haul her against his chest and hold her close. But what he wanted wasn't what she needed. He brushed damp hair away from her forehead with a shaking hand. "Rose, your fever is too high."

She looked at him curiously. "How do you know how high my fever is?"

"I'll explain later. I've got to go deal with that bastard. Then we'll get you out of here."

He stood up to find Solomon transfixed by the sight of his father, cross-hatched with cuts, held captive by a rogue drone.

Jackson called to the teenager, "You've only got a minute before that thing stops and he's free. Find someone to help you hold him down. I'll be right there."

When he crouched again, Rose tugged at his collar. "Don't let Solomon kill his father. I think he wants to but he shouldn't be the one."

"You don't need to think about that." He leaned in for a quick kiss, fully intending to hold himself in check. He couldn't do it. When her soft mouth clung to his, he deepened the kiss and poured his heart into it, claiming her as his. He couldn't pretend anymore. Not after almost losing her.

She held on to his shoulders and kissed him back just as fiercely. Then he sighed against her mouth and gently disengaged. She reached for him again and he kissed her fingers before releasing her, hoping she understood what he was trying to say. He was sick and tired of having to let her go. But they weren't done yet. Not by a long shot.

He stood up and called out to Solomon. "Be ready. You've got thirty seconds. Not too close though. Count to twenty and then go in and restrain him."

Mutan heard him of course. His stance suggested he would retrieve his gun the moment the Hummingbird dropped dead.

The heavyset lady standing by observed all this with interest.

"This is Doris," Rose said. "Doris, this is my friend Jackson."

"Stay with her," Jackson said to Doris. "I'll be back as soon as I can." Then, looking down at his beloved's flushed face, he bent down and kissed her one more time.

Just before he hopped down from the truck, he spotted a long line of armored vehicles coming over a rise in the distance. That would be the government convoy he'd seen on the drone's feed. Those soldiers would be seasoned fighters, primed and ready. The regular army was not known for its mercy. They treated anyone suspected of insurgency with equal brutality.

The remaining men and boys around the train had also seen the coming convoy. Some scrambled to find defensive positions and others fought over the best hiding places. Two boy soldiers fled into the desert. They couldn't have been older than twelve.

A panicked squad leader, only slightly older than those he commanded, had them in his sights. The boys looked back but kept running. They knew what was in store for them when that army arrived. Automatic rifle fire rang out. The boys fell forward, spread-eagle. Their squad leader hesitated, looked around, then ran off into the desert himself.

Jackson reached Solomon's side a few seconds later just as the Hummingbird stopped spinning and plopped to the ground, spent. Solomon lunged to grapple with his father, who put up a serious fight. Several other kids came out from under the train, only too happy to help subdue him. It took four young men to restrain the general, whose arms were wet and slippery with blood.

Jackson found the gun on the ground. He would step in if necessary but these kids had things well under control. He scanned the vicinity for a way to tie up the general.

One of the young recruits said to Mutan, "Your men raped my sister."

"And my cousin," Solomon said.

Mutan panted and fought the hands that held him. His eyes blazed with fury.

Solomon got in his face. "Where is my brother? What camp did you send him to?"

"It doesn't matter," Mutan spat back. "All recruits are on their way here. They will do their duty and die for their country. They are not traitors like you. You're not my son."

"That is the best thing you have ever said to me," Solomon said. "I've been spying on you for months. The real generals know you're the one who forced the Red Boys to join the insurgents. They know all about you." He pointed at the highway. "Do you see them? They're coming for you now."

Jackson felt a tap on his shoulder and swung around with the gun braced in both hands. Rose stood there, wobbling but upright, with Doris propping her up. He lowered the gun. "Honey, don't ever do that."

Rose's face was as pale as it had been flushed a minute ago. "Were those boys from Raymond's group?"

"No," Solomon said bitterly. "I don't know where he is."

Jackson wanted to scold her for coming out here but she looked so sad he bit his tongue and put his arm around her instead.

Rose unwound her scarf. "Here. Use this to tie him up."

"Allow me," Doris said, snatching it. "You said he is the one who took our girls?" She bound Mutan's wrists tightly behind his back. Then she removed her own scarf and used it to tie his ankles even tighter. She stood back to admire her handiwork then held up one finger. "Don't go anywhere." She trotted away.

Solomon extended his hand to Jackson. "The gun."

"Hold on a second." Stalling, he retrieved the Range Rover keys from Mutan's pocket. "Let's see if we can come up with a better plan."

"What could be better?" Solomon said, eyes welling up with so much despair and rage that Jackson had to look away.

There had been a time when he despised his own father. Though he would never like the man, he no longer cared enough to hate him. Thank God he hadn't ever had this choice because he just might have taken it. Rose was right; Solomon shouldn't carry this burden.

"Watching him suffer?" Jackson suggested.

Just then, three trucks filled with returning train passengers rumbled in. The drivers immediately abandoned the trucks.

"Rats from a sinking ship," Rose said. She looked at Solomon. "There's an army coming. Why not put him front and center to face the music?"

An anguished look crossed the teenager's face. "I don't know."

Doris came back with her soup pot. "You are a good boy. I know what to do. Follow me." Together, they dragged Mutan to the center of the highway so that he lay in the path of the approaching convoy.

"If we're all going to die," Solomon said. "I want him to go first."

"You won't die," Jackson said. "You're coming with me."

"What about them?" Solomon said, indicating the boys who'd crawled back under the train. "They're as good as dead when the government soldiers get here. You can't take all of them."

Rose said, "I have an idea." She and Doris went to speak to the train passengers. Several of the women quickly rounded up the youngest soldiers and helped them rip off their berets, weapons, and uniforms. Anything incriminating went under the train. Then they hopped into the cargo beds and blended in with the civilians.

Solomon stood above Mutan gripping the soup pot in his right hand. "This is for Raymond." He held it high and hesitated.

Jackson kept Rose back, half-expecting her to charge in. She didn't though. Instead, she fit herself under his shoulder.

"It's out of our hands," she said. "This isn't our fight."

Somehow Jackson managed to refrain from telling her, "No shit."

"Wait." Doris stepped in to take her pot away from Solomon. She tied the handle to Mutan's leg and grinned at Rose. "It is worth the sacrifice." Then she climbed into one of the trucks. The crowd parted, giving her a wide berth.

Mutan sprawled on the hot asphalt and glowered up at them with undisguised contempt. "You are stupid sheep, waiting to be told what to do. Even my own son. You let others dominate you and steal what is rightfully yours. You will all have the country you deserve."

"And you will have the fate you deserve," Solomon said to his father. His voice was calm and clear. "These people will bear witness. This is where I leave you."

Mutan didn't answer, too busy attempting to drag himself from the highway. But he couldn't do it, not with bound hands and feet and the weight of the pot anchoring him. He jerked his head back and forth to avoid the flies that had started to buzz around him like more bloodthirsty drones.

Jackson swung Rose into his arms. "We have to go," he called to the teenager. "Now."

"Don't forget that thing," Rose said, pointing at the orange briefcase. He grabbed it, picked her up and ran for the car.

"What will the army do to the people from the train?" she asked. "Are they in danger too?"

"I don't think so," Jackson said. "They'll know they were captured when the train was stopped. As soon as the track is cleared, they'll load them onto the train."

A minute later, the Range Rover barreled onto the highway with Solomon at the wheel. Jackson sat in the back with Rose and kept her close. She was his now. If she didn't know that yet, she soon would.

He looked out the back window at the rapidly receding scene. The fallen general awaited the government convoy, his body jerking in futile attempts to escape a hungry cloud of flies.

## 24

WHEN ICY COLD invaded her bones, she shook with chills. Then a delicious warmth enveloped her. He tugged his shirt around her and she sighed in contentment that didn't last long. Soon she was boiling hot again. And achy. Even her eyeballs hurt. Had she fallen asleep at the beach? No, that couldn't be right. There wasn't a beach here, not this far inland. She opened her eyes and saw a blurry orange fireball through the car window.

"What *is* that?" she said anxiously, struggling to climb off his lap.

He pulled her back. "Just your last setting sun in Africa."

"Are they coming after us?"

"No one bothered to chase us," Solomon said from the driver's seat. "They've got other problems."

"You're safe," Jackson said. His hand felt cool on her forehead.

"Are you sure?" She didn't recognize that croak as her own voice. He tilted a water bottle to her lips. After a painful gulp, she asked, "Where are we?"

"On our way to an airstrip. My boss sent a jet for us. We'll be there soon."

"This will cost a fortune," she fretted. "I'll pay you back, I promise."

He stroked her hair away from her forehead. "Go back to sleep."

So she did and if she didn't sleep like a baby, she woke up like one some time later to find him cradling her. The car wasn't moving and they were alone. The peace and security she felt in his arms was the best feeling in the world.

"Your fever broke," he said. "Feel better?"

"Much." She nuzzled his shirt.

She heard the smile in his voice when he said, "What are you doing?"

"Smelling you."

"After the day we had, I must smell pretty bad."

"Only a little bit," she said, unbuttoning a couple of his buttons to slide her hand inside his shirt. "I love how you smell. I even like your sweat. Crazy, huh?" She pressed her lips to his smooth, warm skin.

He lifted her off his lap and adjusted himself. "Our privacy's not going to last. Solomon went to get something to eat."

She looked up at his calm, sculpted features. "Why do you have to be so gorgeous?" she asked plaintively.

He bent down to kiss her pout and she ended up back in his lap with her arms around his neck indulging in the long and languorous kisses she craved.

Finally, he pulled away with a rueful sigh. "Our ride is due to arrive any minute now."

She took stock of their surroundings. They were parked near a deserted runway. There were no planes in sight, just a couple of small buildings and one hangar. It was early evening. Faint traces of pink and orange streaked the sky. The first star had appeared. She made a wish.

When she turned back to him, he was watching her with a slight smile. "Yes?"

"My wish was for you."

"What do you want for me?"

"No, I mean I wished for *you*."

"You already have me." He looked more at peace than she'd ever seen him. Those brown eyes that noticed everything were calm and reassuring. "*It's going to be fine*," he told her silently.

"I love you, you know," she said, almost defiantly. Better to get it out there in the open. She forestalled him. "You don't have to say anything. Just think about it." Oh, he definitely loved her back. She knew it quite well, but she also knew he might not ever say so. He never had been one to talk about his feelings. Neither of his parents had been openly loving. From what she could tell, his adult life hadn't exactly been warm and fuzzy either.

"I love you more than you'll ever know," he said quietly.

She stared at him in shock.

"I always have," he said. "Even when I hated you." He ran his finger along her lower lip, making her shiver. "I loved you first and I loved you best."

She reached for him but he didn't lean in to meet her. "You really think I didn't love you back?" she asked.

"No, but I loved you more. That's fine. I've always known." He shook his head and his harsh, almost hopeless expression hurt her. "This is how it's been for me from the start. The thing is, Rose, even if we somehow fuck this up, I'll love you to the finish."

"Why would you say that?" She pulled him in and buried her face in his neck. She wished she could kiss all the bad memories away. He could benefit from a touch of amnesia. He really could.

Because just as Beatrice had said, amnesia had been a gift. For so many years she'd allowed her memories to define her. Guilt and shame had driven a wedge between them and kept her in a self-imposed exile. That was the paradox of the amnesia. Released from her past, she'd found her future and rediscovered her oldest, truest friend. If she hadn't been free of all the bad memories, she wouldn't have fallen in love again. She might not even have been capable of it.

They heard the roar in the sky before they saw it. The jet soon appeared on the horizon and made its descent. She'd never seen a more welcome sight.

While the airplane taxied over, Solomon jogged back to the car.

"Is he coming with us?" she asked.

"No," Jackson said. "He needs to find his brother."

When the jet door opened and the pilot lowered the stairs, Rose jumped from the car, putting all her weight on her right foot, only to sink to the ground wincing. Jackson was already there, scooping her up.

She put her arms around his neck. "I think you like it when I'm helpless and pitiful."

"You couldn't be helpless and pitiful if you tried."

She made him put her down so that she could hug Solomon goodbye. "I *will* see you again," she promised. Solomon kept his face blank and after a carefully indifferent nod, got back in the car. He must have heard a lot of promises in his life. She vowed she'd keep this one.

Jackson carried her into the jet, which was air conditioned, thank you Jesus, and lowered her onto a cream colored leather seat.

Three people waited on board: a second male pilot, a stony-faced woman in a suit and a friendlier one in scrubs. As they introduced themselves, Jackson stood in the aisle beside her, keeping himself between her and the others. She felt his tension.

She nudged his hip. "What?"

"I didn't expect anyone except the pilots," he told her, studying each member of the welcoming committee in turn.

The woman in the suit, a Ms. Harrow, spoke up. "When we heard that Mr. Holloway was sending a jet, the State

Department contacted him and he generously agreed to let us ride along." She glanced at Rose. "After our employer notified me of your, um, mental health problems, I arranged for a nurse."

"How did they know?" Rose asked.

Ms. Harrow smiled thinly. "Diplomatic channels. We knew there must be trouble when you didn't check in. Given the instability here, we couldn't risk more assets until the time was right."

"And when would that have been, exactly?" Jackson said.

Ms. Harrow ignored him. "No time for a post-mortem now. We need to get in the air. Passports?"

Jackson reached into his backpack and handed one over. "It won't pass muster but it's all she has at the moment."

"My real one got lost after the truck bombing," Rose said.

Ms. Harrow sniffed as if Rose had been somehow careless. "Lucky I came prepared."

Rose rested her head against the seat back, feeling unwell and unsettled. She wouldn't relax until they were out this country's airspace. Then she studied Ms. Harrow more closely. "You mentioned *our* employer. Yours and mine? Who do we work for?"

The woman gave her a sharp look. "So it's true about the amnesia. You weren't faking it. We do have a situation then, don't we? Well, we should have plenty of time for debriefing on the flight. Don't worry. This is standard agency procedure."

Debriefing? Agency? Rose exchanged a glance with Jackson. *What fresh hell is this?*

His mouth quirked in a slight smile and he touched her cheek with the back of his fingers.

Aloud, Rose said, "I was working for the government all along?"

"This assignment was never intended to be more than a one-off," Ms. Harrow said quickly. "Due to your previous aid work experience, our superiors considered you an ideal operative." Her tone made it clear she did not share this opinion. "They thought you the perfect unlikely spy. But you took much too long to determine that three of your colleagues, including Dr. Oliver Pedersen, were taking payoffs from multi-national "interests"."

"In exchange for?"

"In exchange for relaying pertinent intelligence to those interests. Which they'd been doing for some time."

"Why didn't anyone come for me? You must have known about the coup attempt."

"Frankly, after your team was kidnapped and murdered...." The woman's voice trailed off.

"You thought I was dead. I would have been if I had gone to work that day. Instead, I woke up completely disoriented and went to the embassy. That memory loss saved my life."

Her head felt very heavy. She closed her eyes and heard Jackson say "She's got a high fever, probably an infection."

"That's why we have the nurse," Ms. Harrow said irritably.

Rose opened her eyes to find Jackson staring down at her with a worried frown. He still had not found a seat, nor, come to think of it, had he produced his own passport.

"No worries," the nurse piped up. "I'll stay with her the entire trip and will personally accompany her to California. Right to her parents' door."

"Take good care of her," Jackson said.

Rose glanced back and forth. "Why are you talking as if..." With a sudden intake of breath, she understood.

The sad apology in his eyes confirmed her suspicion.

"You're not coming with me?" She heard the tremble in her voice as if someone else had asked the question. This couldn't be happening.

Everyone scattered. The two women withdrew to the back of the plane and the pilots went back to the cockpit.

Jackson sat in the opposite seat and gripped her hands. "Believe me, I'd like nothing better. But I can't. I can't leave men behind."

"You mean Markus."

"Raymond, too. He's in the most danger at the moment."

"Can't his brother find him?" As soon as the words left her mouth, she felt ashamed.

He met her eyes. "That's not like you. He'll need help."

She wanted to argue, to wail and gnash her teeth. After everything they'd survived together, it couldn't end like this. They were finally safe. And free. They had come so close. She felt her face crumple. "But I need you, too. I've been alone for a long time. Now that I finally have the sense to claim you, you're leaving me."

All she got from him was a slow shake of his head.

She looked out the jet window at the darkening sky and struggled to contain her emotions. Her worry and conviction that he was tempting fate and really fucking pushing his luck overwhelmed her. Why did it have to be so hard for them? Wasn't it finally their turn to fly off into the sunset?

"Markus is being held by the government," Jackson said. "He'll be the perfect scapegoat, the perfect symbol of a meddling foreigner. I know how this works. He won't get out unless there's someone negotiating on his behalf with local officials. Someone they can't ignore."

If she weren't so sick, she would have jumped out of her seat to give him a good shake. "This isn't right. You've

already done so much. What if they arrest you, too? What
if—"

He held one of her hands flat against his heart. It beat
warm and strong under her fingers. He had more heart
than anyone would guess. This was who he was. No way
would he leave this country with his friend imprisoned. Just
like he would never leave her behind if she were in trouble.

But she wasn't in trouble anymore. She had her own
private nurse to pamper her, give her medicine, blankets
and juice with a cute straw. She was going to be fine, and
they both knew it. Those they'd left behind needed him
more than she did.

This really sucked.

"So you understand." He held her face between his
hands and kissed her three times, each one soft, tender and
true. Each kiss made a promise. He loved her. He had
never forgotten her. He would do his best to come home.

He promised all that without saying a word.

"You be careful," she said, crying openly. "You better
be really fucking careful Jackson Lee. Because I need you.
And you need me, if only to make you laugh now and then.
And just so we're clear? When this is over, you are *mine*. I
don't care who else needs you."

His smile was lopsided. "I know sweetheart. If I don't
make it back—"

She clamped her hand over her mouth to hold in a sob.

"Sorry love," he said. "I have to say it, if only for my
own peace of mind. Do this for me. If I don't come home,
find someone who gets you. Live your life. Be happy."

She took a deep breath to compose herself. "Of course
I'll live my life. I managed without you this long. I'll
survive. I might even marry someone else. But understand
this: I won't give up on you. Alive or dead." She paused to
give him a fierce look. "Don't you dare laugh. We *will* be
together. In this life, or the next one."

He stood up and slung his backpack over his shoulder. His face softened when he looked down at her. "We're already together."

Every time she thought she knew him, he surprised her. "I know that. I just wasn't sure you did. I'll be waiting. For the next fifty or sixty years, if that's what it takes."

He bent down and kissed her eyelids closed. "Dream of me. When you wake up, you'll be on your way home."

She didn't smile. She just couldn't do it. "You have my letter still?"

"Always."

"Someday," she said, memorizing his face, "we will look back on this and laugh."

A steady light shone in his eyes. "You will. You always do."

Then he was gone.

## 25

SHE MUST HAVE READ the text Jackson sent to her mom's phone about fifty times.

"She's in the air and on her way. Details to follow."

Except no details did follow. Not from him. He didn't text again and he didn't call. Every time she tried his mobile, she heard, *"The number you have reached is no longer in service."*

The State Department had no explanation for his silence, or if they did, they weren't telling. The intelligence agency who'd employed her offered no help. Ms. Harrow had been only too eager to close the book on an ill-fated mission and accepted Rose's resignation with insulting speed.

Rose gave her parents an abridged, glossed-over version of her time in Africa. Her dad's prognosis was good, but neither he nor her mother needed any more sorrow. Though careful not to say so, her parents had worried they'd lost another daughter.

She too kept her anguish to herself. When her brothers arrived for Christmas with their families, she played with their kids and changed the subject when they asked about her experiences. However, her longing and worry for Jackson were constants, always lurking under the surface. She had witnessed too much evil to have confidence in happy endings.

When her fears became overwhelming, she walked the half mile from her parents' house to the beach and watched waves roll in. The beach was the only place where she didn't have to pretend. The rest of the time, she simply faked holiday cheer.

Two days before Christmas, Rose looked up the Holloway Foundation and called their office in Seattle. Mr. Holloway himself returned her call almost immediately.

"You haven't heard from him at all?" Will Holloway asked. He spoke in a cool, emotionless voice. "They got out two days ago. Things went very badly for Markus. He was detained and held by the secret police. They're known for their rough interrogations. It's going to take him a while to recover."

"Was Jackson held too?" she said anxiously.

"I don't know the details. All I know is they got out by the skin of their teeth. Maybe Jackson is just taking a well-deserved break." His voice became less frosty when he added, "My wife tells me I'm not an easy boss, but even I don't track employees during the holidays."

"Wait. You didn't fire him?"

"I believe I'd remember that," he said dryly. "I'll admit I wasn't pleased about the setbacks to the autonomous delivery program. However, as my wife reminded me, our global charter *is* to improve health and quality of life for women and children. As I understand it, you two did both for dozens of people. Hundreds if you count the refugee camp that's now been returned to the United Nations' control. All those displaced women and children were released and are back where they belong. You and Jackson make an interesting team."

When he put his wife Camille on the phone, Rose heard sincere concern in her voice. She was as warm as her husband was cool.

"I'm so sorry we can't help," Camille said. "I understand you were put through the wringer over there. How are you now?"

"Much better. I'm being treated for malaria. With a newer drug than the one that caused the memory loss, thank goodness."

"He'll be coming home to you," Camille said. "Don't worry."

"I thought you said you hadn't spoken with him."

"Oh, I haven't," Camille said. "That's my...intuition talking."

"You have more confidence than I do," Rose said.

"Give him time. Tell me how you two met."

Rose recounted their history. Camille asked several questions about her background and experiences. Rose thought she was just being polite and, while she appreciated the chat, all she really wanted to talk about was Jackson.

Hungry for any crumbs at all, Rose pumped her mother for her insights at every opportunity. There were still so many things she didn't know about Jackson, things she'd never thought to ask, things she'd missed in their years apart.

"He always loved you, hon," Mom said. "From the get-go. You meant everything to him. As little kids, you two were joined at the hip, remember? He spent most of his time with us, especially after his mother died."

"What happened to her? Did she die in a car accident?"

"I thought Jackson would have told you by now. She took her own life. An overdose that simply could not have been an accident."

With a pang, Rose thought about his reaction when the young girl blew herself up at the checkpoint. She felt even worse when she remembered how he'd also witnessed her sister's suicide. Back then, she'd been so caught up in her own devastation, she never considered the tragedy's effect on him. Then again, no one had ever told her about his mother.

Her mom went on. "I took him under my wing after that. Since Mr. Lee travelled a lot, he hired a string of housekeepers to run the house, but that was all they did. Jackson was a darling little boy but so quiet. We could hardly get him to say a word. When we moved away the following year, I begged Mr. Lee to let his son come for a visit. I offered a plane ticket, offered to come get him myself but the bastard refused. That's why I was so glad when you two started dating years later. Then, after we lost Katie and you went off to college, I lost track of him. Eventually I found him again, and we kept in touch."

"Why didn't you ever tell me?"

Mom smiled sadly. "Rose, you never wanted to talk about him. After Katie died, you changed overnight. We were all drowning in grief, but you, especially, changed in ways I never anticipated. You shut down.

"Still, I always thought you and Jackson would find each other again." She beamed, sadness forgotten. "And you did. You grew up and became the people you were meant to be. Now you've had adventures, learned and achieved things you wouldn't have otherwise. Consciously or not, you've been heading back to each other for years. You each made choices that put you on similar trajectories and eventually, back into the same orbit. This is your time now, dear. You were meant to be together."

"I hope so, Mom. But where *is* he?"

~

The late December sun shone weakly through the fog as it crept back into shore. Rose sat in the oversize lifeguard chair and wrapped Jackson's shirt closer. She still hadn't washed it and she didn't intend to. His scent still clung to the Oxford cloth.

Christmas had come and gone and still no word from him.

Her brothers and their families had returned to their homes this morning. Though she'd enjoyed their company and playing with her baby nieces and nephew, the peace and quiet of the beach were a welcome change.

This was where she and Jackson had fallen in love ten years ago. Then too, they'd found each other again. Now that she had regained her memories of that summer, she intended to hold them close. Whatever happened next, no one could take that time away from her.

Though they'd been best friends as kids, as young adults she and Jackson had discovered they couldn't keep their hands off each other. At least that was how she recalled it. How strange to think that all those people—the two children who snuggled close on a beanbag, the two lovers who made out on the beach—all were gone forever.

Hadn't he told her, warned her that first night at the safe house? *"We can't go back. It doesn't work that way."* What if it were true that "you can't go home again?" As heartbreaking as that was, she might have to accept it.

Tears slipped down her face and she let them, glad she didn't have an audience. For days she had done her best to keep her unhappiness to herself. At least here she didn't have to pretend. She could be what she was: a woman still trying to make sense of the twists and turns her life had taken.

She'd give herself a few more minutes to feel sad and then she would climb down the ladder, plaster on a smile, and walk back for a quiet dinner with her parents.

A movement out of the corner of her eye caught her attention.

She looked up to see a tall man coming down the sand, outlined against the setting sun. She blinked the tears away, afraid he was a mirage. Without her glasses, she couldn't see his face. When she saw long dark hair and broad shoulders, an involuntary cry escaped her.

She dried her face with her sleeve and leaped off the tall chair, nearly knocking him over. He staggered backwards and held on tight while she blubbered into his chest for a minute, too overwrought to speak. He stroked her hair and swung her around in a circle before bracing them both against the lifeguard chair. She refused to let go, just in case she really was dreaming.

When she finally leaned back for a good look at him, she saw her own joy mirrored there. "Jackson, where the hell have you been?"

He kept his arms locked around her. "You look healthier."

"You didn't answer my question."

"You're not going to believe this," he said. "I came down with malaria."

"Me, too. How bad was yours?"

"Bad enough that I couldn't keep travelling. I made it as far as Senegal and somehow put Markus on a plane. Then I hunkered down in a hotel room in Dakar until I was well enough to board an airplane myself."

"Why didn't you call?"

"I did. I left a message on your mom's phone a few days ago. It was the only number I had."

"She didn't get a message. She would have—" Rose broke off and tipped her head to sigh at the sky. "Mason. My brother let his two-year-old play with Mom's phone for two days straight. He must have screwed up her messages."

"I didn't want to get your hopes up until I knew for sure when I'd get in. I called her again when I landed at LAX this afternoon. She told me where to find you."

Rose inspected him head to toe and ran her hands over him compulsively. "You lost weight."

"I'm fine, a little weak but that's to be expected. You?"

"All good. My foot's almost healed. What's happening with Markus? Is he all right?"

"He will be eventually. They roughed him up pretty good. I had my hands full, dragging his sorry ass out of the country. We ended up driving across half the continent."

"And Raymond?

"Solomon and I found him on the side of the highway. The truck he was in broke down and he missed the battle entirely. Both boys are with Beatrice now. They're safe."

She looped her arms around his waist, half-afraid she'd somehow lose him again. "Did their father survive?"

"Government soldiers executed the general right where we left him. The old regime regained control and the insurgents went scurrying back to the outer provinces. Things are back to normal."

"Whatever that is," they both said simultaneously and then smiled at each other.

"Are you free now?" he asked.

"God, yes. I resigned from that agency gig. Not a good fit."

"Understatement. But I still don't understand why you agreed to do it."

"I've been asking myself the same question." She paused, then said slowly, "I think that after years of aid work, I'd seen too much. I can't tell you how many pallets of food, medicine and supplies were unloaded onto tarmacs and docks that never made it to people who needed them. Maybe it was burn-out, but I was perpetually angry and disgusted. When the agency approached me about investigating corruption in the NGO, I decided, why *not* clean house?

"But even I didn't expect to learn the extent to which basically decent people could be corrupted. In fact, General Mutan was right. That aid organization really *was* stocked with spies who wanted his country's oil and mineral deposits."

Jackson turned to stare out at the ocean and she felt his uneasiness as if it were her own.

"What?" she demanded.

"When I asked if you were free, I was actually asking about the douche bag."

"Who?"

"Your fiancé."

"Oh, him." She dismissed the idea with an airy wave. "I made him up. As I thought."

"Why?"

"To keep guys from hitting on me. I mean, some still hit on me but the lie did make my life easier."

A shadow crossed his face. "What about the Danish doctor? You didn't mind him hitting on you?"

She hated that she'd caused him unhappiness and would have preferred to kiss him senseless until he forgot all about it. She could do it, too; she could make him forget. For a while. But he deserved better.

She met his troubled eyes. "I wish I could tell you that affair with Oliver didn't happen. But it did. We had a brief fling a few months ago. I thought he was different, that he couldn't possibly be anything other than what he appeared to be. After all, he was a doctor working in the toughest conditions imaginable with very little prestige or pay. How could someone like that not be a hero? Some spy I was, right?"

His detached, blank expression frightened her. Despite the cool ocean breeze, she broke out in a sweat. They had to put this to rest. If he couldn't get past her mistakes, they wouldn't have a chance.

She went on. "I was lonely and confused. That's not an excuse but it is a reason. I'd seen a lot of bad things and I needed to believe in someone. I picked the wrong someone. I broke things off with him even before I realized he was no hero. Then I found out I was pregnant. The doctor I saw last week said it's possible the medication side effects played a part—in both the pregnancy and the miscarriage. Oliver never knew about the baby. I told him I'd had a scare and left it at that." She paused to catch her breath. "I know this hurts you. I'm so sorry."

"It's in the past," he said gruffly. "You're okay now? No long-term effects?"

She shook her head. "I'm okay. Only thing is, one doctor confirmed I might not ever get some of my memories back from that last week—like Beatrice said. I don't care. I don't want those memories anyway. They can stay buried."

"We won't talk about it again, unless you want to."

"I want to talk about the future."

His answering smile, slow and sweet, made her giddy.

"I heard you spoke to Will and Camille," he said. "What did you all talk about?"

"You, silly."

"You made quite an impression."

"Really?"

"They want to offer you a job."

She bounced in place. "Where? Doing what?"

"It could be anywhere. The 'what' remains to be seen. Their foundation has projects all over the world. Most involve integrating technology to improve health and quality of life, sometimes training local entrepreneurs. Once things settle down, I expect they'll be funding Beatrice's work with displaced kids."

"They know about her?" When he nodded, she reached for his hand. "Because of you. But why do they want me?"

"Two reasons. First, they value versatility and people skills. Since you have international aid experience and charm out the wazoo, they think you'd be a good fit."

"They do?" she asked, pleased. "What do you think? Are you okay with this?"

"Of course. You know what I think of you."

"Do I?" she asked wistfully. Then she waved. "Never mind, what's the second reason?"

"I'm not done with the first one. You're determined, strong, brave, and caring. Not to mention beautiful inside and out." He lifted her hair and kissed the back of her neck. His mouth sent shivers up her spine and his words gave her the loveliest sense of belonging.

To him. She belonged to him. She closed her eyes in gratitude for this second chance. *I love you so much.*

"It's mutual," he whispered into her hair.

She turned in his arms for a long, satisfying kiss.

He lifted his head and grinned down at her. "Now we come to the second reason. I should warn you. It's not an easy gig and typically not as exciting as what we just experienced. The work is predictably unpredictable. Challenging but rewarding. We'll be living out of suitcases more often than not. I don't know many people who can cope with that lifestyle. You should take your time and think about this."

"I already have. What's the second reason?"

"I told them, from now on you and I operate as a unit."

"Unit." She mock-sighed. "Such a romantic."

"Partners. Is that better? I didn't want to tell them we're getting married before I ask you. Anyway, I'm not leaving you behind for weeks at a time. We've been apart long enough."

"You really don't mind if we don't settle down?"

He looked wary. "I don't know what that means. I know I'm not letting you go. If you're talking about staying in one place and going to an office every day, well, I'm not so sure. We can talk about that. Either way, I won't let work separate us. If you need to stay—"

"Not at all," she exclaimed, delighted. "I was worried you were going to quit a job you loved and then hate me for it."

"Never." He wrapped his arms around her to share his strength and heat. They stood entwined to watch the last traces of sun melt into the ocean. "If we're together, I'll be happy."

"That's it?" she teased. "That's all you need? No devices, no data?"

"If you want the long answer, I want to work hard. I want to create things that make the world a better place. I want to wake up to your smile every morning and hold you close every night. I want to make you happy."

"You will. We have so much to do. Let's have some adventures. Together." She looked up at her beloved's face. "You still owe me a trip to Fiji. What do you say?"

\* \* \*

# Author's Note

*I don't know what it is about amnesia stories. Maybe it's the appeal of a fresh start? For whatever reason, I can't resist them. Thank you for reading Jackson and Rose's story. If you can, please offer your opinion in a review— short, long, or in-between. That makes a big difference in the book's discoverability and I do appreciate any help in spreading the word.*

*Join my readers group at noellegreene.com for exclusive offers and giveaways.*

# Also by Noelle Greene

*Lover's Intuition (Blue Mill #1)*

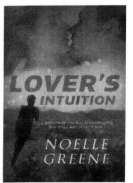

A psychic must save
the skeptic she loves

*Warrior's Intuition (Blue Mill #2)*

A small town cop's intuition
leads him to a widow with secrets

*Sailor's Warning*

A single dad fights his attraction
to a scientist in trouble

# About the Author

Noelle Greene lives in Northern California with her husband. She grew up in Memphis, Tennessee and Milwaukee, Wisconsin, earned a degree in advertising at San Jose State and has lived up and down the West Coast, including the Pacific Northwest and Southern California. Her background includes work in Silicon Valley marketing communications, running an elementary school library and raising two sons. She loves action-packed stories and classic romance themes with a twist.

# Acknowledgments

For a real-life story of amnesia and the author's brave journey back, check out *The Answer to the Riddle is Me* by David Stuart MacLean.

My editor Jena O'Connor sets me straight time after time and always helps create a far better book. Thanks also to the talented Scarlett Rugers for a wonderful cover. Rebecca Amthor, Carlene Garrison, Gwen Grasso, Rachel Amthor, and Susan Shyu were extremely helpful beta readers. You guys are great. Several advance readers—you know who you are—gave last minute input that I'm grateful for. David Muench, Rachel Amthor, and Jack Muench offered suggestions and guidance about aid work and cultural details in various countries. Any inaccuracies are my own doing. This book's setting is a composite one and not based on any one country. Rose Simon posted my first ever review on Amazon. Her generous spirit inspired me to name this heroine after her. Joji Ruhstorfer contributed marketing advice, as always. My dear husband patiently listened to my poor-man's audio drafts while commuting and put up with nearly a year of me obsessing over this story. Even better, he never asks me why dinner isn't ready.